A WALK ON THE BEACH

The breeze had picked up a little and was fluttering the Windsurfers' sails that lay in the sand, adding a soft fluting sound to the slow crashing of the waves. One sail in particular, a steely blue one that in the moonlight shimmered like water, was swollen with wind, as if ready to cut across the ocean.

I stopped and stared. *There wasn't enough wind to swell anything.* Besides, the shape was all wrong. The sail must be stuffed, I thought, with a rock or a piece of driftwood. Slowly a cold weight sank deep in my stomach. The sail rippled . . . deflated a little . . . then settled over a long, narrow shape. Clammy sweat coated my neck; I clenched my fists, recoiling from the idea of touching that sail.

I kicked at it, trying to lift it. Something hairy brushed my toes. I held back a scream and gave the sail another shove. It slid to the left a couple of inches, letting the moonlight pick up a white streak, then a naked shoulder. It was Iguana. The blade of a machete was imbedded in the thickness of her hair. Her skull had been split open like a coconut.

A SIMONA GRIFFO MYSTERY

THE TROUBLE WITH TOO MUCH SUN

TRELLA CRESPI

ZEBRA BOOKS
KENSINGTON PUBLISHING CORP.

ZEBRA BOOKS

are published by

Kensington Publishing Corp.
475 Park Avenue South
New York, NY 10016

First printing: June, 1992

Printed in the United States of America

CAST OF CHARACTERS
in order of appearance

SIMONA GRIFFO — Transplanted Italian, who tries to make sense of things, but doesn't always get it right.

LUNDI — A two-year-old French boy, who grabs more than hearts.

COCO — Harvester of coconuts and dreamer of freedom.

PAPA "LA BOUCHE" — Coco's crusty father, who spins revealing tales.

BOB HALSEY — Club Med's Aerobics G.O., who provokes gasps, sighs, and doubts.

MANOU — Excursions G.O. from Corsica, who has only some of the answers.

NICK DOLIN — Clothes stylist, who lies about more than her name.

ELLEN PRICE — Model for a French cosmetics firm, who considers beauty a handicap.

PAUL LANGSTON — Broody photographer, driven to make a bad buy.

ERIC KANZER — An expatriate, looking for the action of Vietnam days.

TOMMY BOYLE — Groupie to the advertising crew, who hands out tidbits of useful information.

IGUANA — Lundi's young and desperate mother.

CRISTOPHE BEAUJOIE — Guadeloupan police commissioner, who likes to examine every possibility.

PETER — A bookseller, full of remorse.

HM — Hair and makeup stylist, in love and jealous.

JERRY — Paul's assistant, who stays out of it.

ZAZA — Iguana's friend, who wants to be warmed by *le beau soleil*.

STAN GREENHOUSE — Simona's ex-lover, who looms large in her mind.

Plus an international assortment of G.O.s always ready to help, G.M.s ready to have fun, and Guadeloupans who won't stop smiling even when faced with disaster.

ONE

I was buried up to my neck in the gloriously welcoming, warm sand of La Caravelle—Club Med on Guadeloupe, while Mozart's *Jupiter* Symphony was allegroing over the sound system to the rhythm of creaking tree frogs and breaking waves. In the past three happy days the late-January sun had warmed, burned, and finally tanned me.

Now it was sunset time, a quiet affair in the Caribbean. No fireworks of colors in the sky, just a slow, dimming withdrawal as the sun slipped into the cloud bank that hid the Soufrière volcano on the other side of the island. The light was soft, restful to the eyes. I let myself relax.

After sweating an hour of Club Med's high-impact aerobics, my muscles were beginning to unknot and melt. My chest had stopped heaving; I smoothed the blanket of sand that covered me and closed my eyes. A well-earned peace.

A child screeched—a shattering sound delivered with one hundred percent intensity. I bolted upright. The screech continued, drowning out Mozart, the frogs, the ocean. I scrambled to my feet and ran toward the sound, thinking: please shut up, please don't be hurt,

7

please go away.

He stood, as naked as a peeled fruit, at the edge of the water next to a purple kayak at the western end of the beach. His face, too thin and too tanned, was still red; his screams had turned into trickling tears. Dirty hair stuck to his ears and to the folds of his neck. He was French, around two years old. I had seen him on the beach in the afternoons after we came in from shooting our BEAU SUN print ads. Several American women, G.M.s—a club guest is called *gentil membre* or G.M. for short—stood nearby with their arms outstretched as if to catch him. Except they weren't looking at him.

"Arnie, get the camera quick!" A large woman, her face hidden behind an umbrella-sized straw hat, jangled her bracelets in excitement. "I told you this was better than Florida."

A swelling wave of people was coming my way. But not to save the boy who now stood with his mouth hanging open, sand visible on his tongue and around his mesmerized eyes. The coconut man had stolen the show.

The tall black man carefully crossed a few feet of beach to the next coconut palm, a machete swinging loose in his hand. He sliced sand with each lift of the giant saw-toothed blades that seemed to grow out of his green rubber boots. As he dug the metal into a new tree trunk with a deft ankle stroke, I heard a collective gasp.

"Coco," the boy called out, opening and closing a fist in salute.

"Coco, Coco," Umbrella Hat picked up, flashing her bracelets as she clapped to the rhythm of some imagined steel drums. The G.M.s made a wide circle under the tree, picking up the chant of "Coco, Coco." Arnie took pictures.

For a moment Coco's long-legged body leaned away from the tree, his knees pressed together, the blades at his ankles gripping the tree trunk like claws. His dark sculpted face looked out to the ocean without a smile. His blue shirt billowed in the wind. There was something glorious and defiant about him, and I imagined a sea captain at the mast of his captured ship, ready to sail his brothers back to Africa. Too much sun can do that to me. Coco was more realistic. He lashed the leather belt around himself and the tree, threw his machete high into the trunk, and started his rapid climb toward a cluster of coconuts fifty feet above him.

We all gaped at Coco's gracefulness, at the thinness and length of his body. He was aware of his audience, exaggerating his movements, every few feet stopping to collect his *sabe*—the Creole word for machete—from where he'd last embedded it, in order to fling it with an elegant flick of his arm as high on the tree as he could. With each step upward, Coco suspended one saw-toothed blade in midair for an instant, as if to reflect the last rays of the sun before sinking the metal back into the trunk. When he was only a few feet from the top of the sixty-foot tree, he whipped out a rope and lassoed the new cluster of coconuts. A swift whack of the *sabe* and the coconuts were his. He got a big round of applause.

Below, a green truck waited to fill up with the tropical fruit. BOUE COCO—drink coconut milk—was neatly lettered on its wooden sides with the *O*'s of COCO replaced by two childlike drawings of pink and yellow madras suns. A short old man with legs as curved as Coco's claws stood next to the truck angrily whipping his cane against the base of a squat palm tree. Did he disapprove of Coco's show, of our applause, of some private fact? There was no way of telling.

The boy let out another scream. He was facing the

ocean, one hand pulling his small mouth into a grimace, the other pointing toward the waves breaking at an angle to the left of us, at least three hundred feet out to sea, beyond the coral reef.

My skin was scorched from the sun; my muscles were whining for rest; I was dying for a Piña Colada, and kids make me feel awkward. But the boy kept crying.

"What is it, *Doudou?*" I said in French, using the Creole equivalent of "honey" that I'd heard said by the local women who worked at the Club. He whimpered, pointing his finger toward the buoy with the persistence of a child spotting a candy shelf. There was nothing to see except the roll of white foam, the splash of the waves breaking, an orange buoy bobbing. The surfers had left for the day, and no Windsurfers' sails colored the horizon.

I stooped and wrapped an arm around his waist. "Are you looking for *maman?*"

His mother was part of a group of half-naked women who tanned themselves almost black, then gathered under the shade of several palm trees in front of the white gazebo sitting on a short, concrete pier. The women smoked, chatted, and twisted their stunning bodies into new bathing suits and beach clothes to model their wares. Every hour or so, one of them would attach the clothes to a belt, loop the belt over her shoulder and walk the length of the beach in search of a sale. The most popular item was a colorful rectangle of cloth, called a pareu, that could be wrapped over a bathing suit in a dozen different ways. A few male friends, equally good-looking, would come by to replenish the stock, kiss all the women, then stretch out on pareus and fall asleep.

Iguana, that's what her friends called the boy's mother—an odd name for someone as smooth-skinned and lithe as she was, tall, with a mane of curly brown hair that she tied on top of her head, letting it spout to her waist like fountain water. Thin, not a hint that her body had ever carried a baby, except for her breasts which were so long and pointed they made me think of baby bottles. I'd watched her in the three afternoons I'd sat at the beach, watched all of these French women and men who'd come from the *Métro,* as they called France. I'd asked Zaza, a petite black-haired woman, what brought them across an ocean, while she tried to convince me to buy a yellow, crushed velvet monokini.

"Le beau soleil, une belle vie." The beautiful sun, a beautiful life. My reason for crossing the ocean from Italy three years before had been less ambitious. I wanted a life—the word "beautiful" was beyond my imagination. Coming from a bad divorce, I needed a place to breathe, to start again. I had spent some wonderful college years in New York so back I came, unaware that the Big Apple doesn't easily market *une belle vie.*

"You must remove the city, the worries, the clothes from your body, and breathe in the light," Zaza had said, lifting her perfectly shaped breasts to the sun. "Naked except for a hibiscus of velvet to hide *le pubis."* She spread out her short but shapely legs, showing me a purple monokini the size of a barette. *"Très érotique."*

On her. For me to even think of that two-inch strip of velvet on my body, I would have to hack off ten years from my age and ten pounds from each hip. Besides, I didn't have anyone to be *érotique* with since my detective friend and I had parted company to "find ourselves." It had seemed like a great idea four months ago. All I had found was fat.

The little boy had walked up to me that time. He'd been left with Zaza while Iguana surfed, one of the

11

three or four dark stick figures balancing on the ocean. He was then, as now, dark with dirt and sun, sand whitening the lashes of his brown, birdlike eyes. He'd seemed perfectly content. After giving me a solemn glance of appraisal from head to toe, he had wrapped an arm around Zaza's thigh and rewarded her knee with a drooling kiss.

A very unhappy boy now, as he punched his finger at the sea. I took his hand and we wobbled toward the gazebo, festooned with "wet paint" signs, looking at the emptying beach, at the graying horizon. The classical music hour was over, the sun had dropped behind Basse-Terre—the mountainous, lush wing of the butterfly-shaped island. The *Métro* women had gone home. I picked up the boy, hoisted him on my hip, and walked beyond Club grounds to a small cove where the nudists hung out. The sand was less clean—black seaweed piled against the shoreline like gathered fishermen's nets. Huge tree trunks, stripped of bark and branches, lay victims of Hurricane Hugo. The water, as it splashed against a man-made limestone jetty and the coral reef beyond, made much more noise.

The boy stopped whimpering as he played with the Club beads I wore around my neck, each color a different cash value. The old black man who had seemed so angry ten minutes ago now stood calmly smoking under the feathery leaves of a poinciana tree, called *flamboyant* locally because of its bright red March flowers. Seeing us, he dug into a trouser pocket that reached below his knees and came up with a crumpled French sailor's hat. Flicking the red pompom with his fingers, he bowed in our direction. I bowed back and walked on.

No sign of Iguana. Beyond the end of the beach, the village of Sainte-Anne turned on its lights. We walked

12

past a row of Windsurfers. Their multicolored sails lay flat against the wind like felled butterflies. I shivered, maybe from too much sun, maybe from a childlike fear of the approaching darkness. I turned around, the boy's weight grinding into my hip bone, and hurried back to La Caravelle—Club Med.

TWO

"Bob! Thank God you're here," I cried out as I got to the bar, crowded with G.M.s drinking pre-dinner rum punches. "What am I going to do with this boy?"

"I just met you, you can't pin him on me." Bob laughed. He was the aerobics G.O. from California who gave me impure thoughts every time I saw him. Blond to the point of iridescence, with eyes the color of a David Hockney swimming pool and a hazelnut brown tan, he was as handsome and muscled as Michelangelo's *David,* with the same curls falling over his forehead. Now the tan was gone under a thick layer of white body paint. He was naked except for a white ribbon on his forehead and a white bikini not much wider than the ribbon.

Bob caught my appraising glance. "I'm a marble statue. Watch." He curled his body, flexing his muscles by putting one hand to his forehead, the other behind him, as if he were about to throw a discus. "Tomorrow's Olympic Day. I'm the captain of the white team."

The boy let go of my beads and reached one arm out to Bob. "Do you know him?" I asked hopefully.

Bob moved away, as if afraid the boy would mess up his paint. "He's always hanging out on the beach."

14

Behind Bob, a couple of professional dancers leapt onto a platform facing the bar and started dancing *la biguine,* the national dance that consists of hips grinding together to a one-two rhythm guaranteed to whip your hormones into a froth.

The boy squirmed in my arms. "I found him," I said, "and now I don't know what to do with him."

"How about letting him walk?" Bob said.

"I tried but he kept plopping down on the sand and waiting for me to pick him up."

The boy stuck out his tongue and grinned as if to let me know he was putting one over me. I held him closer and resisted an urge to kiss the top of his head. We were getting along fine.

"Have you any idea where his mother lives?" I asked.

"No, I don't, but try upstairs at the excursion desk. I'd help, but I've got to be in front of the dining room and get people to join my team for tomorrow. How about you?" He offered me a thin white ribbon to wear next to the blue ribbon Club Med handed out to identify us as guests.

I wouldn't mind being on your team, I thought, if trying to seduce a very supple marble statue at least ten years younger than me would get me anywhere healthy.

"No, sorry. I can't," I said, handing back his white ribbon. I liked fantasizing, but when it came down to facts, Greenhouse still had a firm grip on my sexual loyalties. I shifted the boy to my other hip and walked away just as the woman *biguine* dancer lifted her purple and pink madras skirt to hug her partner's waist with a long, sleek, ebony leg. I could hear the taffeta slither.

"With you I would have won," Bob called after me.

Sure, I was hefty enough to win the tug-of-war. I smiled back at him. "Thanks, but duty calls."

Duty was shooting a print ad campaign for BEAU

SUN, a new line of sun products from Janick, Inc—a medium-sized French cosmetics firm and my advertising agency's biggest client. We were going to start advertising in glossy women's magazines first: *Vogue, Harpers Bazaar, Vanity Fair, Cosmopolitan,* a two-page spread with a strip of sea scent. They had even thought of adding a tiny transmitter that would emit the distant roar of the ocean, but gave it up because of the cost. HH&H, my agency, planned to come out next with store-sponsored ads in newspapers. Our last persuasion was going to be through the television medium. No dialogue or movement, just pictures, the ones we were shooting now. Photo after photo would flip on the TV screen with no commentary except the sound of the ocean. At the end of the commercial, yellow letters on a sky-blue screen would read:

ENJOY A SUNNY SKY
WITH
BEAU SUN

Still pictures were classier, the agency felt, and would give the television viewer a sought-after relief from all the fast motion, hard-sell commercials. The same relief that comes with sunny vacations. Peace, serenity, the tranquilizing influence of the sun's rays—that was the message we were trying to convey. We had suggested the concept of "Caribbean Pleasures." Our client had preferred the snobbier *Les Plaisirs des Caraibes*. We were starting in Guadeloupe, and if the campaign went well we would come back to do all the islands. Well, I was pretty sure the "we" wouldn't physically include me. Art Buying, which is what I do officially, usually entails organizing from behind a small, cluttered New York desk, sending the crew off with my blessings and hoping the telephone won't ring

16

to say that the heavenly location I so painstakingly researched is being bulldozed to hold a new Holiday Inn.

This time I had gotten lucky and been asked to come along to be the art director's assistant. The official reason for my presence was that Guadeloupe was a department of France where people spoke either Creole or French. I knew French, my boss and the crew did not. The real reason was that my boss was grateful I'd gotten him out of an ugly situation a year ago. Along with the yellow roses he had sent me then, this was my thank you. Now he was gone, called back to New York because of another client's sudden need to review the agency. I was left in charge—not scary so far. Everything was going more or less as planned. Except for the boy, who still refused to walk, apparently too happy with the forty dollars worth of beads he was chewing.

"Manou, help," I called out when I got to the excursion desk. *"Un enfant* for sale."

Manou, who was from Corsica, trekked willing G.M.s all over the island. She was the historian, *la spécialiste* of island lore. She was also handsome, with wide palm green eyes and lots of curly black hair flying free—the "hurricane look."

I explained the situation to her. She'd seen the French vendors, but didn't know the boy.

"What is his name?" she asked.

"He won't say."

"Comment t'appelles tu?" she said, pressing her face against his.

The boy went for her hair; she ducked.

"Michel? Jean? Luc? Philippe? Paul?" Her voice scaled upward as if the names were notes.

The boy pushed her nose away and turned to me. I could swear he was asking for help.

"Today's Monday, isn't it?"

"Mais oui."

"His name is Lundi, then. I'd call him Monday, but that would be denying his nationality."

Manou's green eyes widened.

"You know, like Friday in *The Adventures of Robinson Crusoe?* Never mind. Where should he go?"

"The Club will take care of him." She reached out her arms, her expression stuck in the bafflement mode.

"Ciao, Lundi, see you at the beach." I leaned him over toward Manou. He howled and grabbed my neck. I dangled part of my necklace. "Here, you can have some of these. Take them." Lundi shook his head, big fat tears coming down. He was pulling every trick in the book and he was winning. No one had cried for me since first grade; it felt good.

"How would the Club go about finding his mother?" I asked.

"Call the police."

Logical, but I didn't like it. "Maybe I should keep him a little while longer," I said, nestling his head against my shoulder. "His mother's bound to show up. Spread the word that I've got him, in case she calls up or I don't see her. Thanks."

I carried Lundi toward my room which I shared with Nick, the clothes stylist. Only Ellen Price, our model, and Paul Langston, the photographer, were important enough to have rooms of their own. Henry Marsdon, called HM because of his name and the fact that he was the hair and makeup man, roomed with Jerry, Paul's assistant.

I didn't enjoy having a roommate. I always feel silly having to ask permission for things like, "Do you mind if I read until three in the morning?" "Do you care if I

18

take a thirty-minute shower?" "May I ask you, for your own good, not to use the bathroom for at least another fifteen minutes?"

I didn't enjoy the situation, but I liked Nick. I'd met her only once before coming down here, but she'd been working with Paul for the past year. She had a real flair for combining clothes, a flair she didn't use on herself. Nick was six feet tall, model-thin without the looks or the grace, straight dark hair cut boy-short, a lock of it always falling on her forehead. I'd asked her her real name once, but she said Nick was the only name she answered to. She seemed straightforward, reliable, and eager to do the best job possible.

"You're going to be late for dinner," Nick said, as she strode down the length of the baby-blue corridor, aiming a forefinger at me. She was dressed in wrinkled khaki bermudas and a white T-shirt—a uniform with her—bottomed off by yellow high tops. She gave Lundi a nod, but raised no eyebrows.

"Want me to take him? I'm real good with dogs."

Lundi opened his mouth in a grimace, ready to do his protest bit again.

"Guess he doesn't like the comparison. This kid needs to eat," Nick said, always practical.

"That's why he clings to me. With my fat, he knows food can't be too far away."

"If you don't like the way you look, you can always do something about it."

As I said, practical and straightforward. She was right, of course, but I wasn't about to think of self-esteem problems now. It would kill my Club Med stay. I told Nick to go ahead, that I'd join the crew in fifteen minutes.

Lundi and I showered together. He happily peed as soon as I turned on the water, then sloshed his feet while I soaped him and shampooed his hair. He blathered away, the first time he'd spoken except for his emphatic "no's" when anyone except me tried to touch him. I'd no idea why he'd taken to me, but the feeling was beginning to feel mutual. I made a resolution to seek him out and play with him every afternoon of my stay, while his mother sold her clothes or windsurfed beyond the coral reef.

I asked him "Where is Mommy?" several times but all I got was a garbled *"Maman est belle,"* which she wasn't according to the impossibly high standards set by the other Métro beauties, but I wasn't going to argue with filial blindness. Besides, he was looking at me when he said it. I'm okay looking when I'm happier and thinner: thirty-six, five-four, hippy even in my slim days, top-heavy since the age of twelve, which got me used to a lot of bad jokes like—"Moo, moo, where's the bell around your neck?" The most flattering description of me is my mother's when I was a baby: *"Cicciotta d'oro,"* which means roughly "fat ball of gold." I liked the idea of fat having a valuable quality. Also I've got dark brown hair and brown eyes, so being made of gold seems fantastic and fairy-tale-like. I could go on but won't.

Wrapping Lundi in a towel, I left him on the bed to play with the Club beads. I looked out of the floor-length window at the nude beach with the vague hope Iguana would materialize with her surf board in tow. I wondered about her odd name, maybe gotten in the same silly way I'd dubbed her son Lundi. The ocean gave out a low steady roar, like a nearby highway. It was not as friendly as the lulling *slosh-slosh* of the Mediterranean. Even the smell of the ocean was different, danker, less sweet. Or was I just being nostalgic? I couldn't complain here. The moon was almost full; the palm trees rustled in the wind; the tree frogs made their odd creaky-hinge sound; the stars sparkled; I was in a glorious, gorgeous travel magazine cliché. A very sensual cliché.

Lundi threw something at me along with a string of incomprehensible words. While I was lost in my reverie he'd left the bed and gone into Nick's duffle bag, pulling clothes out with great relish. Scooping up Lundi, I stooped down to pick up whatever he'd thrown.

Her passport was lying on the floor, open to the heavier picture page. A much younger Nick looked up at me, a scowl on her face. She must have been fifteen or sixteen at the most. She wore her hair long then, tied back in a scrawny ponytail that dripped down one shoulder. I looked at the expiration date. The passport was valid for two more months. Birthplace: Lincoln, Nebraska. Birth date: August 12, 1968. Name: Elizabeth Ashford Dolin. Not Nick, Elizabeth. I should have felt guilty for prying, but I didn't. It had happened so naturally. I closed the passport, scolded Lundi who wiggled away, laughing, and put passport and clothes back in the duffel bag. I hoped she wouldn't notice. I had the feeling she wouldn't like it if she did.

My stomach growled. Food was long overdue. I would worry about finding *Maman* after dinner when all the blood had drained to my stomach. I thought better that way. Slipping into a loose Indian cotton skirt and a black T-shirt, I decided that a stark-naked Lundi wouldn't meet the Club's very lax restaurant dress code. I stuck a clean face towel between Lundi's legs, wrapped it around his waist and tied the outfit together with the Hermès silk scarf the client had given me for Christmas. In terry cloth and Hermès, my date was more than appropriately dressed; he looked like a very chic French Cupid. Now all I had to do was hope his mother would show up.

21

THREE

Ellen Price our model, Paul Langston the photographer, and Nick were sitting in our usual eating spot: one of the four restaurant gazebos overlooking the coconut palms and the beach. HM and Jerry, by rooming together, had apparently discovered love and had gone off to be romantic at the Club's more intimate restaurant at the western end of the beach. G.O. Bob was standing by, flexing his painted white body and telling them all about Lundi.

"He must be so frightened, losing his mom," Ellen said as I approached. Her normally beautiful oval face looked pinched and unhappy.

I sat down next to her, lifting Lundi up on my lap. "I have a feeling he's used to being left alone a lot."

Ellen winced and tentatively caressed his combed, wet head. "He's adorable," she said, in a whisper, as if afraid of sentimentality. Ellen knew all about losing mothers. Hers had jumped from the eighth floor of a New York office building when Ellen was less than a year old. After that Ellen's father had shipped her off to live with his sister in Omaha. I came upon her picture by chance, brought her to New York for a photo test, and she became our client's model. Janick had just renewed her contract for two years at three hundred thousand dollars a year, which wasn't baseball money, but was a little better than the eighteen thousand five hundred dollars she'd been getting back in Omaha as an administrative assistant.

Nick, sitting between Ellen and Paul, brandished half a baguette under my nose. I tore off my favorite part, the *culo*—the ass of the bread—and stoically gave it to Lundi. Club Med had flown in a French genius to do all the baking on the premises. The breads and tarts were irresistible.

"The scarf's a good touch," Nick said.

"Wait till he pees on it," Paul said, always seeing the darker side of things. He looked staid in a tie, blue slacks, and white shirt with sleeves kept buttoned on his wrists.

I scanned the beach hoping to see Iguana. The lamps on the basketball court had been turned on, shining perpetual daylight on a vast square that included the court, rubber trees, and bleached sand. I felt as though I were gazing at an old Hollywood movie set.

"No sign of Mom, huh?" I asked Bob.

"I wouldn't know. I've been recruiting my team. Come on, Paul, how about it. After you're through tomorrow, give me a hand with the team. I can use all the men I can get. So far I have nine people on the team, all women."

"That's because you're gorgeous," I offered. Nick made loud noises with her fork against her plate. She obviously didn't like displays of female longing.

"If Roseanne can do it, so can I," I said in my defense.

Bob winked at me and tried to sell the Olympic Day to the table next to us. He's fun, I thought, not like Paul who was equally handsome but had forgotten to pack a sense of humor, if he had one.

"You should take that boy to the police," Paul said after I asked to change places with him. His chair was in full sight of the beach.

"If his mother shows up, I want her to see us. If she doesn't come by the time the show starts, I'll go to the police."

"How 'bout some more food?" Nick offered. Lundi was handing her back the soppy baguette end. "What do you think a kid that age eats? My puppies really took to steak."

Ellen laughed. God, she was beautiful when she was happy. She had chin-length, dark brown hair—shingled to give it body—and large hazel eyes that mirrored the many roles she had to play as a model. She could look candid, moody, fragile, sensual. Vibrant, most of all. What she felt was harder to determine. In the past week she had stopped laughing, except for the camera.

"I think I'd better take care of the food," Ellen said, getting up, the laugh still sitting on her face almost as bright as the basketball court. She was wearing a Granny Smith–green T-shirt with a mid-thigh-length hot pink tulle skirt that made me think she would do a *grand jeté* across the restaurant.

"Nope, you sit down," Nick said. "The kid likes you." Lundi had grabbed the tulle of Ellen's skirt and was pulling fiercely.

"Everything for me and something healthy for Lundi," I said, distracting the boy with a potato stolen from Paul's plate. Nick loped off on her yellow high tops, her tall body bent forward. I half-expected her to start dribbling a ball.

"Biological clock ticking away. Makes women funny about kids."

I cringed at the sound of that voice. Eric Kanzer, the man from whom I'd hired a van and a jeep for our

24

shoot, was jumping over the gazebo railing like a hero from some bad Western. He tugged at the long hair that wandered all over his head, as if unsure of where to settle.

"I bet you can buy him real cheap," he said, sitting down next to Paul uninvited. He had on his usual dusty combat boots, jeans worn since the ice age, and a T-shirt that told us I'M A F . . . . . . HERO front and back. On his back someone had filled in "arting" with a magic marker.

Eric was thin, scraggly looking, somewhere in his forties, with a face that stayed white despite the tropical sun and an expression that had made me think Hurricane Hugo had caught him between the eyes. Then he'd told us he was a "Nam Special Forces vet," which could have explained the slightly bulging eyes constantly shifting, as if he were still watching out for the enemy. And his need to be considered a hero.

He had moved to Guadeloupe a few years ago, to "keep movin'," and kept a "fleet" of jeeps just outside the Club to rent to the guests. The fleet consisted of three metal carcasses left over from World War II. By paying a daily fee, he could use the Club whenever he wanted. Ever since we'd come, he'd been there every night.

"Hi, everyone, not tired of seein' me, I hope."

Ellen and Lundi were the only ones who welcomed him. She blessed him with one of her smiles—"the instant bloom of a rose," a copywriter at HH&H had called it before getting fired for such gems. Lundi spread out his arms as if wanting to be picked up. He seemed to have a thing for men. He'd done the same thing with Bob. Eric ignored him, as he ignored everyone except Ellen. Staring at Ellen, eating up her smile, his devastated look faded.

"I think I'll get my own food," I said, getting up with

Lundi in tow. My heart was not big enough to like Eric, despite whatever awful experiences he'd been through in Vietnam. He was crass, obnoxious *and* had made fun of me from the moment he'd seen me.

Tonight was *La Gastronomie Française* night. The display was stomach-boggling as it had been the previous nights. Tables and tables of food wound around one side of the huge hall. Young men with toques on their heads sliced pâtés, spooned casseroles, forked small fillets of fish or meat, never forgetting to smile. I accepted swordfish steak *à la provençale* with a mound of *gratin de pommes* for both of us. Lundi then led me to the U-shaped table in the center of the room, laden with bread and pastries. He selected a mango tart by picking it up and almost throwing it on the floor. As I scooped the tart in midair with my plate, I spotted Tommy hovering next to Manou, who was playing hostess tonight. He kept pointing to the gazebo where we were sitting. She was shaking her mass of black hair and pointing to a table where two young women were stranded.

"Hi, Simona," Tommy called out in a high-pitched voice, waving. He seemed very relieved to see me.

"Come on, join our table," I said. "We'd love to have you." Manou shrugged and rushed to harness another stray diner.

Tommy, sweet-faced, bland personality, late twenties, with a heavy butt and the small mincing steps of a very old man, was an Ellen groupie. Too shy to impose himself like Eric, he tried to get near her by finding me first, then hanging around hoping she'd notice him. She hadn't.

"A kid and a man all in one night," Eric said as we approached, Tommy sweetly carrying my loaded plate. "That's fast work."

I bit my tongue. Paul, looking like a dark version of

Kevin Costner brooding in the Wild West, turned his back to the company in general. I don't think he'd smiled once since we'd been down here. Eric wasn't helping.

Tommy eagerly greeted everyone while I sat down to plunge into my food, ready to stuff myself as if I were a goose about to give up my liver to the glory of French cuisine. Lundi sat on the floor, on my Hermès scarf, and wiped his face with the mango tart. Bob was leaning on the railing near Nick. Tommy offered to join his team.

"I'm a CPA, so don't expect too much."

"You'll do great," Bob said. Behind him, on the right side where the sailboats and kayaks were kept, something white was running along the beach. I craned my neck to see better.

"You really look familiar," Nick said.

"You don't. I lived in Milwaukee 'til I was ten," Eric said. "After that you could have seen me anywhere. Where're you from?"

The figure in white had stopped by a palm tree. I picked up Lundi and stood up so that we were in full view.

"Lincoln, Nebraska," Nick said, "but I didn't . . ."

"Hey, I didn't know that," Ellen said. "I'm from Omaha. That's just sixty miles north."

Was it Iguana? The figure was too far away for me to tell. I balanced Lundi on the railing. He dropped his tart and started crying.

"I'm from New Orleans," Tommy said.

"San Diego myself," Bob chimed in. "Simona's all the way from Roooome, Italy." He made "Rome" sound like a football cheer.

Maybe it was Iguana. Maybe she was frightened the guard wouldn't let her come closer. I tried to pick up Lundi but he clung to the railing, burying the tart in the

27

sand with his foot.

"I made some money in Nebraska once," Eric said, "but I didn't stay long enough for anyone to recognize me."

The figure moved forward a few steps into the light, looked our way, then stepped quickly back behind the rubber tree. The waist-long ponytail had been unmistakable.

"Maman," I said, pointing to the tree. Lundi let go of the railing. I picked him up and ran out of the gazebo, his weight hitting me in the stomach. When I reached Iguana she was pressed flat against the tree, like a wary lizard. The guard was standing fifty feet away, not even looking at us. What was she afraid of?

Seeing Lundi, she cried out and snatched him from me.

"Doudou, mon petit Doudou," she whimpered, burying her nose in his neck, the inside of his elbow, kissing his toes, rocking him. Lundi laughed at this new game.

"He was alone, screaming. I looked for you."

Iguana was crying now, and I felt awful.

"You must have gone crazy, not finding him. I shouldn't have taken him up to my room, but I thought the police station would be worse."

"Merci, you are very kind," she said, finally looking at me. She was wearing the usual monokini but she'd covered her chest with a white eyelet top, part of a ruffled outfit I'd seen her sell. The top ruffle had been torn and trailed limply down to her belly button. Her ponytail was pulled down to one side, as if she'd been dragged.

"Zaza promised to take 'im." Iguana looked angry now, jostling Lundi, hopping from one foot to the other as if the sand were still burning. For an instant her shoulder caught a rectangle of light. I thought I saw

28

red welts.

In the bar a guitar started playing a mournful "lost love" Brazilian tune. I wanted to relax, have fun, sip a few Coladas before show time. I wanted to stay away from whatever unhappiness she was going through.

"Are you all right?" I asked. "Do you need help?"

She stopped moving and stared at me, as if wondering who I was. Lundi pointed a mango-smeared finger at my face and grinned with a gurgle. That seemed to help her assessment. She looked at me less fiercely.

"Is there anything I can do?"

"Oui, s'il te plaît. You 'elp me." She dropped Lundi back in my arms. "Keep him close. No one must take 'im. You promise me?" She dug her fingers in my arms. "Promise!" Anger and fear were back, clutching her face.

"I promise, but what are you afraid of?"

"I must do something for our future. Now, *tu comprends?* Now I 'ave the courage." She gave a low splintery laugh, and Lundi started to cry. She patted his back. "Two 'ours, give me two 'ours."

"Okay. Two hours," I said. Lundi clung to my neck now, spitting and crying into my T-shirt. Half of me thought, *Mamma,* who needs this! The other half was suckered in.

"I'll be over there, where my friends are." I pointed to our gazebo.

Iguana inhaled, her breath hissing sharply through her teeth. "'ow do you know they are friends, eh? Tell me that? No, meet me alone. At the cove, beyond the Club. *Chez les nudistes.* Tomorrow you pick any clothes you want." She gave me a lopsided smile, her long narrow face listing, her hair drooping over her shoulder.

"The courage comes and goes. *Comme les alizés."*

29

Like the trade winds. She gave Lundi a quick kiss on his shoulder. *"Je t'aime, mon Doudou."*

Off she went, just like the trade winds, her long legs scissoring across the sand toward Sainte-Anne a mile away. For an instant she turned golden as she streaked through the wide band of light from the basketball court, her long ponytail whipping behind her. Then she disappeared behind a row of sails hung up to dry.

Her nickname's all wrong, I thought. She's more like a frightened gazelle. For a moment I wondered what kind of courage she'd been talking about—probably the courage to break off an abusive relationship. I glanced at my watch. It was eight-thirty. I found myself wishing the two hours had already passed. For her sake, not mine.

I turned back toward the gazebo. Bob waved and Lundi squirmed in my arms. My hand filled with sopping silk. Hermès scarf, *au revoir*.

FOUR

My repeated attempts to get Lundi to sleep on my bed failed. All he wanted to do was to run around the room, wiggling his newly cleaned and freshly wrapped butt to some very personal rhythm. So music and dancing is what I gave him.

Every night in the amphitheater just beyond the bar area, the G.O.s put on a show. The first night, Saturday, it had been *A Thousand and One Nights* which had turned out to be a fancy display of glittering fabric and glistening bodies. Sunday, the sun had wiped me out and I preferred bed and a good Italian mystery. That Monday night we were being offered a cut version of *Les Misérables,* "The Glums" as an English G.O. had dubbed it.

Walking into the theater, I caught a glimpse of Bob and the bronzed captain of the Red Team as they left the stage door. I waved and felt foolish when neither of them saw me. Inside, the stage was dark except for a spotlight shining on Manou's dirt-streaked face. Playing the part of Eponine, the Paris street waif, she was singing "On My Own," with her green eyes wide with hunger and loneliness, belting the song out almost as well as the original English singer. I looked for my gang and tried not to listen to the music, which had made me bawl on Broadway. I gave up spotting them in the darkness of the theater and sat against the wall by the side steps, releasing a wriggling Lundi. He walked to the lip of the stage, stood underneath Manou, and did his dance routine. The audience loved it. A glow-in-the-dark watch ticking near my right shoulder told me I still had forty minutes to go until my appointment with Iguana. Manou left the stage, and the tennis pro came on followed by a chorus of male G.O.s to sing "Drink with Me."

As they held up their wine glasses I made resolutions. I should have been thinking about Iguana and what had led to her anger, her vacillating courage. But I didn't. I was selfishly thinking of my lonely, fat self and how tomorrow I'd forgo the banana shake, the miniature croissants that crumble in your hand and melt in your mouth, and eat only fruit and salad for the rest of the week so that back in my studio apartment in Greenwich Village I might have the courage to readmit men in my life.

In New York a few months back, bad loving had killed a movie star I was working with, threatened a very good friend with jail for life, and devastated several other people along the way. It had set me thinking about myself, my bad Italian divorce, and my future relationships with men. Man, to be precise—an adorable-looking homicide detective, Stan Greenhouse, who couldn't make up his mind about me which was really too bad because he had twinkling eyes and the world's greatest ass, and if I thought about him any longer, I would sexually harass the first man I encountered.

Anyway, as I already mentioned, we had separated. The American self-help craze had gotten to me. I realized I needed to explore myself, to mature, to find

32

my feet in this new American life of mine. No men at all, I decreed, afraid that even a shadow of one would weaken me into depending only on him for happiness. The results were that I had a few stilted conversations with Greenhouse on the phone, hadn't made love in four months, and I'd eaten myself to a twenty pound pregnancy of pasta and pizza. A feminist's nightmare!

Now I was bored stiff with exploring myself, and I really liked this man and didn't care if I did depend on him. Something was always going to affect my happiness, be it career, money, food, friends, the weather. Why not add a man to the list? So first the diet, I decided, then the phone call.

I did wonder, when a danced-out Lundi curled himself against my leg, if a divorce had brought Iguana to Guadeloupe. Was Lundi's father back in France? Sleep was catching up with the boy. He sucked at the hem of my skirt, his hair tickling my calf. He was sweet, I thought. On stage, all ninety G.O.s were marching in place for the grande finale. I spotted Bob in the back, his nineteenth-century top hat slightly askew, his face back to its normal hazelnut tan. The glowing watch showed ten-twenty. Iguana's two hours were almost up. I picked up Lundi, cradled his face against my neck, and slipped out of the theater.

One of the Club Med guards passed me as I walked past the mini-golf course. He tipped his baseball-capped head in my direction, one hand on the walkie-talkie holstered to his belt. I liked the idea that the only weapon needed in this tropical paradise was a word spitter. After a trip to Haiti, friends at work had talked about guards with machine guns.

"Bonsoir," I said to him. A light breeze cooled me; the theater had been hot. The sky held so many stars it

33

looked like a black, moth-eaten blanket held against the light. I noticed the Little Dipper, which reminded me of the pot in which my mother had always boiled milk. I had taken it from her when I came to America as a cozy reminder of home.

Lundi slept, dribbling saliva down my neck. His arms swung loose as I walked past the lone beach gazebo that shone pearly white. We left Club Med territory to *"chez les nudistes"* as per instructions. Moonlight made the rippled sand look like a long, narrow piece of corrugated cardboard. Phosphorescent waves continued to break against the coral reef three hundred feet out. The tree frogs were in full concert, and Iguana hadn't shown up yet. I sat down on a bleached log, as sleek and elegant as a Noguchi sculpture, and prepared to wait with Lundi asleep on my arms. The Club Med anthem hiccuped from the theater, interrupting the low booming of the ocean.

"Hands up, baby, hands up. Give me your heart, give me, give me your heart, give me." I automatically tapped my foot to the beat. The Club always had an infectious finale to its shows. The G.O.s lined up across the stage, singing the same songs each night, each lyric accompanied by a special sign language and feet shuffling thatta way, shoulders lifting thissa way. You had to have studied with the Paris Opera Ballet to get them all. Or stay a month at the Club. It was a clever idea that put you in a good mood and made you forget shyness and the stiffness of city jobs. Dancing, singing, and signing became a common denominator that held us together. You didn't have to join in, but if you did, you might discover it was fun. I pictured standing on an icy New York sidewalk, hands waving and punching air, singing "Hands Up," and being joined by a stranger on the other side of the street. Two crazies signing in Club Med language, laughing with the memory of good times.

Well, it wasn't a good time now. I was tired and Lundi was gaining weight by the second. Where the hell was she? Fifteen minutes had gone by. I got up and walked toward the lights of Sainte-Anne, past the same neat row of Windsurfers I had seen that afternoon. Fifty feet ahead of me, near the thicket of trees that edged the beach, I saw something move.

"Iguana?"

A man with his back to me—an old one judging by the curved cane he leaned on—lifted bow legs one at a time with a quick, jerky rhythm, as if he were stepping on very sharp stones. After a few minutes of labored walking, he disappeared behind a row of trees.

Lundi and I were on our own again. I gave the top of his head a kiss and smelled my shampoo in his hair. A warm feeling came over me, along with thoughts of rushing back to New York, pouncing on Greenhouse on a fertile day, and producing a Lundi facsimile nine months later. This sleeping child was giving me dangerous fantasies. Fantasies which certainly did not indicate mature thought.

Annoyed, I started walking back to the Club. I wanted to call Iguana's name again, but didn't for fear I might wake up some sleeping G.M.s. What was I going to do with Lundi if she didn't show up? Would I really let him spend the night in some grungy police station? Did I dare keep him for the night and look for Mom in the morning? *Porco Giuda!* All I had wanted was to shut the kid up, not get attached to him. That's why I didn't own pets, I couldn't stand the thought of losing them.

Then a timid fear peeked up from the selfish anger. Why wasn't she here? What had happened to her courage?

The breeze had picked up a little and was fluttering the windsurfers' sails that lay in the sand, adding a soft fluting sound, almost like doves cooing, to the slow crashing of the waves. One sail in particular, a steely blue one that in the moonlight shimmered like water, was swollen with wind, as if ready to cut across the ocean.

I stopped and stared. There wasn't enough wind to swell anything. Besides, the shape was all wrong. The sail had to be stuffed. With a large rock or a piece of driftwood. Slowly a cold weight sank deep in my stomach. The sail rippled, deflated a little, and settled over a long narrow shape. I noticed a big jagged hole near the tip of the sail. Moving closer, I realized it was a stain. Clammy sweat coated my neck. I clenched my fists, recoiling from the idea of touching that sail.

Covering Lundi's face with one hand, I kicked at the sail with my foot, trying to lift it. Something hairy brushed my toes. I held back a scream and gave the sail another kick. It slid to the left a couple of inches, letting the moonlight pick up a white streak, then a naked shoulder.

I clasped Lundi, suddenly feeling responsible for his two years of life. In the breeze, a strip of eyelet cotton fluttered like a ribbon in his mother's hair, the end looping around a black wooden handle. The blade of the machete was imbedded in the thickness of her hair. Her skull had been slit open like a coconut.

I ran to the Club, half stumbling, biting my fist to stop from screaming, clutching Lundi as if he were my life. A guard caught me as I was about to fall on my knees. Lundi started crying and I, hysterical, forgetting there were such languages as French and English, tried to tell him what I'd seen with a babble of Italian sounds. He understood the urgency. I remember the crackle of his walkie-talkie. In what seemed an instant, thick, muscular arms lifted Lundi away from me while someone else patted my back. I don't know how long it took before I stopped gulping down heaving breaths of damp, salty air and was able to show the guard what I had found. I stopped ten feet from the sail, mumbled "Iguana," and sobbed.

FIVE

Despite Iguana's death, the next morning was swilling in sunlight, so much so that we all wore sunglasses to tone down the brightness of the island. At 7:00 A.M., Eric, Paul, Ellen, and I were riding in an open jeep to Pointe-à-Pitre, the commercial center of Guadeloupe, to shoot pictures in the market place. Behind us, HM drove a van carrying Nick, Jerry, various pieces of equipment, and Ellen's wardrobe. Paul, who sat next to Eric in the front seat, was harping on the fact that I should have stayed behind to get some rest.

"All I need to see is one sail fluttering in the wind," I shouted back at him over the din of the rusted motor, "and I'll lose twenty pounds with one heave."

That shut him up. Actually, I wouldn't have minded lying down in the sand to have my brain bleached of all memory. I wasn't being a stoic and thinking the show must go on at all costs, although it did help to pretend that the ads wouldn't get shot perfectly if I wasn't there to watch. The real reason I insisted on coming along was that Police Headquarters was just behind the marketplace at Pointe-à-Pitre. I wanted to find out what was going to happen to Lundi.

"Listen, I knew that girl," Eric said, his voice loud, glancing back at Ellen with those bulging eyes of his. She was sitting behind Paul, hidden underneath sunglasses, hat, and scarf. She hadn't said a word.

"Fanm-lasa menné lavi," Eric said. "You don't know what that means, right, Simona?" He grinned in the mirror, pleased with himself, acting as if today were just another sunny day.

"That's Creole for 'that woman led the life'," he went on. "She was trash, slept with half the island, all colors."

"Don't call her trash," Ellen said in a strong, even voice, her expression unfathomable under all her sun protection. "No one is trash."

"Not even murderers?" Eric asked.

Ellen didn't answer. Wind was lashing the loose ends of her scarf across her neck. I turned away to look at the cows and billy goats grazing by the side of the highway, fighting to stay away from the memory of a strip of eyelet cotton.

"Know how Iguana got her name?" Eric said. "Tattoo she had."

I couldn't help but be intrigued. "I never noticed a tattoo," I said, leaning forward. When not modeling clothes up and down the beach, all she had ever worn was a monokini.

Eric's eyes shifted left and right in the rear view mirror, as if he were trying to find Ellen, who had slipped down in her seat.

"In a private part," he said. "You know how you models shave down there to wear those high cut bathing suits. Iguana got rid of all her pubic hair, put a tattoo in its place. Hey, hon, this isn't embarrassing you, is it? I mean, I can shut up."

"I could go for a little silence," Paul said, his shoulders rigid against the seat, the back of his neck red.

39

"I don't mind. I'm a big girl," Ellen said. She sounded angry though.

"You seem to know her quite well," I yelled in his ear, smelling Old Spice.

"She always wanted me to give her and her buddies free rum. After we're through with takin' pictures, you're gonna visit my distillery, see how rum is made. It's dead right now. There's a fuckin' water strike on. Can you believe these Frogs? You'd think they were handing out Perrier or something. It's been bad around here since Hugo, let me tell you. You can still see the damage." He nodded to the right, at a row of gray tree trunks that reminded me of knotted finger bones.

"You'd think nothing bad could come from that sky," he said, "but you'd be wrong."

I didn't need him to tell me that.

"How did you ever get to own a distillery?" Paul asked, his dislike for Eric clear. "That costs money."

"You'll never guess. Anyway, I got me a good business. Pretty soon I'm gonna be able to buy any rum mill I want."

"Going to kill a rich aunt?" Paul said.

Eric hit his horn with the heel of his hand. "Right on, Ansel Adams. You can go right into the voodoo business like the rest of the lazy bums around here. Mix a little herbs, stick a few pins. Come right up, folks," his hand went up in the air, as if waving to the van behind us. "Meet Magic Doc, straight from the U.S. of A. Don't let his white skin fool you. He's just as good as the rest of 'em. He'll guess your future just by snapping a photo."

Paul said nothing. He just hid one eye behind his Pentax. It was something he did often, and I was beginning to think he was only comfortable looking out on a small square of world where he could control the focus.

40

Eric slowed down behind the choking fumes of a truck brandishing a *J' ♥ GUADELOUPE* sign on the back flap. Inside was a solitary calf tethered to the metal railing. I didn't even want to begin to think where he was headed. Eric slipped an arm around the back of Paul's seat, then dropped it to touch Ellen's knee. Ellen, her eyes closed, smiled.

God, was something going on between them?

"Two-handed driving is safer, isn't it?" I asked. It was awful of me, but I couldn't help myself.

Eric's hand shot back up while Paul snapped his head first at me, then at Ellen, who was now sitting up and rubbing her knee as if it hurt.

I decided all four of us needed a rehaul. I hadn't gotten much sleep last night. After the lineup of sails on the beach, I'd been led with very gentle persuasion to a small room on the second floor of the main building. Bare walls, four square tables covered in green baize. Metal chairs with fake leather padding. The Bridge Room, I realized after much concentration on a score card. Someone, a G.O., probably, brought me a neat shot of rum that I didn't drink. After an eternity, an almost bald, ebony-black man walked in. Hungry for details to keep my mind busy, I took in the short-sleeved white shirt, meticulously ironed, the wide maroon tie spattered with white flowers still wet with stains, as if he'd needed to gulp something down before facing me. He was a police inspector or a commissioner; I forgot his title when I heard his name. Beaujoie, beautiful joy. An incongruous name for a policeman, I thought, as he held my hand for a reassuring moment of human contact.

He was big, well over six feet. Broad too. A trunk of a man now going soft, his belly pushing against his shirt. The black leather of his belt was worn; the brass buckle had left a series of notches to commemorate the

41

kilos gained by his waist. During the whole interrogation he never stopped smiling, as if some happy event like a wedding or christening had brought us together. He emptied his pockets of his keys, bits of paper, two matchboxes, a pen, and dropped them on the card table. Pulling out a chair, he sat down, engulfing it with his girth, his pants riding up to show sagging gray socks.

He fingerprinted me personally although I kept swearing I hadn't touched anything, then handed the sheets and the ink pad to an assistant who left us alone. Beaujoie asked me what I knew in a murmuring tone that didn't betray curiosity. We are here to pleasantly pass the time, he seemed to be saying. I must have looked very upset, I thought, for him to be so discreet. I told him about finding Lundi, about making the appointment with Iguana. How determined, maybe even desperate she'd seemed. How someone had obviously shaken her, ripped her top, if not actually beaten her. I remembered to tell him about the old man with the curved cane and the jerking bow legs. Maybe he had seen something.

In between questions, Beaujoie patted my hand or offered me his handkerchief, reassuring me that *le petit* was with his wife who would take good care of him.

"Back in the Métro, the girl is bound to have relatives," he said, in a soft, welcoming French that was easy to understand. "We all have relatives, no? Whether we like it or not. Someone will take the boy." He said that sadly, as if we would all miss Lundi.

When I refused the handkerchief, he used it to wipe his forehead, his almost bald head, to rub his hands. He wasn't sweating and I wondered where his discomfort came from. As a policeman, wasn't he used to death?

"Why was she murdered?" I asked.

He shook his head and looked taken aback by my naïveté in seeking an immediate answer.

"The pretty ladies that come from *le Métro,* they run away or seek something they do not have. We offer the sun, the ocean, the colors of Gauguin, the rum. It is no guarantee of happiness. Now you, you should go back to New York only with good memories of Guadeloupe." From his back pocket he produced another, neatly folded handkerchief and placed it in front of me. "You keep this one. Cry, which is good. After crying a good 'ti' punch, *le petit feu* we call it here. The small fire will burn the memory of tonight and permit you to sleep. In a few hours a new day, a new sun, and always the ocean."

Heaving his massive body off the chair, Beaujoie said *"En ke vwe,"*—I'll see you again in Creole— leaving me to wonder how many times I would have to repeat the little I knew about Iguana's death.

It took three "fine 'ti' punches"—a combination of fruit juices that barely diluted the chest-tingling rum— to knock me out. After what seemed a minute Nick woke me up with two aspirins and a glass of water, telling me I had slept like a zombie and snored like a bear. After shoving me under the shower, and laying out clothes for me to wear, she rushed to the Club kitchen to pick up our breakfast bags for me. Nick was turning out to be more than a good roommate.

Hungry, I dug into my white paper bag with the blue Club Med trident on both sides. We were now driving through the outskirts of Pointe-à-Pitre, and Paul was commenting on the ugliness of the massive apartment buildings in various stages of completion. My hand came up with a baby banana, as green as a salamander. No croissants. How like Nick to hand out healthy food. I sat up and waved to her in the van behind us.

I nearly flew into her face, the banana slipping from my hand. Eric had slammed on the brakes to avoid hitting the side of a truck that now blocked half the

43

road. A scant three inches separated truck from jeep. I settled back in my seat, checked for whiplash and stared at neat white letters wavering on a green background. BOUE COCO, with the *O*'s replaced by pink and yellow madras suns. Cars all around us honked, people shouted. For a second I thought I was at a Neapolitan wedding. I had no idea what was going on.

Eric had jumped out and was yelling at the empty driver's seat of the truck. Coco appeared from the back. They ran for each other, arms grappling, Coco leaning away from Eric, his wide cheekbones like shields picking up the sun. Then I caught sight of a black fist, a white shirt arm, and Eric's head snapping back, his long hair lifting in the air as if picked up by a sudden gust of wind.

Ellen yelled. Eric was flat on his back on the asphalt, blood trickling down his chin. Coco had disappeared behind his truck. Paul and Ellen scrambled out of the jeep and bent down to help Eric. I sat there paralyzed by the violence, by that thin streak of blood, by the image of Iguana, machete dead.

Coco was back in the driver's seat, scraping gears, backing up his truck on the sidewalk. The gears screeched again and the truck lurched forward. For a horrifying moment I thought he would run over all three of them. Instead he swerved to the right, missing Eric's shoulder by inches.

"You owe me," he said in clear French, leaning his head out of the window. "You owe me twice."

Eric reached up with an arm as if to grab Coco's head. The truck sped forward, and I heard the dull *thwack* as the rear fender slapped Eric's hand. The sound reminded me of a large insect splattering on a speeding windshield.

"What was all that about?" Paul asked angrily. He had parked the jeep by a bank; the van had found a space farther down the street. We huddled together watching Eric clean his cut lip with a shirttail doused with rum. We were all a little dazed, I think, even embarrassed.

"Nothin'," Eric said, with his usual devastated expression. He offered us the rum bottle, taking a swig when we refused. One hand hung limply by his side.

"We gamble together, and that guy's a sore loser." This time he jerked the bottle under my nose. "Drink up, you got that haunted look. I know what it's like to kick into a dead body. Did that a lot back in Nam."

"No, thanks."

He shrugged and took another swig. "Hey, hon, thanks for caring."

Ellen was holding out her silk scarf to finish up the cleaning. She had taken off her sunglasses and her face looked contrite, as if somehow she was at fault.

Paul scowled even more than usual. "Kicking into a dead body" had gotten to all of us. "We better get going," he said.

"Sure, that mornin' sun you guys are so hot for isn't gonna wait," Eric said as he threw the bottle back in the jeep. "The marketplace is a five minute walk. I'll leave the jeep where it is. There'll be a spot for the van behind the market."

I watched him take charge again, his small body almost twitching with nervous energy as he gave HM instructions on how to get to the Saint-Antoine market. Standing there in the brightness of the sun, I remembered how Iguana had stayed away from the light as I talked to her, as if afraid to be seen. Not by the guard; he wasn't paying any attention to her. Someone in the Club then. Someone at my table from the way she'd reacted. Eric?

"Is your hand all right?" I asked. It was obvious, by the way he did not move the hand, that he was in pain.

But as I hypocritically asked him how he was, I resisted a strong urge to fire him, gut-sure the scene we had witnessed with Coco had nothing to do with gambling debts, mind-sure Eric was the one Iguana had been afraid of.

"Lissen, this is nothin'," Eric said. "I mean I saw that shitface comin', it was a fair fight." He laughed, his eyes slipping to Ellen. "In Nam, you never knew when you were goin' to get it. Zzzzing!" He mimicked a karate chop with his good hand. "Right in the back! Makes for some bad dreams, let me tell you."

Makes for a dead Iguana, is what I thought.

"I couldn't survive a war emotionally," Ellen said.

I started fanning myself with my empty breakfast bag. It wasn't that hot—it was just that the air seemed suddenly thick with death.

I hurried over to the Rue Frébault, the main shopping street which was just opening up for the day. Every inch of space was dedicated to selling; even the sidewalks were being set up to offer goods. Women set big plastic bags full of underpants or bathing suits on each corner, next to gutters deep enough to catch the streams of rain that came down from June to November. Wood panels covered with rows of watches leaned against the narrow spaces between shop windows. Inside the shops, owners prepared for their customers. At the *Royaume d'Or,* the golden kingdom, an Indian was tidying a pile of blouses strewn on a table. At *Très Chic,* small dark woman, with a face that shone like a pair of new shoes, tried to straighten towering rolls of green, purple, and orange madras. At *La Seduction,* behind a screen of dusty perfume bottles piled high like a house of cards, a mulatto girl held up a dust cloth. Catching my look, she burst out laughing, her task so obviously impossible.

Paul walked ahead with his Pentax raised to his face,

reducing the bustling scene to more digestible portions. As he walked, his shoes scuffed the sidewalk, probably in some kind of protest. I tried with my sandals to see if I could get some release from my own bad mood. All I managed to do was knock off a heel.

Ellen and Eric waited for me while I stopped in front of the old cobbler with cocoa-colored skin who plied his trade on the sidewalk. I handed him my sandal and breathed deeply to take in the smell of shoe polish and dye mixing with the butter and baking dough that came from the pastry shop behind him.

"Did what happened with Coco back there have anything to do with Iguana?" I asked Eric, ready to "agitate the waters" as we say back in Italy.

"Simona!" Ellen said sharply.

"You ever mind your own business?" Eric asked.

"If you don't ask, you never find out." That's something I had learned after my first encounter with a body back in my New York office.

Before I could repeat my question, Tommy popped up from behind me with the perfect timing of someone who is never welcome. Eric walked away.

"Hey, great seeing you," he said, looking pretty silly in bright red bermudas, a Club Med T-shirt, huge sunglasses, and a wide straw hat on his head.

"You look like the sun got to you," Ellen said. She laughed, I think with relief at the interruption.

The cobbler handed my heel back and refused any money. "The next time," he said, his face as wrinkled as an almond. It was reassuring to know that someone so old still thought in future terms.

"The sun kills me," Tommy said, showing off a very pink arm. "Egg-shell fragile. That's Mom's definition." He made a face. "Makes me sound gay."

"Guadeloupe's a great place to pick a vacation then," I said, after thanking the cobbler and slipping my foot

47

back into the sandal. I reached in my skirt pocket and handed Tommy a new jar of BEAU SUN, *crème de protection*. "That's the stuff Ellen is trying to sell with her looks. Smear yourself with it, and you can enjoy endless sunny skies."

"God, that's sweet," Tommy said, beaming a smile. He fingered the beige tube lovingly, as if Ellen had given it to him herself.

"I thought you were going to play on Bob's white Olympic team today?" I asked.

"I changed my mind."

Better to follow Ellen around, I thought. She walked ahead, with the straight back of a dancer. Eric had stopped to wait for her and was now saying something about her feet.

Tommy made no mention of Iguana's death, which surprised me. Everyone was bound to know by now. I was relieved he kept quiet.

"Where's the rest of the gang?" Tommy asked.

I told him about the van waiting for us at the market and asked how he'd gotten to town.

He pointed at the intersection down the block, where Manou with her hurricane hair was gesticulating, surrounded by a group of camera-laden G.M.s.

"It's a Club tour. Did you know Pointe-à-Pitre is named after a Jewish Dutchman who fled from persecution in South America?" Tommy had raised his voice, trying to catch Ellen's attention, reminding me of one of those know-it-alls who didn't wait to be called on by the teacher to blurt out the answers. I had always been grateful for their existence, having done my homework quickly and just as quickly forgotten it.

"His name was Peter and he settled here to sell fish, so they ended up calling the place the Point of Peter."

I was just as grateful to let him show off what he'd just learned, allowing my mind to float on tourist trivia.

"I bet you didn't know there was an independence movement here in Guadeloupe," Tommy said. "I saw a sign painted on a wall coming in on the bus. ANSAMM NOU KÉ LIBÉRÉ YO! That's Creole for 'Together we will liberate them.' I bet they're getting ready to kick out the French any minute."

"That's a load!" Eric spun around, making us both jump. "Without French money, what're these bums gonna do after another Hugo, huh? Patch up the mess with mashed-up bananas?"

We had reached the *Marché Saint-Antoine,* and Tommy quickly changed tack and pointed out the Coca-Cola and Pepsi umbrellas that shaded some of the stalls.

"You'd think they'd have Perrier or Evian umbrellas."

The marketplace was a large, tree-lined square with an oxidized metal fountain in the center, topped by a green cherub. At one end, the market was covered by a red zinc roof surrounded by long tables bearing fruit, beans, rice, edible roots, and rolled-down bags of brown, ochre, and deep red spices. The smell of spices mixed with the smell of the ocean a few hundred feet away. The market women saw us coming and called out for us to buy, ending each solicitation with the typical "doudou." They had soft voices and smiling faces. When I didn't buy, they shook their heads as if to say I was missing out on a wonder.

Tommy followed and touched my elbow, pointing out the madras scarves the women had wrapped to rise above their heads like crowns.

"The corners of the headdress have different meanings," he said, this time lowering his voice so that only I could hear him. "One point means no boyfriend, my heart's available. Two points: too late, heart's been given away. Three points: I'm happily married, and

49

four points: I have a husband but my heart has room for more, maybe."

"Great way to avoid embarrassing questions," I said, spotting Nick at one end of the square and waving to her. I felt Tommy hesitate beside me.

"How many points would Ellen wear?" he asked.

"Oh, Tommy, I'm sorry. I don't know." I did feel sorry for him, remembering the terrible feeling of hope and despair that came with being lovesick. "You'll have to ask her. I really don't know."

I looked at Ellen as she made her way through the stalls, her hat already filled with bags of spices. In the year we'd been working together I had heard of no particular man, but it was not my business to say anything about her private life.

"What about you?" Tommy asked.

"Me? I don't know." I could see myself with a strip of madras trying to decide whether I was available when Greenhouse had only been willing to fill one night of my week. "Maybe we shouldn't decide on our hearts until we know how the other person feels. Easier said than done, I know." Where was I getting the gall to dispense advice to the lovelorn?

An old vendor with three plaid points on her scarf offered me a kiwi to taste. I slipped the cool, sweet slice in my mouth. How many points would I need to say: No boyfriend, stomach available?

"Come on, Ellen, we're late," Nick was calling out, running toward us. "Paul's having a fit."

"I've got to get to work," I said, thinking of Police Headquarters where I didn't want Tommy to follow me. When I turned around to say goodbye, he was gone.

Police Headquarters in the elegant Place de la

Victoire informed me that Beaujoie was usually found a block away, at the local police station. There, a young uniformed policeman, leaning his chair against the thickly stuccoed white wall of the entrance, saluted me with two raised fingers and informed me politely that the *Commissaire* was out for the morning. What did I wish of him?

I asked for Beaujoie's address.

The policeman rocked his chair forward and looked at me curiously. "You know *le Commissaire*'s wife perhaps?" he asked in soft Creole French that sounded as if his mouth were holding water he didn't want to spill. "I cannot give out the address even if you are a friend. You understand, it is not possible."

I asked him if he knew whether the baby of the murdered woman was still with Beaujoie's wife. I wanted to see the boy, make sure he was all right, I told him.

"It is sad with Madame," was all he said, taking off his cap and lowering his eyes, and for some reason I wondered which woman he was talking about.

I went back to the van where HM was putting the finishing tanning touches on Ellen's face. She now had an even, medium tan as though she'd been in Guadeloupe at least a month. A safe tan everyone would envy enough to rush out to enjoy a sunny sky with BEAU SUN.

"I told you to put a folded tissue over your nose if you're going to wear glasses," he said, as he applied concealer to the small red mark on one side of her nose. "Now you've got those ugly little marks."

Nick was unzipping a white short, low-cut cotton piqué dress with a big orange sun stitched over one hip. It had been her idea to have all of Ellen's clothes and jewelry depict a sun to underline the BEAU SUN theme. Our client had loved the idea, and we now had the piqué dress from Byblos, a linen blouse from Valentino with a sun bursting over the left breast, yellow glazed glass earrings from Armani, a smooth silver sun from Angela Cummings, and countless other sun themes from less haute designers like Carole Little and Adrienne Vittadini.

Nick's face was taut, the square jaw pushed out at an awkward angle, making her look older, angry. She caught me looking and bent down as if she had suddenly dropped something valuable. The murder's gotten to her, too, I thought.

The back doors of the van were open to circulate as much air as possible. Two small boys in school uniform peeked in, faces serious.

"*Le carnaval,*" a young woman said, smiling at us apologetically and pulling them away. Ellen waved and gave them one of her knock-out smiles.

At the market, fifty feet ahead of us, Paul's assistant was readjusting the fruit of one long table while Eric was talking to a market woman who laughed and kept shaking her bare head. He was probably trying to convince her to pose for the camera, and I should have been over there, helping, instead of pouting in the scorching heat of the van. I stepped down from the van just as I heard HM cry out.

"What the hell happened to you?"

He pushed Ellen's bathrobe down from her shoulders, and tilted her forward. I leaned back in the van and saw two bruises the size of fried eggs between her shoulder blades. A deep red zigzag marked where the skin had torn and bled.

"Oh, my God, Ellen!"

"It's all right," Nick said. "I can get the dress to cover it."

"Please don't make a fuss," Ellen said. "It's nothing major. Some rocks fell on me."

"Rocks?" I knew it rained pretty hard in the Caribbean, but rocks were something new.

"That's what they felt like. I didn't wait around to check. I'm fine, really." She tried one of her smiles on us but I, at least, wasn't having it.

"Come on, Ellen, give us a few more details please."

She gave me a put-on sigh. "I couldn't watch that show last night so I took a walk and climbed up that bluff at the end of the western side of the beach. With the moon being so bright, I wanted to see the view from up there. I'd just climbed up when these rocks hit me in the back. I scrambled back down and ran."

"Where you under a ledge, a tree?" I asked, that cold weight beginning to settle in my stomach again.

"There were just a lot of bushes."

"Someone threw rocks at you!" I dropped down to the floor. *"Mamma, why?"*

"I don't know. I didn't see anybody and I didn't do anything except walk."

"It's carnival time," Nick said, touching up the sleeves of the white piqué dress. "It was probably some kids playing some evil spirit. Carnival's a big thing down here."

"You think?" I was willing to clutch at anything that sounded good.

"I'm perfectly all right!" Ellen said.

"Yeah, Carnival. Kids or some drunk," HM said, swirling a light, thick cover cream over Ellen's bruise with the tips of his fingers. He dabbed a dollop of cream on my nose. "Hey, don't go connecting it to that murder."

I couldn't help doing that. "Can you remember what time it happened?"

"I left the show right after Bob and that other guy told us about Olympic Day. The minute the *Chef du Village* announced *Les Misérables,* I slipped out. I

53

didn't look at my watch. Now I wish everyone would forget about this."

More than an hour before my appointment on the beach. Iguana had mentioned having to do something. What if she was meeting someone on the bluff? Ellen had shown up; Iguana didn't want her there and threw the rocks to scare her away. It was possible. Women, even mothers, weren't exempt from committing violence. Three years of New York had taught me that. It could have been Iguana or the other person waiting for Iguana. The murderer! But why on the bluff? Iguana had been killed half a mile down the beach.

I was beginning to get confused, maybe even a little panicky, ready to imagine some dwarfed Polyphemus standing by the bluff and throwing stones at anyone who passed. I needed to talk to Beaujoie, needed to make sense of events to find some degree of order that would calm me down.

"Please don't tell Paul," Ellen was saying. "He gets angry so easily. My skin heals very quickly. It really does. Tomorrow I'll be fine."

"Sure thing, sweetheart," HM said. "But if we get hold of whoever did this to you, he sure won't be fine. Tomorrow or ever!"

SIX

For more than three hours, we worked at the marketplace and in quieter, quaint streets lined with two-story buildings old enough to have survived many hurricanes. Above a sturdy first floor built with cement, narrow wood panels were painted blue, yellow, or pink and decorated with gingerbread details. Iron balconies reminded me of pictures I had seen of the French Quarter in New Orleans.

With Nick's help, Ellen slipped in and out of clothes and jewelry, careful each time to cover her back; HM powdered, lipsticked, mascaraed, and combed her to repeated perfection while Jerry and Paul set up shots of Ellen drinking water from the cherub fountain, Ellen surrounded by laughing Guadeloupan market women, Ellen trying on a pert red hat in front of an Art Deco wood and glass vitrine, Ellen sniffing pink bags of spices, Ellen holding a wide basket of tropical fruits and BEAU SUN products. They worked quickly to beat the pace of the sun climbing the sky, while I paced nervously, trying to convince myself that those rocks had been thrown by a kid, hoping that we'd get the scheduled shots done before the sun's glare cut sharp shadows on Ellen's face or wiped out her natural contours. If this was what bosses did—have worries cluster into an ulcer while everybody else did the real work—I didn't want it. I worried about the ad campaign, I worried about Lundi, I worried about Ellen's back, thankful only that Paul never discovered the bruises. Whenever Paul moved on to another shot, I slipped back to the officer resting against the sunny wall of the police station. Beaujoie stayed out of my reach.

At noon, with the work done, Eric drove us across the Salty River that divides Grande-Terre from Basse-Terre, past a tiny isle on the narrow channel that looked as if a storm had left it littered with paper until we came closer and saw the isle was covered with seagulls. On the outskirts of Jarry, Eric showed off his prize.

The rum distillery was a U-shaped building that opened onto an inner courtyard, vaguely reminding me of a Roman atrium. In the courtyard, half-filled with empty bottles and crates bearing the SOLEIL label, hens pecked at a hard floor of bare soil, and a panting gray tiger cat displayed her pregnant belly to the sun. Hurricane Hugo had torn off the corrugated tin roof—typical of all the buildings here—from one side of the U, and wooden beams dropped to the concrete floor in an intricate braid. Shards of glass carpeted one corner of the courtyard.

We all stood in an awkward huddle on the intact side of the building, surrounded by rows of twisting, empty tubes, and the pungent smell of almost a hundred years of rum. That's how old the distillery was. At one end, a ceiling-high pile of coal waited to be used to heat the juice of the sugar cane. Eric reminded us of the water strike.

"Let's go to the beach," Nick whispered in my ear. I rolled my eyes in agreement. Ellen had been the one to

56

insist we all come, seemingly set on pleasing Eric no matter what.

"This place needs lots of money," Eric was saying, kicking dirt with his feet as if he were about to take off. "The minute I turn my aunt into a dead broad and grab her bread," he grinned at Paul who dropped to his knees to snap pictures of the cat, "I'll fix the place up."

A grungy looking white man with a face as crumpled as his shirt ambled into the courtyard with a rifle slung over his shoulder. He jerked his head in the direction he'd come from and Eric, excusing himself, hurried after him.

"Rhum agricole," a voice announced. We all turned around to see a small black man sitting on a high stool, behind a frail contraption that was gluing labels on full bottles. Both he and the machine seemed to be vestiges of another century. I recognized him by his French sailor's hat, the same man who had knocked his cane against a palm tree and greeted Lundi and me with a bow from underneath a *flamboyant* tree.

"We seem to keep running into each other," I said in French. Up close his lined face reminded me of the bark of an oak. It had the same resilience.

He ignored me. *"Rhum agricole,* that is what we produce here," he said in French. I translated.

"It has nothing to do with the rum you buy in other countries. This is the best. Direct from the sugar cane juice. What you are used to drinking comes from molasses which is a residue. Terrible." He spit on the ground. "Your rum is worse than water. Our rum gives our women the softness of their bosom, and our men the strength of their loins."

The old man gripped a bottle and shook it in the air, the tendons of his hands sticking out like roots. "We fill four thousand bottles an hour." The label was white with SOLEIL spelled out in yellow letters, the *O* replaced by a childlike drawing of a pink and orange madras sun.

"The drawing of the sun is pretty," I told him, picking up a bottle with a fresh label. "It reminds me of Coco's sign on his truck."

"My son drew that when he was three years old," he said, his dark forehead furrowing with some unhappy thought as he twisted the cap off the bottle. He offered it first to Paul, who had asked to take his picture and been refused.

"I do the honors around here, Pops," Eric said, striding in and whisking the bottle out of the old man's hand. "This place is mine, remember?" Eric shouted in his face. *"C'est à moi,* okay?" The old man bent down over his labeling contraption and fed it bottles of rum from a crate by his side.

"Don't mind him, he likes to yak," Eric said, breaking away. "They call him *La Bouche,* the mouth. That's 'cause he's always filling kids with a bunch of fairy tales."

"Papa La Bouche, conteur," the man said, straightening up and wagging the red pom-pom of his hat. "Storyteller," he managed in slow English syllables.

Ellen thanked him for telling us about rum-making and wished she spoke French. "I love fairy tales," she said.

Papa cupped her chin with his gnarled hand. *"Tu es belle,"* he said. *"Tu es une belle princesse."* Ellen frowned and stepped out of his reach. I'd have given Papa a loud smooch on his brow for calling me beautiful. Fat chance he'd do that, Simona, or as we say back in Italia: *col cavolo!* With cabbage!

"Why did that guy have a rifle?" Paul asked, his face suddenly cleared of its morning cloud. He was almost smiling. I had no idea what had done the trick.

"Goddamn raccoons. Caught one once tippin'

58

straight from the rum bottle. Would you believe it? Alcoholic coons!" Eric waved to Ellen and walked to a small cinderblock construction next to the entrance. "Hon, come 'ere. I wanna show you somethin'."

Nick, HM, and Jerry started wiggling by the van, as if they all had urgent bathroom calls.

"Go on ahead to the Club," Paul told them with a lift of his chin. "If that's all right with you," he added, turning to me as an afterthought. The crew had already jumped in the van.

"I'd like to go with them," I said under my breath as the van took off in a cloud of dust and ruffled hens. "But I'm not leaving Ellen here."

"I can take care of her," Paul said.

"I'm sure you can, but I'm the one responsible."

His bad mood settled back. I thought I'd finally put my finger on the problem. He didn't like being bossed by a woman. I wasn't used to the number one spot myself, and I was treading softly for my sake as well as his. Anyway, we were both bound to be nervous. This was his first big ad campaign for a major client. If he did this one right, his career would take off. If I did this one wrong, the only thing that would take off was my head.

We followed Eric and Ellen into a small office that hadn't seen a wet sponge in years. On one side was a long shelf filled with different types of rum: *rhum agricole,* banana punch, lime and orange punch, even a sparkling rum.

"This is the *bureau de dégustation,*" Eric said proudly, "where my clients taste the stuff."

Bureau de disgusting was more like it. Piles of old magazines sat under the only window; *Penthouse, Playboy, Soldier of Fortune, Adventure Life,* slid over each other and slipped to the floor as the wooden boards shook under our footsteps. Eric grinned at

59

Ellen who was staring at one very round, naked rear end on the front cover of *Penthouse*.

"Don't like to throw anything away," he said.

"I thought a soldier liked to stay light and keep moving," Paul said, closing the offending magazine with a kick. Under that brood, he wasn't a bad man after all.

"Those wandering days are gone, aren't they, Eric?" Ellen asked, dropping down on an old wicker armchair, her back straight up. I didn't know if that was her ballet training or pain from those bruises. "You look so settled here."

"Are you okay?" I asked her under my breath. She sat up straighter.

"I stay where there's money," Eric said, reaching up on the wall behind a wooden desk that had been painted green, matching the tall grass outside the window. "Look at this, my new label." He showed us a watercolor of a purple and fuchsia label with elaborate gold palm fronds spelling KANZER, Eric's last name. It was ugly compared to the simplicity of the original SOLEIL label. The frame was lovely: a thirteen by eleven inch silver frame exquisitely carved with highly stylized leaves, now almost black with tarnish except where fingers had repeatedly touched it.

"Paid an artist in Key West a lot of bucks for that. The minute that new money comes in, I'm gonna have four thousand bottles of rum with a gold KANZER plastered over 'em. Can you believe it? Me, an entrepreneur!" He shook that narrow, hairy head of his in what I guess was supposed to be amazement. I thought his eyes rattled like dice.

"Where'd you get this wonderful frame?" I said. My fingers were itching to take it and polish it back to its original beauty. It belonged in the warmth of a loving home.

"An old job I did. Great label, huh?"

"You will be dead before you change my son's label," the old man shouted from his perch across the courtyard.

Eric leaned out of the open door. "Shut up, you old crow. If you wanted the place for your shitfaced son, you shoulda kept your hands outta your pocket."

"God, he's awful," I said in a low voice.

"I'll be right back," Paul said, looking out the window as if he'd just caught sight of the picture of the year. He pushed himself out of the door, knocking against Eric's shoulder.

"Eric's not a bad man," Ellen said, looking up at me with her earnest, lovely face. "It's anger, can't you see that? Those five years of that jungle must have been a nightmare. We can't just turn our backs. No one deserves to be given up on."

I wanted to start a you-don't-have-a-mission-to-save-rabid-strays lecture, but Eric had come back in, slamming the door, shutting out any breeze. I turned my back to them, feeling odd man out. I had no proof that he was connected to Iguana's death, and he *had* been through an awful war, but nothing justified bad-mouthing a dead woman and humiliating an old man. And I was getting annoyed at Ellen for making me feel unforgiving.

As Eric rambled on about his new label and the artist he met in a bar in Key West, I went over to the window splattered with dust from yesterday's rain. I missed the solidity of Beaujoie: his looming presence, his reassuringly soft voice, and the handkerchief waving over his face as if in sign of peace. I wanted to hear what he had to say about Iguana, about Lundi, about Ellen being hit with rocks. I wanted him to explain things away, make them good again.

Paul was outside, standing at a corner of the

building. I could only see a long, muscular tanned leg, part of his white shorts, the Pentax resting on one haunch. His elbow was moving as if he were talking to someone. I pressed my nose against the glass, my curiosity taking over as usual. I couldn't see more of him or who was with him so I tried to stick my head between the louvered panes.

"It's hot," I said, in case anyone was watching. My head is too big to fit between anything, but Paul, as if to oblige me, leaned back on his heels. His shoulder came into view, and as he moved I saw the butt end of a rifle. What on earth did those two have to talk about? Shooting raccoons?

"A cock fight. That's where I'm taking you tonight," Eric was saying, opening the door to his office again. I turned around and watched the draft lift the covers of the magazines on the floor. One lapped at my calf. "A cock fight where rum distilleries are lost and won."

"Great idea," I said. "We'll all come."

Eric got on his knees in front of Ellen, ignoring me.

"Hope you don't mind my sayin' so, hon, you're gorgeous but your feet, someone musta closed the garage door on 'em. They are some ugly."

"Toe shoes." Ellen raised her sandaled feet under his nose and laughed. "I'm so proud of them. I love ugly."

I walked out. Three hundred thousand dollars a year because of her beauty and she loved "ugly." Suddenly I needed gulps of sane air.

"Don't believe that *missié,*" Papa La Bouche said, using the Creole equivalent of "Mister." He was standing by the wooden gate at the entrance now and pointing an arthritic finger at the office. "That *missié* is bad. He lies. Le Soleil is my company, my father's, his father before him." He spoke in French slowly, whether for my benefit or because what he was saying pained him, I couldn't tell.

"We were freed in 1848, fifteen years before democratic America freed her slaves, and my grandfather, a young man then, called our freedom 'the sun after a long night.' He worked hard, and when he had enough to own his own distillery, he called it Le Soleil." Papa reached for a cane that hung from one of the planks of the gate. "Kanzer rum!" He spit an inch from his shoe. "This distillery will be my son's one day. He will forget the politics and claim his property before there is none left."

"Coco?" I said.

"Fabien. His mother, God rest her soul," he crossed himself with the hook of his cane, "his mother and I christened him Fabien. Coco is the name of his foolishness, scurrying up a tree like a monkey, flinging his *sabe* to show off to all the naked white women below, making no money. And those claws he ties to his ankles! It is shameful!" His anger had built with each word, reddening his eyes, shriveling his face until it looked like the hard pit of a bitter fruit. "We have always climbed those palms barefoot!"

"Last night a *sabe* split a woman's head in two," I said.

"With my son's name engraved on the handle. I know. The police have questioned him all night long."

And released him just in time so he could knock Eric down on the street.

"Did Coco know Iguana?" I said, my mouth drying out. I had not seen Coco's name engraved on the machete handle; I had only seen blood.

"Ah, no, do not look to my son for that white woman's death. Go to the Club. It was there the *sabe* was stolen. From my son's truck. Yesterday I turned my back and it was gone. Why did the thief not also take the claws? Then my son would have to do his Coco show barefoot. At least that would be something to

63

see." He turned his head away from me, waving at the Club Med bus that had just driven up. The door opened and Manou jumped out with another woman G.O.

"Papa la Bouche!" they cried out in unison. "The whole world is thirsty. *Où est le rhum?*"

Papa laughed and waved his cane, all his anger gone in front of this bus load of tourists pouring into the distillery. He was playing host again.

"Once upon a time," he began in French, slowly walking toward the women with the help of his cane, "there were two beauties who came to a sunny isle . . ."

I watched as the old man left the shade of the corrugated tin overhang, his bow legs lifting with the quick, jerky rhythm of a puppet being pulled by the knee strings. My stomach hollowed out as the sight of last night came back: the shimmering water in the nudists' cove, the row of windsurfers' sails flapping in the breeze, the creaking cry of the tree frogs, the smell of salty, damp warmth, Lundi's sleeping weight against my hip, a thicket of trees at the edge of the beach and a man walking. It was a moment—ice cold in my memory—a moment in which an old man walked away and a woman lay dead under a steely blue shroud.

SEVEN

I phoned Beaujoie as soon as I got back to the Club, but he still wasn't back. "Tell him I have new information regarding last night's murder." That would get his attention.

Now we were walking to Sainte-Anne at a fast clip. Bob and Nick were ahead, way ahead, jogging their muscular legs off. I was waddling behind with Ellen keeping me company out of the kindness of her heart. There had been no five o'clock high impact aerobics because of Olympic Day, but once Bob and his white team had won, he'd offered Nick and Ellen a two-mile jog to Sainte-Anne and back. I had been lying in the sand, drowsily listening to the end of Vivaldi's *The Four Seasons* and wondering why Beaujoie, Zaza, and Iguana's other beach-vendor buddies had all disappeared when Nick handed me my gym shoes and insisted I needed to sweat it out, not bothering to specify the "it." I had assumed she meant the ordeal of discovering Iguana. Now that my feet burned each time they hit the asphalt, and my lungs were about to shatter into shards, I decided the "it" included my steak, *pommes frites,* and a three-foot baguette lunch together with all the lunches, dinners, breakfasts, and snacks I'd consumed in the past four months.

Ellen, undulating next to me on shoulder-high legs, for some reason looked as bad as I felt.

"Does your back hurt?"

She shook her head. "Sometimes I wonder why the locals don't hate us for taking over their paradise." Her voice came out in even, calm tones, as if she were sitting in a living room sipping tea.

Maybe they do, I thought, too out of breath for sustained conversation. The image of Coco had slipped in front of my eyes, smashing his fist into Eric's chin.

"Don't get too close to Eric," I managed to say between huffs.

"I can take care of myself." Ellen lifted herself up on the balls of her feet and started to jog. Trying to keep up, I started wavering.

"You can't give up," Ellen called out with a backward glance. "Slow up, but don't stop." She was running just ahead of me, her every movement floating through the darkening air. "You'll never forgive yourself if you stop."

I slowed to window-shopping speed, although there were no shops to look at, just flat grazing land to my left, with the usual assortment of semistricken trees and farm animals tethered to spikes hammered into the ground. On my right, a graying ocean churned up long, mellow waves.

I wasn't going to stop although every bone, muscle, vein, and vessel was begging me to. It had nothing to do with not forgiving myself. I was afraid I'd miss something just up ahead. After six years of marriage, I'd gotten the urge to explore and learn, above all about people and what makes them act in ways that are not immediately clear. I was hoping, I think, never to be caught unaware; never again to discover that my best friend was really my husband's best bed partner. I

66

wanted to understand, to be able to say, "Ah yes, of course, A did this to B, therefore B does this to C. How perfectly logical." I wanted finally to learn an algebra of life. I had broken off my relationship with Greenhouse back in New York when I couldn't understand his motives for holding me at bay, when I couldn't measure how much I cared for him once he was out of my bed. I was confused then and obviously still hadn't caught on much. Not if I needed to eat myself twenty pounds over my decent weight limit. But I wasn't going to stop trying to understand, just as I wasn't going to stop myself from seeing Sainte-Anne or shambling after the Muscled Three.

Inhaling the breeze that was now blowing in my face, I let my body relax and lengthened my stride again, picking up a little speed. I watched Ellen catch up with Bob and Nick, her dark hair bobbing from side to side, brushing the back of her long neck. Bob and Ellen were beautifully matched, with their contrasting coloring: her almost black hair next to his blond head, her first-day-at-the-beach pale skin side by side his tan. "Handsome specimens" Paul had called them with an ironic tone, as he looked at them through the eye of his camera. He'd asked Bob to model with Ellen at Carbet Falls this coming Friday.

Nick, as if she knew she didn't fit, slowed her pace to let them distance themselves. With her cropped hair, broad shoulders, and muscular legs, anyone would have mistaken her for a gangly boy from the back. Did she resent her masculine looks or did she resent being a woman?

There I was, sticking my nose into other people's business again. Part of the "understanding," I told myself. "Long Roman nose," Greenhouse had decreed the last time I had gotten involved in a murder. The thought of him made me smile. What would the great homicide detective say now that I had another murder literally at my feet? In exotic Guadeloupe no less.

"Stay out of it," that's what he'd say, hating for me to horn in on police work, maybe even worried I might get hurt.

I couldn't do that. I had found her. In a way her death belonged to me. She had trusted me with her son. It was a covenant we had shared. I knew I was being dramatic; I tend to fly off into these operatic states of mind whenever I want to bend things my way. Maybe I was simply itching to look at another person's life again, at the pieces that led to her death. Who? Why? Had she doomed herself? Had she just been in the wrong place at the wrong time, an unwilling witness to some other misdeed, the way I had stumbled into my Rome apartment three hours early to find husband and best friend in bed? Or did someone hate her enough to crack her skull open even though her baby was waiting for her only half a mile away? What operatic degrees of emotions were at work in this case?

Bob had dropped back again. "Come on, slowpoke," he said to Nick, who lagged behind. "Get a move on."

To me, she was going at the speed of a Ferrari.

"Just because you won the Olympics for my team gives you no right to rest now." Bob turned back to me. "Nick's fantastic. We were losing by twenty points when she came in at noon." How he could talk and jog at the same time I couldn't begin to understand.

"She won in archery and rammed that volleyball down the Red Team's throat. It was great." He punched a thumb in the air. "She was the best guy on the team." Bob gave me a California happiness smile that warmed my insides. I couldn't help being so blatantly horny. It had been a long time, and he looked better than a buttered baguette.

"Are you okay?" Bob asked.

"My body is singing happiness. I'm drenched not with sweat, but with tears of joy. Great idea, Bob. Next time I'll lock myself up in my room."

We had reached the outskirts of town by now. Small shops appeared in two-story buildings that had none of the charm of the old quarter in Pointe-à-Pitre, probably because the town had been completely destroyed in the 1938 hurricane. Most of the buildings were made of unadorned concrete or cinderblocks, and the shops offered none of the colorful variety I had seen in Rue Frébault. One dark, cavelike place offered a thick smell of grease and LOVE BURGERS that came with a Paris trademark.

"Leave it to the French to come up with that, huh?" Bob said, walking beside me now and putting an arm around my waist. I must have looked as if I were about to collapse, which I was. It was nice of him, I thought, noticing that I now felt even hotter than before. Ellen had also slowed to a walk, but Nick kept running, faster than before, as if a wind were pushing against her wide back.

"Look at her," Bob said, letting me go. "She's something, isn't she?" I looked up at him sharply. He was hooked. It was clear by the soft sound of his voice, by the look of awe in his face. Boyish, loose-gaited Nick was Bob's choice.

I laughed with embarrassment, selfish disappointment, even relief. Bob was out of my reach. I could once again direct all my sexual thoughts back to Greenhouse in far away New York City. Safer, at least. I watched Nick's graceful run and wondered if she knew how Bob felt, whether she cared.

"Hullo, Nick," a man called out, leaning out of a shop doorway a few yards in front of us. Nick kept running as if she hadn't heard.

"You can't run from your old friends, love," the man

shouted with a strong English accent. "It just won't do."

Nick had stopped now and turned around, working her feet up and down like the paws of a sucking kitten. Sweat dropped from her chin. Without coming closer, she made a rolling motion with her hand, as if to say, "Later." Then she spun on the balls of her feet and took off again, swinging down a side street.

The Englishman looked disappointed and stepped back into his shop. Wiping my face dry with an arm, I followed him. The itch in my long Roman nose was unbearable. Ellen and Bob kept on in a slow jog.

"What a wonderful place," I said, looking around at rows and rows of shelves crammed with old and new books in a space not much larger than my room at the Club.

"Hm," the man answered, as if I had stated the obvious. He was bone thin, with elegant pleated slacks and a peony pink polo shirt, and I imagined him more at home in the West End of London or in Soho in New York than in Sainte-Anne. The store was also incongruous, stuffed as it was with books in all languages. Very few tourist books. A lot of art books; one on the Sicilian Baroque by Anthony Blunt that I knew had been out of print for years.

"Do you own the shop?" I asked, fingering a Roberto Olivieri mystery I hadn't read.

"Yes." He was riffling pages of a telephone directory and not being friendly, which made it harder for me not to appear like a snoop.

"I'm working with Nick," I offered, pretending to scan Olivieri's dust jacket. "We're staying at the Club."

"Super gal," he said, finally looking up with a wan smile. "I'm glad to see she's back. Do tell her to stop by."

Back? So they had met here. Why hadn't Nick

70

mentioned she'd been here before?

"Will you be wanting that book?"

"I have no money with me," I said, hitting my hips to show the absence of crackling paper and jingling coins. For how long had he known her? How long ago? Months? Years?

He took the book out of my hand, and polished it with a cloth as if I had germs.

"Very well, I'll put it aside for a few days, shall I? Not much call for Italian mysteries right now. There've been mostly Canadian and Métro tourists of late." He set the book down on a shelf under his desk, and then looked up with a polite face that had adored the sun too long. His skin reminded me of burlap steeped in dark tea.

"Perhaps Nicoletta can pick it up for you."

"Nicoletta?"

"Nick. Nicoletta I like to call her."

Did I dare stick my Roman nose into Nick's life and ask him for more information? I had no valid reason for it.

"I'm afraid I have to close now," the Englishman said, walking to the door to hold it open like a tired host at the end of a dinner party.

"Sorry. I'll give Nick your message. And thanks for holding the book. One of us will pick it up." As I left the shop I glanced above the doorway, hoping to find his name as part of the store sign. Something like Bob Grey's Books or Chris Markland's Book Shoppe. All I got was the anonymous LIVRES.

After fifty yards or so I turned back to see two tourists walk in. He hadn't closed the store after all.

Ellen and Bob were waiting for me up ahead, both of them leaning against a wall, arms spread out above them. They looked as if they were about to be frisked by the police, but they were only stretching their calves,

71

pushing the heels of their feet into the sidewalk. The tendons of Bob's ankle were as taut as rubber bands about to tear. Nick was nowhere to be seen.

"You are very courageous," a familiar voice said in a lilting French. I turned to see Beaujoie overflowing from the driver's seat of a blue Renault 5, a car that by old American standards could comfortably seat only two ten-year-olds as long as they weren't on the basketball team.

"You got my message!" I said, leaning down, ready to pour all my doubts in his ear. "Papa La Bouche, he was there on the . . ."

"I know, I know," he said, a patient smile on his face. The steering wheel was propped on his stomach like a book he was reading.

"Why am I courageous?" I asked, only slightly annoyed.

"You risk exhaustion, I am sure. May I offer you a 'ti' punch by the beach for your effort?" He reached out a hefty arm and opened the car door on the passenger side.

I slipped in gratefully. "How's the boy?"

Before he could answer, he stopped the car in front of Bob and Ellen.

"I take your friend," Beaujoie told Bob in slow English. Bob frowned, then gave me a weird look, as though he was scared.

"It's all right, I'm not being arrested," I said, guessing he had recognized Beaujoie. Bob plastered a smile on his face.

"Have fun," he said, for the first time sounding as if he didn't mean it.

"Don't forget the rehearsal," Ellen added. In a moment of Club Med enthusiasm, we had both signed up for the G.M. show that was being put on tomorrow night. I was due for rehearsal at seven. It was now five of six. I had plenty of time.

Beaujoie swooped back into traffic without bothering to look first. Behind us, brakes screeched, but to my surprise no one honked. That blue Renault was known.

"You are the real danger," I said in French, when he finally braked the car one inch from a large wooden sign that read A CLEAN COMMUNITY = HAPPINESS AND LOVE OF LIFE. The five-minute ride over to this public beach had been hair-raising, with Beaujoie weaving in and out of traffic at top speed like some twelve-year-old Roman on his first drive. I got out of my seat on shaky legs.

"I always wanted to run the Grand Prix," he said, setting his round face on me with a smile as he maneuvered himself out deftly. "I drive well."

I didn't argue. "How's Lundi?"

Beaujoie stood with legs spread apart, looking out at the smokey ocean with an expression of love and awe, as if it were his first time.

"His name is Marcel," he said.

Hearing Lundi's real name made him a stranger. I didn't like that.

"He is well. He does not know—how can he know at that age?—that maman will not come back. For now he is well." The look of love and awe changed to sadness.

"Is he still with your wife?"

"No, no." His handkerchief appeared and he wiped his perfectly dry face. "Sometimes it is bad to hold what you cannot keep, do you not find?"

Yes, I did find. Sometimes I thought I'd stopped seeing Greenhouse on a hunch the man was not for keeps.

"How did you know about Papa La Bouche?"

"He came to see me this morning, when he heard I was questioning Coco. He told me about seeing you with the boy pacing the beach last night." He spoke reluctantly, as if his mind were miles away. "Papa also confirmed the theft of the *sabe* yesterday after Coco harvested the coconuts at the Club."

"A father would defend a son. Did you hear about Coco knocking Eric Kanzer down this morning in the middle of the street?"

"Ah, yes, the American Vietnam hero. All of the Antilles has heard." There was a hint of a smile on his face that he removed with a shake of his head. "Coco and Iguana were good friends. He is not our man. Five of his companions have sworn he was with them the evening long."

That's when I told him about Ellen and the rocks that bull's-eyed between her shoulder blades. "I was wondering if it was connected with Iguana's death."

"It comes easy to create links that satisfy us into thinking we have a tied-up package. The murderer is on the bluff, throwing rocks at a beautiful young lady. Why?" He both spoke and walked slowly, as if following the tired rhythm of the waves seeping up the sloping bank of sand.

"The bluff is two kilometers from where Mademoiselle Verdin was found," he said. "How do they connect?"

"Verdin?" There were so many changing names. I took my sneakers off and let the sand, as pale and fine as face powder, slither between my toes.

"Lucille Verdin, born in le Cateau, a small town near the Belgian border. A cold town, I would say. The cold brought her to the Antilles three years ago. Once here Lucille became Iguana. The long ponytail down her back was like the crest of the iguana. That is how her friends explain the nickname."

"She had a tattoo," I said.

"Yes, a tattoo," he confirmed, not at all surprised I knew. "Despite the dragonlike appearance, iguanas are

74

timid, defenseless animals. A protected species now."

We had reached a wooden shack no bigger than the hot dog stands on the street corners of New York. A teenage girl, her face carefully covered with feathery streaks of blue and green makeup, curtsied when she saw us. On top of her tight rows of braids, she wore a yellow satin cap pointed at one end like a beak. She was like a girl from a fairy tale, caught in the magical moment of turning into a parrot.

"Martine, you have fun with the Carnival?" Beaujoie asked. He put some money on the counter.

"I love to dance," Martine said, dropping below the counter in one fast motion, as if she were part of a puppet show.

"My friends think Ellen got hit by kids high on Carnival."

"Perhaps." Beaujoie looked at the sky. "It is almost the full moon, the bluff is secluded. There are bushes, soft sand. Perhaps Mademoiselle Ellen interrupted . . ." he stopped when Martine bobbed back up, clutching an enormous mason jar half-filled with pieces of fruit floating in an amber liquid. Using a soup ladle, she quickly filled two paper cups, making sure we each got a piece of fruit.

"*Carambole*," Martine said, looking at me. I didn't understand.

"*Carambole* is the name of the fruit," Beaujoie said. "Many different fruits can be used for a 'ti' punch. Lime, passion fruit, coconut. Martine always gives me *carambole*. It means car crash."

I looked back at the toylike Renault and thought Martine very clever.

We made our way to the edge of the water with our paper cups. Beaujoie drank and closed his eyes with pleasure. I took a tentative sip. The drink burned, the strength of the rum barely masked by the sweetness of the fruit. I went for a longer sip and chewed my slippery piece of *carambole*.

"Délicieux, n'est-ce pas?" he said. "Martine's mother makes her own. The best 'ti' punch on all the islands. I have tried them all."

"What's 'ti' mean?" The first time I'd heard a G.O. mention a "ti" punch, I'd thought of a nice cup of English tea laced with rum. After all, the English had conquered Guadeloupe from the French at least three times, although they never managed to hold it for very long.

"A lazy way of saying *petit*. Small," he said in halting English. "The sun drains the energy. So does the rum."

I was with him there. "What were you going to say about Ellen back there?" I asked, careful not to slur. That drink was making my bones feel as though they'd sopped up liters of heavy liquid.

"Lovemaking is what I believe your Ellen stumbled onto." He looked inside his now empty paper cup, starkly white in his black hand, regret on his face— maybe for the rum he'd swallowed too quickly, for sexual urges gone by, for time past. It was hard to tell his age—somewhere in the late fifties, early sixties. There were gray specks on what little hair he had left, as if he'd sprinkled himself with ashes. He had the sad, kind look of a penitent, too. Or maybe I was letting the rum and the darkening sky turn up my melancholy dial.

"I am sorry she was welcomed so ungraciously," Beaujoie said. "I hope it was not too painful." He crushed the empty cup and slipped it into his pocket.

"Bruises, a little blood. She won't say how much it hurts."

Beaujoie turned to me. "I need to ask one more question. Then you must promise me to forget this death."

76

"I'll answer if you'll answer." I wasn't going to make any promises.

"I cannot answer questions about my suspicions. We are investigating, that is enough."

"No, it's not enough. I found her. That gives me some rights in my opinion. Was she killed on the beach where I found her? You're not going to risk anything by telling me that."

"A few feet back, behind the trees, where it was harder to be seen. In the underbrush we found blood. He then dragged her under the sail and covered his tracks by wiping the sand with a leaf, a hand, it is hard to tell."

"He?"

"It could be a woman," Beaujoie said. "The blow was strong, but not impossible for the muscles the woman of today seems to have." His tone was disapproving.

"Why not leave her lying in the underbrush?" I asked.

"Who can understand? Perhaps he felt the need for a shroud." We walked a little closer to the water. The damp sand was smoothly compact.

"We are left with no fingerprints, no clues," Beaujoie said, watching his own prints being washed away.

"When was she killed?"

"Between nine-thirty and ten-fifteen when Papa La Bouche came to the cove."

I had reached the cove at ten-thirty.

"Last night, did you tell many people when and where you were meeting the girl?" The words came out in a casual mumble, as if Beaujoie were too distracted to care. He kept his face set on the ocean and the sky, both almost equally dark now except for a patch of fading light over the clouds to the west.

"Pardon?" I said, not understanding. He repeated the question and I felt a whiplash of adrenaline.

77

"Is someone at the Club involved?"

He waited, without an added word. The light shrank to nothing, and we were left in the dark. My face felt wet from the heavy damp air, from a small fear that was weaving itself through my ribs.

"I told my table," I said, recalling how the conversation had changed when I went back to the gazebo. Paul asked Eric questions about Danang and whether he knew what "Lurps" meant.

"Long-range recon patrollers," Eric answered with his ugly laugh. "They'd smear black grease on their faces, swallow a fistful of pills to get that extra kick that can save your life in a tight spot, and creep up to VC bases at night." Paul looked surprised by his answer.

"What is this, some kinda test?" Eric asked.

Paul had looked up and noticed me. "What did she have to say for herself?" I had mentioned the appointment and left, needing to change Lundi.

"Who was at your table?" Beaujoie asked, keeping his casual tone.

"Paul, Ellen, Nick, Eric. Have you looked into Eric?" Beaujoie said nothing, but I could hear his breathing, heavy and slow as if it was difficult for air to chug through his weight and height.

"Bob was wandering around our gazebo recruiting for Olympic Day. I don't know if he heard me. And there was Tommy, too." Tommy who had whispered to me that Paul didn't like Eric, as though it wasn't blatant. "Tommy Boyle. He's a sweet, nerdy guy, who follows Ellen around like a stray. There were three other tables at that gazebo, but I didn't notice who was sitting there. Mothers and fathers with children and lots of ice cream being eaten. They might have overheard. Is it important?"

"To kill her, someone had to know where she would be."

"She could have had an appointment," I said. "Iguana was determined to do something or meet someone last night. She spoke of finally having courage." To do what?

"It is time to go," Beaujoie said with audible regret. He turned slowly as if he were unwilling to let go of that ocean sight. "You have a rehearsal."

"You will tell me what you find out about the murder?" I said, when we reached the car, brushing my feet free of sand. Across the street a neon sign—LE COQUILLAGE—blinked on, dropping garish yellow on Beaujoie's face as if it were the pollen of some giant lily.

"You are a young, attractive lady. Why do you wish to mix yourself up with violent death?"

"It comforts me to know that if I work hard enough, I can come up with solutions."

"I see." Beaujoie unlocked the car door on the passenger side and held it open for me. It had been a long time since I'd seen that. "Like the sign here above the garbage can," he said. "Cleanliness equals health and love of life. You wish to follow the cleanup."

I laughed as an image of me with a broom popped in my head. "I usually wish to do the cleanup myself."

EIGHT

At the Club entrance a guard raised a hand to salute Beaujoie and went to lift the gate.

Beaujoie drove in. On each side of us, scattered beneath the palm trees, white wrought-iron street lamps held frosted balls of glass that looked like glazed coconuts. Their light streamed into our laps.

"You have been involved with murder before?" Beaujoie asked, as he parked the car next to a huge plow painted black.

"Twice. Does that make me a suspect?"

He squeezed out of the car. I got out before he had a chance to open the door for me. He looked disappointed, and the signature handkerchief popped out of his pocket again, staying bunched up in his hand like an unwanted letter.

"Independent, curious," he said, examining me under the lights. "With a need for cleanliness."

"My studio apartment's a mess, I stain my clothes just by looking at them, I'm totally dependent on friendship, but you got one thing right—I can be annoyingly curious."

I overheard the radio in the guard room announce the arrival of sixty-five children from the Parisian suburbs to learn skin diving on Guadeloupe.

"Does the boy have a father in France? Relatives?" I asked, my rum-sloshed imagination picturing him pale and shivering, his tan washed away by a freezing winter rain. "Will he be sent back?"

"We have traced the grandmother. She is anxiously waiting for the boy." He didn't sound happy, and I was sure that his short contact with Lundi had left him hooked, too. "A nice woman on the telephone," he added. "The boy was born here. He will miss the sun."

"Any idea who the father is?"

Beaujoie glanced at his watch. "You must hurry now. You are late for your rehearsal. Tomorrow night I shall come see you perform. And do not worry about Mademoiselle Ellen. Your friends are in no danger. There are no connections. *Au revoir, Mademoiselle Simona.*" He waved me away.

Low strains of *Swan Lake* drifted our way from the theater. I started running; the next number was mine.

Just before turning into the main building, I saw Beaujoie still standing in the driveway, his feet planted wide. His lips, open in a wide grin, shone pink like the inside of a conch. I waved, liking his paternal, comforting warmth, his underlying sadness. My friends are in no danger, I repeated to myself. There are no connections.

Nick was waiting for me backstage with the costume she'd helped put together. It was a gray velvet flapper dress that barely made it over my hips. Ellen, her bruises covered by the netting of her bodice, danced across the stage in a white tutu and toe shoes. A Lawrence Taylor look-alike from Washington, D.C.

followed her around in a black tutu, the black flippers on his feet thwacking on the floorboards as he mimicked her ballet steps with the grace of a Frankenstein. Everyone was in stitches, me included. Then I remembered Iguana and stopped.

"Nick, I can't go out on stage wearing this," I whispered when I finally noticed that the hem of my costume came within six inches of my groin. I'm by no means a prude but I had to do the Charleston in that dress, and I didn't particularly want six hundred people to be aware that my thighs overlapped.

"Be patient," Nick said, just as the Club photographer sneaked by and immortalized me with a blinding click of his flash.

"I'll sue," I yelled at him, which got me a cynical Gallic laugh in response. *Swan Lake* blended into *Black Bottom,* and Nick gave me a push onto the stage. Two other women and I started to do our number, wiggling our asses, winking one eye at the black void of seats in front of us, circling a hand as if we were washing windows. I didn't feel much like prancing but Nick had said, "busy is good when you're upset."

She was right. I was having fun. I forgot what I looked like, remembered to keep the count so that we would flap our legs out together; slap our uplifted feet with a resounding whack; twirl around, shaking our head plumes; cross our arms to open and close our knees. On one side of the stage Nick looked on with a satisfied grin on her face. Her dresses were holding up under the strain of wobbling flesh. On the other side, Tommy, in clown face, grinned at me, punching the air with his thumb. The music was ending. The three of us turned to the left, stuck a hip out at the imaginary audience, repeated the gesture on the other side, this time throwing our arms up triumphantly on the last note. We skipped off stage to scattered applause and a "bravo" from the G.O. director.

"You look like you enjoyed that," Paul said backstage as I walked by on my way to change behind a curtain. Nick handed me a welcome towel.

"It was great," I said, wiping my face. Nick picked up discarded costumes and walked away.

"A good release," Paul said. I looked back at him, surprised at his understanding. He wore his usual brooding expression. Was he sad, angry, nervous?

I tried a smile on him. It didn't work. What the hell, maybe he was lonely, too. I got behind the curtain and inched out of my dress.

After putting on my shorts and T-shirt, I walked out next to Paul. "What did everybody do last night after I left?"

"What do you mean?" he whispered. HM and Jerry were on stage now, doing a mime act called *Les Rues de Paris*—Parisian streets—with the Club's entertainer playing a rake. Jerry, thin and small, played a lady of the night dressed in mesh stockings, a short red skirt, gold high heels, a gold blouse with enormous false breasts. A blond curly wig sat askew on his head.

"When I came back down last night I looked for you guys, but I couldn't see anything," I whispered back. "The theater was too dark."

"I went to my room. I don't know what the others did. What did that cop want?"

"More questions about what Iguana had said." Yves Montand, in his gravelly, sexy voice was singing "A Paris" on the tape deck.

"That's all?"

"That's all." Why did Paul care?

HM lumbered across the stage like a zombie, dressed in a French policeman's uniform, his eyebrows blackened and a huge handlebar mustache glued on his face. He rolled his eyes and twirled his night stick

83

with great menace.

I thought I saw a flicker of a smile on Paul's face. The rake, unaware of the policeman's presence, stretched his hand behind his back in search of Jerry's derriere. Seeing those wiggling octopus fingers, Jerry quickly removed one of his foam rubber breasts and stuffed it in the rake's hand. Paul started laughing and didn't stop until the end of the act.

"It's good to see you having fun," I said over the applause of the stagehands and the other G.M.s and G.O.s involved in the show. "You've been very tense in this shoot."

"Eric Kanzer gets me. I'm not going to any damn cock fight tonight with that man." Paul slapped Jerry's back as he ran by. "You make a great whore," he said.

Jerry laughed, fluttering his false eyelashes. "You ought to try me sometime."

"Come on, Paul, let's all go," I said. "Ellen's set on it and I don't want her to go alone." I wasn't going to take any chances after the "rocks" incident.

"What the hell does she see in him?" Paul said. A string of male G.M.s with white clown faces slid on stage from the left wing. Dressed only in a tails jacket and bow tie, each held a top hat over his groin and mouthed the words of the song *Je suis un homme*—"I am a man." Tommy was the third from right, his top hat not large enough to cover his dough-ball belly. I felt a wave of sympathy for a fellow fatty.

"Eric's a first-class creep," Paul said.

"I agree, but he did find us that neat little cove on the northern side of Grande-Terre that no one knew about. You took some great pictures there." Some rushes had been FedExed back to us along with my boss's raves.

"Yeah," Paul said. "That's where those Indians threw themselves off the cliff rather than be enslaved by the white man. Cheerful place. I had to stand on my head to get Ellen to smile."

"Did you ever try smiling first?"

Paul gave me a dirty look. The men on stage, Tommy included, moved very cleverly, removing and replacing their hats fast enough so that we never saw anything indecent. Had it been me out there I would have probably dropped my hat, turned around in shame and then bent down to retrieve it, mooning the audience.

"All the French think about is sex," Paul said with abrupt anger in his voice.

"I think that's narrowing it down a little," I said, trying to make light of it. "You're doing fine, Paul. Our difficult French client is very pleased with your work."

"Janick was *enchanté* with the last photographer who worked for him until he fired him in a New York minute."

"Shhh," someone whispered from the other side of the stage.

I took Paul's arm and dragged him back toward the exit door, which was propped open to let in some air.

"Listen, the last photographer overstepped some boundaries. I'm not free to go into it, but you've got nothing to worry about."

"I know perfectly well what happened. The man dared to fall in love with Ellen, and eight years of good work for Monsieur Janick and the great HH&H got wiped out."

"It wasn't love. It was just a vulgar pass."

"How do you know that? Did you ask him how he felt? Maybe the man didn't know how to say it so he tried to kiss her instead."

"I don't see why you're so worried about it."

"I'm just tired of men being thought of as ogres, being blamed for everything that goes wrong. I tried to pay for dinner once and my date, who'd been wonderful up to that point, gripped my credit card and said, 'Don't expect pussy for free steak.' Another time I tried to adjust the fold of a model's blouse, and she slapped my face. I wasn't even aware I'd touched anything except fabric."

"For every inadvertent touch, there are a hundred right on target," I said, having ridden on many an Italian bus. "Women have had enough."

When I got one of those love pats, I never slapped or got huffy; that gives the jerk too much power. I'd throw myself against him and then innocently call out for all the bus to hear, "I hope the hand you had on my ass didn't get hurt. It would be every woman's loss." I'd even hold the hand up, if he was still anywhere near me. Worked to perfection.

"I understand they've had enough," Paul said, "but it's gotten to the point where I don't dare get near a woman unless she's the first to act. And even then I'm not sure. And with Ellen, I freeze." He looked utterly glum.

"Well, keep freezing," I said, "because your photos are great. It's what got you the job."

That and the fact that Ellen liked him. Janick swore by Ellen, thought she was responsible for his runaway success with the perfume *Free* which she had launched a year ago. *Free* had even hit Moscow three months ago and was outselling Big Macs. Well, almost. Ellen had incredible power which she didn't even realize. Paul knew it and obviously didn't like it.

"Don't give up on women," I said. "You think we're unfair now, we think you've been unfair for centuries. Give it a few more decades and both sexes will find the right balance."

"I'm thirty-two years old. I don't want to wait until I'm an old man."

"You're a great dancer, Simona," Tommy said,

86

walking by still in white face, with a Club Med T-shirt over his chest and a towel wrapped around his plump middle. He was not a monument to elegance. "I'm impressed."

"I just heard about that woman being killed." He hovered over me, his jowly face ghoulish-looking with that white makeup streaked with sweat, red skin showing underneath like a layer of old paint. I couldn't tell if he was genuinely upset for me, or whether he was waiting for details to spread to the uninitiated.

"Was it awful?" he asked. His breath smelled of spearmint. Maybe he was just being sweet.

"It took courage to do that number," I said. At that moment, Nick and Ellen walked past the stage door, already dressed for dinner. Nick was in her usual T-shirt and bermudas and Ellen wore a black stretch skirt with a saffron yellow strapless top. Tommy straightened up with a sharp intake of breath.

"Hey, Ellen!" Paul said. "Where you rushing to?"

Ellen stopped and smiled one of her specials. If she kept that up, there were going to be a lot more holes in the ozone layer. "I thought everyone was already at dinner."

"Forecast says it's going to rain tomorrow," Nick said, sticking a thumb up at the black clouds covering the stars.

"Don't believe it," Bob's voice said. "The sun always shines on Club Med." He walked up behind Paul, looking great in white jeans and a baby-blue polo shirt. His matching blue eyes were so bright they looked washed in ammonia. Tommy had fled.

"Did you see my act?" Ellen asked, still smiling at Paul. She was so lovely I understood why Tommy felt hopeless.

"It was good," Paul said, smiling back.

"Fabulous," Bob boomed for the whole Club to

hear. "No one as beautiful as you has ever been on that stage."

"Come on, Simona," Nick said, now thrusting a thumb in the direction of our room. "Let's go change for dinner."

What the hell for? No one was going to look at us.

NINE

"Eric's taking us to a cockfight," I said, walking out of the shower.

"Not me, he isn't." Nick was throwing her room key up in the air and catching it with a loud slap of hands.

"Come on, Nick, let's stick together. Cockfights are part of the island lore." I wanted us all to go, to diffuse Eric's blather, to create a curtain of bodies around Ellen. He was obsessed with her and I didn't like it. Had he been obsessed with Iguana? Could he have killed her? I thought of Beaujoie and the reassurance I felt in his bearlike presence. He would never leave us exposed to danger.

"Eric's not that bad, is he?" I said. "Sometimes I think he's odious, but I guess Ellen's right. We have to give him points for Vietnam."

"I ignore Eric. His hormones are way up because of her." Nick was sitting on the bed now, kicking a leg against the night table. "I just refuse to see animals being killed. I know I shouldn't care if two dumb animals slash each other to death. And cocks are dumb, let me tell you. They remind me of sorefoot Tommy and Eric and Bob, who see a woman and suddenly their brains turn into peckers.

"I shouldn't care. Not when I love fried chicken. That's the same thing isn't it? The chicken's got to die to fry, but I don't want to think about it. I sure don't want to watch it." Nick slipped her long legs up on the bed and hugged them.

"This ugly memory popped back into my head today." Her eyes widened.

"What memory?"

"A couple got murdered on my block back when I was in high school. They had a mutt that got killed, too. The burglar shot him through the ear and for weeks all I could think of was that black and white mutt. I guess I prefer animals to humans."

"I get that feeling sometimes." My ugly memory was a little more recent and I didn't feel like dwelling on it ever again. I slipped on an extra large T-shirt that came to my knees. Gold letters across my chest commanded, "Kiss me, I'm Italian." No one had taken me up on the offer.

"Come on, Nick, come to the fight and keep me company."

"Sorry, no cockfights for me. And no show. I'm dead after that rehearsal. I got myself a good book from the Club boutique to bore me to sleep."

Nick stretched out on the bed as I quickly applied makeup on skin that after four days in the sun looked like beef jerky. That BEAU SUN cream we were touting wasn't great stuff. From the mirror I could see Nick reach under the night table and hold a glossy book against her face. SNOSIOP LACIPORT.

"Mystery title?" I was thinking of the bookshop owner who knew Nick and the mystery book he was holding for me.

"*Tropical Poisons*. It's a neat book. These islands are full of poisons. I'm surprised Iguana's murderer bothered with cracking her skull. He could have made

90

her drink a brew of oleander leaves."

"I think we'd better go to dinner." I didn't like her macabre humor.

"I don't want dinner and you could use a break from food. Just wait a minute." She was leafing through the book trying to find something. "Here, listen. The Calbasse tree, that's the one with the green fruit that looks like a huge apple—they dry the fruit and make maracas out of them, you know, cha-cha-cha music. Then there's the deadliest of them all, the mancenillier tree."

"Elizabeth is a beautiful name. Why don't you use it?"

Nick looked up, a surprised expression on her face. I don't know what made me say it. Maybe I was annoyed at her for being callous about Iguana's death, for refusing to keep me company.

"I'm sorry, Nick. Lundi took your passport out and I saw the name. And I also don't know why you never mentioned being here before. That English bookshop owner is waiting for you to visit him. He asked me to tell you that."

"Peter's South African, not English. I didn't say anything because I didn't think it was anybody's business." Nick dropped the book on the floor and smiled, as if to make peace. She wasn't a very good faker. Her foot was twitching as if an Energizer battery had made contact in her sneaker.

"I didn't mention I'd been to the Club before because I was afraid Paul would expect me to know places or speak French, and I didn't want to come off as a perfect nerd. I was here on vacation a couple of years ago, that's all. And as for my name . . ." she kept smiling, trying hard to act real friendly. I didn't know what was bothering her: my knowing her real name or discovering she'd been here before.

"An Elizabeth is what Mom wanted—a girl in pink ribbons. I never looked like an Elizabeth, not even in the crib. By the time I was twelve, I was five feet eight and playing center on the guys' basketball team. I told my parents they'd picked the wrong name, so Dad suggested I get a nickname. He offered Liz or Beth. I chose Nick. You know, nick name. When I was fifteen, I was five-eleven with not a bump in sight except for my nose and knees so I knew 'Nick' was right. Mom never got used to it though. She still sews Elizabeth on the labels of the sweaters she sends me from Lincoln."

"What did your father think?"

"He started roughing me up a little, trying to get me to drink beer with him. He liked the idea of having a son. I hated it." The foot stopped twitching and she looked up, her face drained and rather sad. I got the urge to hug her. "Just forget this conversation. All of it. Okay? I really don't like to talk about myself."

"All right, I'll go chew on an oleander leaf for dinner. That's all that's going to be left by now anyway. Are you coming?"

"No, I'm sick of ogling Ellen's gorgeous face along with the rest of them. Oh, shit." She threw herself down on the bed and covered her face with an arm. "I just feel hideous."

"If it's any consolation, so do I," I said, sitting down next to her. "But there's nothing we can do about it. We'll never get those looks, so forget it, I say. Make the most of what you've got," I said, repeating my mother's words. Nick sat up.

"Look who's talking," she said, pinching a good three inches of my waist fat between her fingers. We both laughed. She shoved me off the bed. "Go get some weight down on your feet or you'll topple over."

"And you try some of my makeup and see what that does to Nick's image. You've got great bones, you know."

92

"That's all I've got."

"Like hell it is."

"Yeah, I know," Nick said, falling back down on the bed. "A sweet personality." She mimicked someone else's voice, probably her mother's.

"Where was everyone last night after I left?" I asked, halfway out the door.

"Paul looked pissed off and said he was going to his room. Bob left to present Olympic Day on stage. The rest of us went to the show, except that Ellen left as soon as it started, which meant Eric took off. I got stuck seeing the show by myself."

"What about Tommy?" Something crackled under my sandal. I looked down. Jutting beyond my toes was half of a white envelope with "na Griffo" scribbled on it.

"Tommy went with the wind and you," Nick said. "What did that policeman want? An account of our whereabouts?"

I lifted my foot and found the rest of my name, then picked up the envelope to see what was inside. "Nothing important." A torn piece of newspaper revealed a phone number to which Beaujoie had added, "My home number. In case you need me." I slipped the number in my pocket and saw Nick looking at me quizzically.

"Beaujoie just wanted to go over what Iguana said to me." I felt the back of my neck heat up. Why would I need him?

"How's little Marcel? Is he going to be okay?" Nick was leaning over her knees, untying her sneakers so she didn't catch the look of surprise that must have been on my face. I almost asked her "Marcel who?" but caught myself in time.

Marcel—Lundi's real name. She had pretended not to know him last night. What was she trying to hide?

TEN

"Wait 'til you see the island of Marie-Galante in the morning," Eric said as he drove Ellen, Paul, and me to the cockfight. "It's got a hundred windmills, a real old château, beaches you'll never want to leave. Hey, Paul, bring plenty of film along 'cause your finger's gonna itch to click."

"Thank you for the advice," Paul said through his teeth. "I'll try to remember. Should I also bring the camera?"

Sea green with jealousy. Why else does an intelligent person turn into a moronic eight-year-old? Paul's conversation with me back at the theater now made perfect sense. So did his brooding. Paul was in love with Ellen. Painfully so by the look on his face.

Thank God Greenhouse wasn't here. I'd lose him to Ellen, too. Not that I had him to lose, not that he would have come, not that I should have been thinking of him at all, not that my life . . . oh, never mind. The jeep bounced and shook over the ruts in the road. I felt my ratatouille, mahi mahi, and chocolate mousse dinner whirl into a Cuisinart marvel.

"Hon, you want me to dump this guy overboard or what?" Eric asked. Yeah, along with dinner and my thoughts.

"Let's just go where we have to go, all right," I said. We were just in the right mood for the sight of cock blood.

Eric veered the jeep inland, up a dirt road that curved along the edge of a banana plantation. Crickets and tree frogs had taken over the musical entertainment, and the curtain of clouds flickered open now and then to show a patch of sky that looked like a Diamonds Are Forever ad. Eric swore that the moon was full.

A full moon might explain why everyone was a little off tonight, starting from Nick on down to Eric, who seemed more nervous than usual, not shutting his mouth once for the twenty minute ride, repeating over and over again how he liked action, how he made things happen to stay on the edge.

"What about murder?" I said as the jeep slowed, and my food settled down to a float. "Is that action enough for you?"

"The Italian's funny, isn't she?" Eric asked no one in particular, stopping the car in the middle of a flat stretch of grass.

Eric's headlights picked up the gleam of a few bicycles. Nearby loomed a big truck with wooden railings, its top covered with flapping tarp.

"Nobody's gonna pin Iguana's death on me," Eric said, "no matter how hard that lump of French fried police fat tries. I killed enough gooks to last me."

Beaujoie did suspect him! Was Ellen in danger?

"There are no connections, no connections." I kept repeating Beaujoie's words to myself like an incantation to safety.

"Ellen, you sure you want to go through with this?" Paul asked just as Eric doused the headlights.

She slipped out of the jeep, a shadow in fluid motion while Paul and I cranked ourselves out. Without benefit of headlights the only thing I could make out

95

was Ellen's yellow jacket and a white construction up ahead.

Eric talked to Ellen in a low voice. "Do you ever get to Key West? That's where I hang out with a buddy of mine during the rainy season. I don't get drowned in the Keys, but I'd still get that soaked air. It weighs me down, makes me feel my bones. That's a good feelin'. Reminds me I'm still kickin'. In Nam—Jeezus, it was always rainin' down there—sometimes the feel of my bones was the only thing tellin' me I was alive."

"Why don't you tell us about the Ho Bo woods," Paul said, his hostility as thick as the clouds.

Eric stopped in his tracks. "Lissen, snapshot man, I'm sorry you didn't get to fight in 'Nam, but just 'cause you don't have stories to tell women, doesn't mean I wasn't there. 'Nam isn't somethin' anyone would invent. Operation Desert Storm maybe, but not 'Nam."

"What's the matter with you, Paul?" Ellen said, not waiting for an answer, walking away with a yellow satin arm linked to Eric's. I hurried after them.

"What gets me is that he's using the war to get sympathy," Paul said, not bothering to lower his voice. "My father fought with the 173rd at Dak To, and he hasn't said a word about Vietnam since."

"I'm sorry," I mumbled, caught off guard by the rawness in his voice.

"War, no matter for how good a cause, is not something one should cash in on. General Schwarzkopf strutting on TV with Barbara Walters—signing a book deal for five million bucks! What about the families of those who died over there? What do they get out of it besides a folded flag and a hole in their hearts? Makes me sick! Eric makes me sick!"

I agreed with him about capitalizing on war, but I couldn't help wonder how much jealousy played into his feelings about Eric. We'd reached the building by now, which was roughly one thousand square feet, built with sheets of plywood that had been painted a garish white. Thin wooden beams held up the usual corrugated zinc roof. One huff from the big bad wind and the whole thing would collapse.

Eric and Ellen were in front of us, already making their way through the semicircle of bleachers facing a green pit. Across the entrance I saw Nick's South African bookseller talking to a handsome black man dressed in a tan linen suit.

"How'd you get hold of Nick?" I asked Paul.

"What do you mean?"

"How did you hire her?"

"I thought you were pleased with Nick's work."

"I am. I think she's great, Janick thinks she's great. I'm just curious how you got hold of her." And curious to know the real reason she didn't tell you she'd been down here before. Why she'd kept Lundi's actual name a secret.

"She dropped in my studio one day, without an appointment, insisted I give her five minutes, and showed me a great portfolio. Really great. I hired her on the spot."

"Ah yes, the mysterious portfolio from her work in California."

When we'd picked Paul to be the photographer for the campaign, my boss had been a little skeptical about using Nick. We like to pick our own stylist just as photographers like to hire as many of their own people as possible, not only because some of them skim off the top, but because having their own crew gives them an edge over the agency. It's all done subtly, of course, or else we'd probably fire the photographer, but the only interference my boss accepts is a whispered suggestion or two I manage to sneak in during his rare moments of confusion. The Janick clothes stylist was seven-months pregnant and refused to fly. Paul had insisted Nick was great, showing us ads they had done together as proof. Of Nick's past work there was no trace. The "great" portfolio had been stolen out of Nick's apartment along with a TV and a radio. I'd accepted the story three months ago, mostly out of relief that I wouldn't have to kill myself finding another clothes stylist that would please Ellen, Paul, my boss, *and* the *capo* of *capos,* Jean Janick. Now I wasn't so sure.

Eric was waving to us to hurry up. He and Ellen had picked seats behind a green metal partition, on the other side of the room. Front row, dead center. With a great view of the bloodletting. The South African bookseller had disappeared with the man in the tan suit. Had Nick been afraid of meeting him here? Was that why she'd stayed at the Club?

"Did you check her references?" I asked.

"Jerry did," Paul said. "What is this? What's the matter with everybody down here? Why the third degree on Nick?"

"I hope you realize you haven't been exactly charming," I said, not liking what I was doing either, therefore shifting the blame like a kid. "You seem to have both your eyes and ears stuck behind that camera or under a black cloud of your own making. Go easy on Ellen. This morning you worked her to the bone. If you're jealous, try being nice to her for a change."

Paul slammed his hand against a beam, his face turning liver-red. "Why do you women always assume that men fixate on you?"

"Wishful thinking." I zapped him a smile that made him drop down on the bleacher a good four feet away from me. I moved closer to Ellen.

The place wasn't very crowded, maybe forty or fifty people. The majority were men of all hues, going from ebony to cinnamon to butter burnt from too much sun; men with different shaped faces and hair of varying textures; men who descended from the different peoples that had settled in Guadeloupe.

Back in the second or third century A.D., the Caraib Indians had conquered the Arawaks and had given the Caribbean its name. Then Columbus and the Spanish came in 1493 and were quickly driven away. The French started settling along with the Dutch Jews expelled from South America. Then the English arrived. With the white man came the African slaves, mostly Senegalese and Angolans, to work the sugar cane fields. When the Africans were finally freed, Hindu Indians—"coolies" as they call them here—immigrated to become the new manual laborers. During this century Syrians and Lebanese joined the others.

In this fascinating cauldron of people, we seemed the only tourists. We had that raw, too bright look that makes the tourist stand out—our tans were not deep enough and we were nervous. Everyone else was barely excited, as if the cockfight was just another TV sitcom. I felt awful. The plywood and the metal roof wavered in the heat. I was in a microwave oven set on HIGH, and suddenly I hated myself for being suspicious and nosy. Iguana's death was none of my affair. Lundi was taken care of. *Basta. Il gioco non vale la candela.* The game was not worth the price of the candle.

"When great cocks are scheduled," Eric said, shifting his rear end as if it were burning, "this place can get packed worse than a Saigon whorehouse. Cockfighting is big business here. Trainers get great pay. I tried it last year, but this dumb ass bird zeroed in on my hand and chop chop." He turned over his right hand to show us where the finger pad of his middle finger had been sliced off.

"I thought that happened in the war," Ellen said. She sounded disappointed. In the entrance, across the pit from us, a cluster of eight muscled young men strutted in and hugged the cock trainers who had just brought in their covered cages.

"When's Ellen going to wake up?" Paul grumbled, hunched down over his knees. The new arrivals were causing a stir in the room. I could hear a ripple of whispers as they made their way through the spectators, nodding and shaking hands. Eric started craning his neck left and right, just like the cocks the trainers were lifting out of their cages.

"I grabbed that bird's neck," Eric said too loudly, "and in six seconds flat he was a goner. A real fuck-up on my part 'cause I paid a lot for that Texas cock. Texas is the best." As he talked, Eric held his hand up to salute a few men who looked our way. He grinned broadly at eyes that quickly cut away. He didn't get a single vote.

"The only way you can judge a cock is in actual combat." Eric picked up the speed of his words. "You gotta watch how he raises his feet. If he throws 'em above his head, that's a good sign. He's gotta have lightnin' motion of legs. Always favor the high flyer when you bet 'cause he's the fastest with the damage. Style's nothing. The main thing here is to win." Eric started laughing, his cackle coming out in even shorter nervous bursts. "I like that 'cause I never had style. Not like you, hon. You got it to give out."

Paul groaned loudly while Ellen looked as kind and mournful as Mother Theresa.

As the eight men seated themselves on the highest row of bleachers, a man on the other side of the pit shouted, *"Tu as vu Coco?"* Have you seen Coco?

Eric craned his neck to one side as if to hear better. He'd stopped laughing. One of the eight, in a bright

100

yellow shirt, returned a flow of Creole words. I caught "Basse-Terre," the rest was lost in the sinking softness of the language. Whatever he said pleased Eric, who leaned back to point to the far side of the pit.

"See that glint of steel on the birds' legs?" he asked Ellen. Two pitters were holding their cocks while the trainers attached something long and thin to the birds' left legs.

"That's a gaff, a six- or seven-inch, razor-sharp blade that gets tied to the natural spur. That's what the cock uses to kill his rival. You gotta make sure the blade's slanted inward, that it follows the direction of the natural spur."

One bird was a "light syrup" color, Eric told us, the other "a black syrup." Traditionally the hue of the bird's feathers was defined by the colors of sugar cane.

Someone brushed past me from behind. Eric snapped up, then relaxed as the "rifleman" from the rum distillery leaned down to whisper in his ear. At least he was unarmed this time. Eric shook his head at whatever the man had said, his eyes darting to Ellen and me. I stared at the rifleman's face as he walked past me, wondering if one of his duties, besides shooting alcoholic raccoons, wasn't keeping an eye on Eric's back. He winked at me, which served me right, and nodded at Paul.

Everyone seemed to stop talking at once. Near the pit, the pitters approached each other, their birds held in front of them. Two beaks touched, neck feathers billowed out in anger or fear, the heads darted out, pecking to kill. The audience cheered. Both trainers quickly stepped back to separate the birds, and the referee nodded approval.

"That's called billing," Eric said. "It gets them in the fightin' mood. The whole point of the game is for those birds to fight each other to the death. Cocks'll fight

101

even if blinded in both eyes."

My full stomach was slowly climbing to my throat. I wanted air. I wanted out.

"It's a sex game," Eric said, while I kept my eyes on the audience. The rifleman had disappeared.

"I guess they don't want any other males around," Ellen said. All of a sudden I felt as if I'd been thrown into the pit of the New York Commodity Exchange. All around me, men made strange, rapid finger signs, shouted incomprehensible gibberish. The betting had started.

Paul stood up abruptly. "I'll be back," he announced.

"Can't take it, huh?" Eric said, enjoying himself again. He actually inched closer to Ellen, who looked oddly pleased with herself. If she was hoping to be alone with Eric Kanzer, she was making holes in the water as we say back home. In other words, I wasn't budging.

The betting stopped and all heads craned toward the pit. The pitters rubbed the back of their birds to quiet them down.

"How you pit the bird is important," Eric whispered. "The earlier you pit the better, so the cock has time to get his balance." The fight was about to start.

The pitters released their birds and stepped back. I saw a flurry of dark and light feathers. Then the darker cock flew high in the air, thrusting the blade of his left leg forward. I closed my eyes, heard the beating of wings and Ellen's sharp gasp. Voices rose in one bloodthirsty yell, and my stomach almost exploded in my mouth.

It was over in less than a minute. The shouting decreased to talk and laughter, someone touched my hand. I opened my eyes to see a deflated heap of feathers, light syrup in color, lying in the grass green of

102

the pit. There was very little blood.

"He goes straight into the pot for good ole chicken soup," Eric said. Ellen held my hand and blinked, as if she too had shut off the sight.

"There's Papa La Bouche," I shouted, happy to be distracted by the old man. He was sitting on the top row to our left, where the eight young men had sat before the fight. They had vanished, leaving Papa perched on the empty white row like a tired old bird on a fence. I waved to him. He stared at Eric, his face a tight mask of hate.

"I want to go," Ellen said.

Eric stood up and held out his hand. "He likes to haunt this place. That's how he lost his distillery, betting against me over a scrawny bird his dead wife's fuckin' brother had trained."

We left the front row the way Paul had, squeezing past obliging knees while Papa's gaze followed our every move. I was glad to be getting out of there, away from that bloody game, away from the intensity of Papa's bloodshot eyes.

"He bet his life's work! That's nuts!" Eric said, wrapping an arm around Ellen's waist to help her through the narrow passageway behind the bleachers.

"What did you put up?" I asked him. I spotted Paul waiting by the exit and waved to him.

"My jeeps."

"Just as nuts."

"I won."

He had a point.

Ellen slipped out of Eric's arm as she saw Paul.

"Did you have fun?" Paul asked her with a surprising look of satisfaction on his face. He'd probably just been to the bathroom.

"No, thank you. I didn't," Ellen said, looking angry.

Eric shook his shoulders and turned back toward the

empty bleachers where Papa La Bouche was still sitting. "Sometimes I think that old man has put a hex on me."

"Voodoo!" Ellen cried out just as the crowd started yelling at a new fight. "I'd forgotten all about that."

I ran out, plunging into a night black with clouds. I breathed in the damp heavy air and waited for my eyes to adjust to the change.

"Voodoo is no joking matter," Eric was saying behind me. "People shrivel up and die here for no known cause."

"That's nonsense," I said. "You've been here too long."

"I'll take you, hon, if you want. I know a real good one. I've had a bum knee since 'Nam and he gave me some grease that rubbed the pain right off for good. They call 'em *quimboiseur* or *Papa Diable*."

"I'd like that," Ellen said. I could see her yellow jacket from the corner of my eye.

"Lissen, you don't need to stick any pins. Just tell me. I'll take care of anyone who gets in your way."

Like you, Eric baby.

"Thank you," Ellen said simply.

"We'd better get back to the Club," I called out just as the din inside the building ended. Another poor bird dead. "We've got a long day tomorrow if the weather's any good."

"It's going to be a great day," Eric said, stepping out of the doorway.

"Oh, yes, it is," Ellen said, the yellow rectangle of light catching only a glimpse of her happy face as she quickly followed Eric into the dark. In that instant she looked as if she were beaming over a secret all her own. I hoped it had nothing to do with magic potions, because—as we say back in the ole country—she was going to come up with a fistful of flies.

104

ELEVEN

We walked quickly down a path of beaten-down grass, along the edge of a dense thicket of what Eric declared were banana trees. Once we walked around the bend all I could see were varying shades of black. Ellen's jacket, the lightest patch, led the way while I brought up the rear. The frogs and the crickets, out to deafen us all, monopolized the sound. I relaxed as my body cooled in the fresher air of the trees. The cockfight was over and I had learned that closing my eyes I could survive anything—even the long, slimy blades of grass that were now slithering across my feet as I walked.

Something rough and thick jerked my ankle, pitching me forward. My face hit soft, dripping grass, then hard, dung-smelling ground. The crickets and the frogs didn't bother to stop their racket. No one else paid attention. The sudden fall had been so surprising, I hadn't even let out a gasp. I lifted my head to feel a blast of heat on my face, then the nuzzle of something gooey. I yelled and scrambled to my knees.

"What's wrong?" Paul called out from somewhere ahead of me.

I was too busy inching my hands in front of me to see

what I was up against to answer. All I could make out was a heavy long mass of something apparently unmoveable—a small car, maybe. I felt a sharp tip hit the palm of one hand. Ah ha, the handlebar of a motorcycle!

Suddenly the mass moved and nudged against my stomach. My butt hit the ground; my face got another blast of hot, fermented breath.

"You won't believe this, but I've crashed into a cow," I said to whoever was interested. I heard Eric's cackle. As the cow grazed by my knees I stroked her brow in the calming way I had seen the pitters do back at the cockfight.

"I never touch meat," I whispered, backing off on my rump, praying it was only grass my skirt was rubbing over. The cow mooed, and I envisioned a New York sirloin with French fried spuds sitting in blood red juice. "You have to believe me, *bella*. Only vegetables."

My back met something hard. I howled.

Paul was at my side in an instant, lifting me up, worrying over me.

"Thanks." I felt awkward with relief that someone was there to help. "I'm such a klutz."

"Are you all right?" Ellen called out from my right. Eric expressed his concern by rustling banana leaves somewhere to my left. At least he wasn't cackling.

"I tripped over the cow's tether." Paul had let go of me and stepped out of my sight. I was on my own again, safely gripping a door handle. "Then I guess I hit a car and panicked." Fair punishment for lying to the cow.

The wind had finally opened a space in the clouds allowing a little moonlight to shine on the car door next to me—white with the blue Club Med trident painted neatly in the center.

"Did any of you see any G.O.'s at the cockfight?" I hadn't, but then I wasn't sure of being able to recognize all ninety of them. Paul and Ellen said no.

"How about you, Eric?"

"Listen," Ellen said. "Isn't that jazz?"

All I could hear was a sudden, heavy silence. For some reason the crickets and the tree frogs had shut up.

"The music is coming from that hill behind the building." Ellen's voice, sounding curious and excited, was farther away now. I thought I heard a swishing sound, as if her skirt were brushing against branches. Far below me, down on the main road, a truck scraped gears as it rounded a curve.

"Where's the jeep, Eric?" I was edging my way toward Ellen's voice, making sure of lifting my feet high from possible tethers, spokes, and cows. I was ready for a fast ride back to the Club.

"How romantic!" Ellen said. "A nightclub in the middle of a banana plantation."

"No dancing tonight," Paul said in a tight voice.

"Oh god, let me live!" Ellen cried out. "If I want to dance, I'll dance. I don't care if I look haggard and ugly tomorrow. I don't want to be beautiful, I want to have fun. Eric, take me to that nightclub."

That's when I heard the bellowing notes of a trumpet. At the tail end of the notes, the crickets and frogs jumped in with their bit, as if they'd only paused for a union break like any respected musician. Everything was back to normal, except that Eric wasn't answering.

"Eric?" Ellen called out again, panic already in her voice. "Eric?"

"Eeerrriccc!" I yelled furiously. "Damn it! Where the hell are you?"

"Playing Jungle Jim to impress Ellen," Paul said.

"Eric, don't," Ellen pleaded. "Please don't play games."

"Come on, Ellen, leave him to the snakes and the

apes," Paul said. "We don't need him."

"We've got to find him. He's got the car keys." I reached Ellen and put an arm around her to reassure both of us. "He's either gone to get the jeep or he went back to the building for some reason. Ellen and I will try the building. You find the jeep."

"Don't let her out of your sight!" Paul growled. I grabbed Ellen's hand, and we ran back to the clearing behind the banana trees, slowing down only as we reached the rectangle of doorway light.

A fat man stopped our entrance with a beefy, ringed finger held to his pursed lips. Behind him the pitters were stroking two new cocks while the spectators watched in motionless silence. I felt as if I had walked into a vacuum, all air sucked by anticipation. Ellen freed herself from my grip. I peered around the semicircle of bleachers. From the corner of my eye, the pitters threw down their birds, and the crowd stood up with a smacking sound of excitement. Eric was nowhere. Neither was Papa La Bouche.

It struck me then that men had come and gone before my eyes all evening.

I backed out of the doorway with Ellen, afraid of the blind, animal violence in front of me, even more afraid for Eric. My imagination was racing—I thought of Iguana's split skull, Coco's anger, Papa La Bouche's hate, of those swaggering young men who had walked into the cockfight like warriors thirsty for victory. Eric—with his Vietnam past, his twitching face and thin nervous body—trying hard to be someone. None of the spectators had looked him in the eye. Why?

"He's not at the jeep," Paul said, joining us in the light. "I went all around the outside of the building, too. He's gone, taking the car keys with him."

"Something's happened to him," Ellen said, looking

at Paul as if it were his fault. "Eric wouldn't leave us stranded."

"Eric can take care of himself," I said in a blustery tone to convince myself as well. "The only thing we can do is wait for the fights to end and bum a ride with someone going to back to Sainte-Anne." It was too far to walk. "Maybe we should hang out by that Club Med car."

"It's too dark back there," Ellen said.

"If you two promise not to move," Paul said, unzipping his camera case. "I want to take some shots of this slaughter."

"Why now?" I asked.

"Now I'm relaxed." He fished in his bag for the Pentax. A silvery gleam slipped through his fingers.

"What's that? A fish?" Ellen asked.

A sharp "No!" popped out of the dark behind her, crashing my heart against the top of my skull. Even Paul jumped as Papa La Bouche literally walked out of the shadows as if he were part of a Roger Corman zombie movie.

"The flash of camera is bad for *les coqs,*" he said. He was smiling, his lips rising to one side of his face. One front tooth jutted over his bite.

"Bonsoir. You wish help?"

Why did he look so pleased with himself?

"How did you know?" Paul asked in a belligerent tone while he tore at the stuck zipper of his camera bag.

"We need a ride to the Club," I said.

"Your boss dumped us," Paul said. The zipper finally gave in and sealed the black leather bag.

"Je suis le boss," Papa said, slapping his French sailor's cap on his small head, as bald and dark as an avocado pit. "I take you *au Club.*"

We followed him for what seemed forever, first along the banana tree path, then through the now crowded car park as he carefully picked a path between cars and bicycles with his cane. His legs jerked up as if hit by a doctor's hammer. The wind had drawn back more clouds and a barely nicked fat moon lit our way. During that slow walk we hung close to Papa, all three of us probably afraid he, too, would vanish. Finally he stopped in front of the truck I had seen when we drove in. Eric's empty jeep sat parked a few feet away.

"There is room for two of you in the front," he said in slow French for my benefit, opening the door on the driver's side. "The young man will have to sit in the back with the rum bottles. I regret they are empty. The ride will be very bumpy."

The driver's seat seemed impossibly high for a man who barely reached five feet, but Papa hooked his cane on the top ridge of the door frame and, with two powerful hand grasps, lifted himself up. Once at seat level, he gripped the large steering wheel with one hand and swung himself into the seat.

Bravo! I thought, and scrambled up the passenger side to sit in the middle. Paul had already hoisted himself into the back of the truck, leaning an angry head over the wooden railing like an animal raging over his imminent slaughter. I heard Ellen offer to ride with him. He refused. I moved over to make room for Ellen.

"Where is your son tonight?" I asked in French as we rode downhill over the ruts and rocks of the dirt road, the headlights catching expanses of green, then night black. The thwack of Eric's hand hitting Coco's truck sounded in my ear, and I made a mental note to tell Beaujoie of Eric's disappearance the minute I got back to the Club.

"I expected to see Coco at the cockfight," I said.

"He prefers some light-skinned woman with her breasts offered to the wind." It was clear from his tone

110

that he considered gambling a better pastime.

"Why have you tourists no modesty?" Papa asked, as the lack of shock absorbers drubbed a couple of inches off my rear end.

"Don't look at me," I said. "My body gets buried under sand." I crossed my arms to keep my breasts from tearing off. I could just see the headline in *Self:* FITNESS GURU GRIFFO TOUTS TRUCKING TO THINNESS. I might even earn enough to leave my studio for a one bedroom.

Once we careened onto the asphalted main road to Sainte-Anne, my weight settled gratefully, and I waved back at Paul for encouragement. Even Papa seemed mollified by the smoother ride as he sat back, his head barely clearing the steering wheel.

"On the beach children should hear stories, not see nudity."

"What kind?" I asked, remembering he had announced himself *conteur,* teller of tales.

"Old stories of magic, of evil fighting good, of disguises that give you power. Dreams of change. When we were slaves, stories kept our souls from dying."

I translated for Ellen, who still clutched the window frame.

Papa leaned over.

"Mademoiselle said she likes fairy tales. As it is night, there is no danger of our turning into bamboo baskets if I give her a story."

"A superstition?"

Papa honked his horn with a quick punch of his fist and laughed. "Perhaps, but it is best not to risk. To become a basket is not a change good for the soul." He slowed the truck and shifted down into second, as if his story needed a prescribed rhythm.

"There was once a little girl called Annette who lived

111

with her old, unloving godmother in a one-room hut. Each night, when Annette fell asleep, the godmother changed herself into a night bird and flew away, leaving Annette to face the dark alone.

"One night, Annette, intrigued by the pretty feathers she always found when she swept under the bed in the morning, pretended to sleep. With half-closed eyes she watched her godmother turn into a sleek, silvery bird and rise to the sky. Wanting to do the same, Annette repeated the words she had heard, uncapped a pink glass vial, and palmed the magic liquid over her small young body. Seconds later, bright colored feathers sprouted from her young skin. She held out her arms to see them spread into wings hued like the flora of the tropics. Flapping her new wings, she flew out of the window like her godmother had done before her."

He paused to let me translate. Ellen let go of the window and I closed my eyes, lulled back into childhood. His voice rumbled on about how Annette flew over mango trees, over the rain forest, over Carbet Falls, how the moon was shaped like a hook that night and she climbed up "longing to swing from the deep gold crescent." Before she could reach it, the moon had faded into the day, and she didn't know how to come back down. She had not heard the magic words that would turn her back into a little girl.

"Annette prayed," Papa said, with reverence in his voice. "And as she muttered her 'amen,' a hand, as soft as a cloud, lifted her and brought her down, down, down into the thick branches of a sea grape tree where no one could see her. She felt a slight breeze on her forehead, like a mother's breath before a kiss. *Voilà,* the night bird was now a pretty little girl called Annette."

He paused and I opened my eyes.

"Annette never tried to imitate her godmother

112

again," Papa added. "Her flight taught her that God has much more power than magic has."

I thanked Papa, masking my disappointment with the ending. I'd hoped Annette would fly away to some wonderful birdland full of fruit trees where she'd never have to sweep under a bed again.

Ellen was more up-front than I. "I think that's a typically repressive story aimed at training female children to become women chained to their limiting domestic roles, relegating all power to a male God, be he a priest or a husband."

I didn't translate, but just as we turned into the Club road, Papa leaned his head toward Ellen, his jutting tooth giving him a cagey beaver look.

"Come to the *flamboyant* tree tomorrow night," he said in slow English. "Many children, many more stories. You will find one you like."

Papa slammed on the brakes. We'd made it to the Club.

Nick was waiting by the guard house. "Hi, was it fun?" She scanned our faces as we dropped out of the truck. "A scream, huh?"

"You're real close," I told her, my knees buckling as I hit solid ground. The evening had been rough for Nick, too. Her face was scrunched like a cried-up handkerchief. She ignored my "Are you okay?"

Ellen and I said goodbye to Papa, thanking him profusely for the ride and the story. Paul leaned against a ficus tree and shook one leg after another to check for broken bones.

"It's been a night to remember," I said, eyeing the guard room telephone. I had to call Beaujoie.

"Yes it has," Bob said, walking up behind me in navy blue slacks and shirt that blended with the dark. "Where have you been? I've been looking all over for you." He was staring straight at Nick. "You wouldn't

113

think someone so tall would be so hard to find."

"I'm not so tall and I'm not someone," Nick said furiously.

"You are someone and you are tall." He made it sound like a declaration of love.

"Eric's disappeared," Ellen blurted.

"Z'oiseauz," Papa shouted as he backed out of the driveway at full speed. "The birds. He flew away with the magic birds."

Eric was right. The moon just had to be full.

TWELVE

I waited for everyone to leave before asking the stocky guard to use his phone. I had a *message très important* for the police commissioner, I told him, and the phone room at the Club was closed. After several seconds of examining me under lids drooping with missed sleep, his thick mustache spread into a smile.

"Be brief," he said in a tone that was too nice to mean it and stepped out of the tiny room.

I dialed the home number Beaujoie had given me. Someone picked up after the first ring, without speaking. I introduced myself and asked for Beaujoie.

"The boy, I want the boy," a woman whispered in French, the words whistling in my ear. "He has no one but me. Please, please bring him back. Cristophe does not understand. No man can understand. Please, mademoiselle. My son. Bring him back." The woman took a long, quivering breath, then began sobbing softly.

Was she Madame Beaujoie? A maid? I didn't understand. I didn't know what to say. I hung on to the phone, my discomfort increasing as the sound of the sobs swelled and pushed their way into my chest.

"I'm sorry, madame. I'm sorry," I managed to

115

mumble. Had something happened to Beaujoie's son?

The crying stopped abruptly.

"Solitude," she said. In the silence that followed, the word seemed to hang in the air. "My mother gave me the name of Solitude. A great cruelty." She hung up.

I lowered the phone on the desk, letting the buzz of the dial tone fill the tiny, glass-enclosed room, somehow hoping the sound would dispel the sadness the woman had left me.

"Has something happened to *Monsieur le commissaire?*" The guard was leaning over me, his eyes now wide with worry.

"No, no." I had no idea what had happened. "Has he children?"

"Not officially. Unofficially, who knows?" He shrugged heavily as if to decline any responsibility. I dialed the Pointe-à-Pitre police station.

"Is Commissioner Beaujoie there? No? Then please let him know that Eric Kanzer has disappeared."

"Everyone disappears at Carnival," was the answer I got from the policeman on duty. I insisted he tell Beaujoie and gave him the details as best I could, fatigue and a bad mood shrinking my French to elementary words. The woman—whoever she was—had depressed me, even frightened me. Her plea had been so desperate, her name chilling.

And where the hell was Eric?

I thanked the guard and walked slowly toward my room, smelling the salt, hearing the soft crash of low waves. More than anything I wished Greenhouse were next to me, propping me up with a word or a gesture.

I called him as soon as the telephone room opened in the morning. I wished him a cheery good morning from the Caribbean.

116

"Simona?" Greenhouse asked, his voice mushy with sleep. In New York it was 6:00 A.M.

"Have you forgotten my voice so quickly?" I had wished him Happy New Year only four weeks ago.

"I'm just surprised."

We fumbled with "how are you's" and "What are you up to's" for a while. I filled him in on the Guadeloupe trip, wasting costly minutes on Ellen's booming modeling career and Paul's photographic talents, hunting for that slot of comfort I was hoping was still available to me. I left space for his words, which came cautiously, mostly about Willie, his thirteen-year-old son I'd never met. I stayed clear of any mention of Iguana, not forgetting how he hated my meddling with murder.

"I'd love to see you again when I get back," I finally said, seeing Nick press her nose against the telephone booth. She looked sunny and that egged me on.

"I've missed you horribly," I told Greenhouse.

A pause, then a guarded, "Me too." I smiled at the familiarity. Greenhouse was never the initiator when it came to declarations of emotions.

"We're flying back to New York on Saturday," I said. "Come to dinner on Sunday. I'll come up with a new Griffo pasta concoction." I always hand out food when I'm on shaky ground.

"It's about time you offered," Greenhouse said, sounding awake, strong, and eager. The slot of comfort gaped open and I slipped right in, wishing myself under the covers with him in his cold New York bedroom. Acceptance was what I'd been looking for, not comfort.

"Make it late, though," he added. "I'm taking Willy down to visit his grandmother in Naples."

"That's pretty far for a weekend trip."

His laugh reverberated in the pit of my stomach.

117

"Naples, Florida, not Italy. Nine o'clock okay with you?"

"Perfetto." We said goodbye, and my whole body grinned as I hung up.

"What was in that phone booth?" Nick asked as I came out. "You look like you've just swallowed the missing Eric."

"Him I'd spit out," I said, wiping what must have been a horny smirk off my face. I had no desire to worry about Eric at that moment. "And what happened to you?"

Nick was wearing my purple Indian cotton skirt, belted high on her waist with a long red and yellow scarf, leaving most of her skyscraper legs exposed. Her feet were bare.

She looked down at herself, following my gaze. "I didn't think you'd mind after last night's lecture."

"I don't." I noticed she had a trace of lipstick on her broad smile, and her cheeks were suspiciously pink. "I see the bad memories are gone."

"No, funny enough that dead mutt's still hanging out in my head, and I'm not even sure it has anything to do with Iguana's death."

"You look great." We walked out of the phone room.

"Did you see the photos of last night's rehearsal?" Nick said. "I look like Tommy Tune except his hair's longer than mine."

"Oh, God, that photographer flashed one of me, too! Where are they?"

I followed her downstairs to an alcove behind the Ping-Pong tables where a very pretty G.O. sat, waiting to answer questions and sell pop-it beads.

"Hi," she said in perfect American, as I pushed behind her to stare at the rows of proofs tacked on the bulletin board. "You can place your orders with me."

"Ellen's everywhere," Nick said, hanging back.

118

She was right. There were rows and rows of Ellen, on stage, at dinner, at the bar, walking on the beach with her back to the camera. She looked gorgeous as always, but she also looked lonely, as if her beauty isolated her from the rest of us.

"Hey, not bad!" I said in a false cheery note. I'd found me in one corner, looking like a wrapped party sausage ready for the grill. It was the kind of picture you could only send home to Mamma. "Where are you?"

"I cut it out. It was really awful."

"I wish people would stop doing that," the G.O. said, standing up and jerking her head with indignation. "On Tuesday someone took four sheets of proofs off this board. And the photographer can't even find the negatives. I think that's awful."

Nick gave her an appraising look. "I bet you're photogenic."

"Well, yeees."

"There's no way you could understand."

"Nick, there's nothing wrong with your looks," I said.

"Not now, there isn't." She stuck one leg and did an awkward imitation of a model posing. "Let 'em flash!" She laughed outright. The G.O. sat back in her chair and gave up on us.

"Thanks for your help," Nick said as we walked away. She reached in her pocket and offered me a napkin full of bite-sized croissants.

"What help?" I locked my hands together to keep from taking those buttery curls of flaked pastry. "Is Bob still looking for you?"

"What do you mean by that?" Nick's jaw stuck out in defense.

"I'm teasing you because right now I'm gushing over a certain detective, and maybe you are just as much of a sucker for a certain G.O."

"Well, Bob and I did agree that being tall has lots of advantages, and that it's okay for me to outshoot him on the court." I won't say she blushed, but she might as well have, judging by the embarrassed look on her face.

"You know, I bet those stolen sheets were all of Ellen," she said, "and some guy is moaning over them right now."

"Sounds like something Tommy might do."

"Are you going to eat these or not?" She was still holding out those delectable croissants.

"Nope." I took the full napkin out of her hand and shot it toward the trash can in what I thought was a smooth Magic Johnson movement. Croissants flew everywhere. "I've got to lose twenty pounds by Sunday."

I had four days. *Col cavolo!*

At the beach Ellen came running up, her green trapeze coverall flapping.

"Have you heard from Eric?" she asked. Her face looked as if it had been stuffed in a tight pocket all night. That's when I noticed that the sky was a solid lead gray blanket, and even the water had a wrinkled put-upon look. I felt ashamed of my good mood.

"No," I told her, "but the police are looking for him." At least I hoped they were. I wasn't even sure Beaujoie had gotten my message.

"If he's dead, they'd have found him by now," Nick said in her practical way.

"Stop it!" Ellen said.

"Yes, please." What if Iguana was only the beginning, what if Eric's body was lying buried in that thicket of banana trees? Ellen and I looked at each other for support. Neither of us wanted to believe another death was possible.

"There's our boat," Paul called out as he walked up from the shoreline. He was pointing beyond HM and Jerry, who were standing knee-deep in water. Two hundred yards out to sea, the fifty-foot sailboat Eric had rented was waiting for us. The captain and a sailor were busy lowering the dinghy. There was no sign of Eric.

"I wouldn't risk going out to Marie-Galante in this weather," I said, wondering if the captain knew anything.

"It's too dark to shoot anyway," Paul said. We walked to the water's edge. "Let's sail to Gosier, instead. It's just around that bend, so even if it pours it's not going to be that bad. Maybe it'll clear up later and we'll get some face shots. What do you say, boss lady?" He looked at Ellen, smiling and relaxed for once.

Ellen shook her head. "We can't just go and have fun."

"Oh, yes, we can," HM said, wearing a SILENCE = DEATH T-shirt over his bathing suit. He wrapped a proprietary arm around Ellen's neck.

"Sweetheart, no makeup's gonna do anything for that face of yours if you don't start smiling. What's going on with you? Don't worry about the ferret, that's what Jerry and I call him—Erit the ferret. You know, like in underground rat? He's such bad news he's bound to show up again."

"The boat's ours for the day," I said, as HM gave Ellen a loud kiss on the cheek. "You might as well take advantage of it."

The dinghy was rocking a hundred feet from the shore, waiting. Jerry had already paddled out and was chatting with the sailor.

"That little hussy," HM said, pursing his lips.

"Have you seen Eric?" I yelled at the sailor. He

121

waved a "no." Where was that man?

"Come on, all of you, go," I said. "Gosier's supposed to be fun. All the fancy hotels are there, great lunch places, nice boutiques. If it rains, you can shop and pig out. Best way to spend a day." I wanted them out of my hair, wanted suddenly to breathe the sharp air of New York, where you know from the start that the odds in your favor aren't great. *From the start,* those were the key words. Here in Guadeloupe, the bad news had come unexpectedly, in the midst of lulling, sensual beauty, leaving me with a sense of horror mixed with an even more frightening sense of insecurity.

"Off you go, it's an order!" I said, waving them away, laughing more than was warranted, hoping Ellen would have a good time.

With a cry of "Chaaarge!" HM scooped Ellen up in his arms and sloshed into the water.

"She hasn't had any more incidents, has she?" Paul asked in a low voice, the smile gone for the moment.

"What do you mean?"

"Like another rock being thrown at her."

"How did you know?"

"I see a lot through my Pentax. Jerry got the rest from HM."

"She thought you'd be angry with her."

"She did?" He looked dumbfounded.

"She's fine now." HM, butt high in water, was threatening to dunk Ellen. She squealed. Paul followed them in, smiling again. He looked incredibly handsome in his new happiness, pressing his precious camera bag against his chest like an eager lover.

"Aren't you going, Nick?" She was looking at the sailboat, her face now as pale as the sand.

"Not to Gosier."

"Why not?" I asked too abruptly, puzzled by her change in mood.

122

She caught me staring at her. "Hey, can't miss stretch with Master Bob, can I?" She loped off in my purple skirt, leaving me wondering who Nick really was.

I tried Beaujoie at the police station. As usual he wasn't there, and I didn't want to call his home and maybe hear another chest-tightening plea. I went to the Club's rental car office and put a van and a sedan on hold in case Eric didn't show up, then I wandered around the grounds. I wanted to feel happily airy about having reconnected with Greenhouse, instead I felt useless and as gloomy as the weather. I joined Nick in the Stretch to Start class. My muscles squeaked as I tried to lean my torso over my straightened legs. Nick's chest, I noticed, lay flat against her knees. Two other women just sat and watched Bob's body.

The class was being held on the upper floor of the main building, open on all sides, the roof a wavy slab of thick concrete meant to look like a fluttering tent or bad Le Corbusier. I commented on the building's ugliness, and Bob, between a deep knee bend and a waist stretch, explained that in a place where winds whipped up to 135 MPH, sturdy was the only goal. I looked at the concrete columns—two feet in diameter —holding up the roof and knew I should feel safe from all storms. I didn't.

When my muscles became wobbly, worn out rubber bands, I slid over on my rear end next to Bob to ask if any one of the G.O.'s had said anything about Eric's disappearance.

"Why should we know anything at all?" He had stopped his neck gyrations and was fast-forwarding his tape.

"I noticed a Club Med car in the parking lot near the cockfight as we were leaving last night. Maybe someone saw something."

Madonna's "Physical Attraction" was replaced by

Streisand singing "Send in the Clowns," and I wondered if he was trying to tell me something.

"Haven't heard a thing."

I turned to Nick, who had stretched out her legs at a perfect one hundred and eighty degree angle.

"Do you know where Zaza lives?" Somewhere in the back of my mind I assumed that if she knew Lundi's real name, she might also know Zaza.

"Why would I?" Nick bent over one knee, covering her face. What was she trying to hide?

"You might have met Zaza on the beach on this trip or the previous one."

Bob stood up and announced, "That's it."

"The hour's not up yet," one of the women watchers complained.

"I only do forty-five minutes," Bob said, snapping off the tape.

"Do you know where Zaza lives?" I asked him, scrambling off my comfortable butt.

"I don't know any of those peddlers. Why do you want to know?"

"Maybe she knows something about Eric that would help." In the past half hour I'd convinced myself that Eric's disappearance tied in with Iguana's death in some neat, easily discoverable way. "Besides, I'm curious to know more about Iguana." And I kind of liked the thought of seeing Lundi again, too.

"Leave it alone," Nick said, getting up with the grace of the natural athlete. "There's nothing you can do. I thought about that murder back home for three months. I even sent my allowance to the police every week hoping they'd catch the killer. They never did. Take my advice. Leave it alone and forget it. It'll save wrinkles."

I didn't want to leave it alone. I don't know what exactly had changed my mind. Probably the eerie woman pleading for her son over the phone, my finding the courage to invite Greenhouse over for dinner, Nick's sudden shifts of moods, realizing Eric could be dead. Who knows what other combination of thoughts, perceptions, and facts convinced me that I needed to know what had gone on, what was going on. Finding out would help the arithmetic of my life and *that* game was well worth the price of a candle.

"So you think the vicious dog killer is going to come after you?" Bob asked, half smiling, folding his mat with slow, deliberate movements.

Nick looked at him. "I like animals more than people. They don't make fun of anyone."

"Bow wow," Bob said, his arms snapping up in dog-prayer position.

I was glad to run after Manou.

"You wish to go to the rain forest?" she asked as she marshaled a group of G.M.s down the stairs. Her eyes were greener than ever in that stormy day, and her hair looked like lightning had already struck.

"We are going on a day excursion to Basse-Terre. Lovely, you must come." At the Club entrance she stopped by the first waiting bus and started taking receipts. "This bus for Italian and French," she announced in a cheery tour guide tone. "The bus behind for German and English."

"Do you know where Zaza lives?"

"Is she not on the beach?"

"Zaza hasn't come to the beach since Iguana died."

Manou frowned at an old man, who was hoisting himself up the bus steps with difficulty despite his Nikes.

"*Monsieur,* you are American. Your bus is behind." She pointed. "This is the French and Italian bus."

"Which bus are you goin' on?" he said, eyeing the hand she'd placed on his arm.

125

"This one. My English not good."

"This one's the one I want then. Ain't nothin' you can do for my ears, little lady, but you sure can do a lot for these peepers." He laughed and heaved himself up.

"Je regrette," Manou said, after laughing back at the old man, obviously considering his comment a compliment. An American woman would have felt insulted, I thought. "I do not know where Zaza lives."

"Basse-Terre," the driver said, leaning over his steering wheel. He was twenty years old at the most.

"Where exactly?" I stepped up into the bus. "Basse-Terre is big."

"Basse-Terre, the town." He held a cigarette outside the window. "Behind the market. Above the fabric store."

"Come with us," Manou said behind me, her fingers counting heads. "We get to the town just before lunch. The tour costs *seulement* three hundred and fifty francs."

Renting a car was going to cost more, but I wasn't willing to jostle along in a bus for hours and get the tourist scoop on the mysteries of the island. I was in a hurry to hear what Zaza had to say.

THIRTEEN

Fifteen minutes later, I was ready to tear off for parts unknown, armed with a map and a 204 Peugeot the color of sand. Just as I shifted into first, Tommy scuttled up to the car, wrapped in enough cloth to surprise a Bedouin.

"Can I come, too?"

"I'm only going to the town of Basse-Terre and back."

"Good choice. It's got a great little market facing the Caribbean Sea." He started loosening the towel around his head.

"I was planning a quiet drive to sort out some work problems," I said in a heavy tone meant to imply the future of my ad agency was at stake. What I'd really been hoping for was to float on thoughts of Sunday night pasta with Greenhouse. Tommy stooped down to the car window and peered at me. His face was swollen and burnt raw in spots.

"God, Tommy, you've got to stay out of the sun!" He looked like he'd used dioxin as a suntan lotion.

"Oh, this isn't the sun." He removed his sunglasses to show me what had once been eyes and now looked like last month's *gnocchi*. "Allergies." He sounded proud.

"Will you take me? I can't afford the tour."

"Sure, get in." I relate to scrimping. Besides, how could I say no to that suffering face?

He ran in front of the hood to get in on the other side and bounced into the seat with the eager grin of a starved kid about to lick the frosting bowl. I certainly relate to that.

"You be the navigator, but no unnecessary talk, okay? I really need to do some thinking." Just the idea of Greenhouse filling my tiny apartment with his wonderful, edible self might sweat off an ounce or two.

Tommy never shut up. First I got the whole history of his allergies—baby formula on up to malt whiskey—and how his doctor thought it was a miracle he was still alive. By this time we had crossed the Salty River into Basse-Terre. I took a sharp left onto a rutted dirt road on the outskirts of Jarry. I'd decided to make a sudden visit to Eric's distillery to see if he was there.

"*Le Soleil* rum is good stuff," Tommy said. "Rum's the one drink I'm not allergic to. Rum and coke."

"How did you know where I was going?" There was no sign indicating that the half-crumbled building three hundred yards down the road was anything but a hurricane ruin.

"I took Monday's tour with Manou, remember? You're a little edgy, aren't you?"

"Sorry. I guess I am." It started to rain, heavy drops that hit the car roof like metal pellets. I stopped under the overhang of the distillery entrance and got out. Across the courtyard Papa La Bouche's rickety contraption was rolling bottles and gluing labels on its own. His stool was empty. The rum-producing machinery that lined one side of the building lay idle. Still no water probably, except from the sky. The office door was locked.

"Is anybody here?" I yelled. A young, startled head

pitched forward from behind a stack of empty crates in the glass-littered corner of the courtyard. I asked for Eric.

"Haven't seen," he answered, retreating his head back under the cover of a corrugated tin sheet that created a small, dry area. Between us, the rain poured, pitting the ground, giving that old courtyard a machine-gunned look.

"No show, huh?" Tommy asked me when I got back into the car. "How much longer are you guys gonna be here anyway?"

"Saturday." Where the hell was Eric? The rain was coming down in streams now. I was glad I wasn't on that sailboat with Ellen and Paul. If this rain kept up, we might not be able to leave. With only two and a half days left, we still had to shoot on Marie-Galante, Les Saintes and Carbet Falls. I drove slowly, feeling the tires beginning to spin in the mud. Suddenly I felt completely out of control, my emotions a scrambled mess. How could I even think of making sense of a murder? And once I'd stuffed Greenhouse with pasta on Sunday, what were we going to say to each other? How were we going to breach a four month gap? Tommy's flapping mouth wasn't helping much either. He was talking about Ellen now, how he'd never been close to a celebrity before.

"You guys ever think of shooting in New Orleans? The house from *Gone with the Wind* is right on St. Charles Avenue."

"Not for a while. Estée Lauder's old *White Linen* ads saturated the plantation market for a while. You don't sound like you come from New Orleans." We were back on the main road. The rain had stopped as abruptly as it had started, and I rolled down the windows to let in the musty smell of hot wet earth.

"I don't. It all depends on where you grow up. I mean

Paul says he's a New Yorker, but I'll bet you anything he grew up somewhere else. I grew up in Columbus, Ohio." A patch of sunlight hit the water to my left. The trade winds were pushing hard to clear the day.

"I guess I'll have to come into New York if I want to see you guys again, huh? Take in some shows. I love musicals."

I kept thinking of Greenhouse, of the wisdom of my move. I missed him too much not to want to keep seeing him. I'd walked off in a huff, thrown by my discovery of American feminism. I'd gotten all wound up with my needs, my fears, my rights, and like any new convert, I'd lost my sense of fairness, of proportion. Now I wanted to go back and enjoy his company, his lovemaking. If I relaxed my fears, maybe he'd relax his.

I looked over at Tommy who was still talking, visions of a night in the Big Apple with Ellen probably dancing under his swollen eyelids. He looked awful.

"Have you gone to the infirmary?"

"Yep. They gave me cortisone. I'll be fine. It's that white makeup I put on last night for the show rehearsal."

"What makeup did you use?"

"Same stuff everybody else in that number used. Bob smeared himself with it to advertise the white Olympic team. I'd be in the hospital if I'd done that."

"What are you going to do for tonight?"

"Put on lots of cold cream underneath. Thanks for worrying. I mean, you've really been nice to me. I'll be fine."

"That's crazy. Leave your face alone. Don't put anything on it."

"Thanks for worrying," he repeated, his sloughy face turned toward me long enough to make me uncomfortable. For some reason I felt as if I were being peeped at from behind half-closed blinds. It was his swollen eyelids, I decided, they left only a sliver of eyeball showing.

I slowed up the car at the Temple of Changuy, a blazing white stuccoed Hindu temple covered with bright colored statues that made me think of Mexican dolls. I imagined an equally strong-colored, happy-looking interior, where people would dance and sing in prayer, very different from the hushed, smokey churches I'd prayed in as a child under the glassy-eyed stare of gilt-clad statues of saints. A green-tailed rooster paraded in front of the gate as though he had been an honored temple guard in a previous reincarnation.

"What did you think of the cockfight?" Tommy said.

I speeded up again. "Were you there, too?"

"No way, but I was close by. Manou finagled a Club car and took a few G.M.s to a great jazz place just up the hill from there." He made it sound like a privilege for a special few.

"That explains the music we heard." And the Club car in the parking lot.

"I wasn't supposed to say anything because of the car. Manou just grabbed the keys from the office. It costs a fortune to get there by cab."

"How'd you know I was at the cockfight?"

"Nick sneaked into our group at the last minute." Tommy rubbed his nose, now just a peeling bump in the general swelling of his face. "She came with Bob."

And here I'd thought Bob had been looking for Nick all evening and she'd been crying out of loneliness. Wrong again, Simona. I glanced over at Tommy who seemed pleased with himself, as if he'd made me privy to a juicy secret. I wondered if he'd been the kind of kid that ratted on his classmates. Ratting and allergies, great attention-getting combo.

I drove on, noticing that the sky was now a pure

Wedgewood blue except for the clouds over the Soufrière volcano. Tommy kept busy stinking up the car with a yellow cream he was spreading on his face. I rolled down the window. At least the landscape was beautiful. Tommy had spotted a shortcut on the map, and we were winding our way up and across the bottom edge of the rain forest through wet multihued green canyons. I felt as if I were driving through a menthol cigarette ad.

"You're really in thick with that commissioner, aren't you?" Tommy said, after about twenty minutes of blissful silence. "It's still got to be rough for you. Finding her, I mean. I'm sorry. I've been worried about you. Really." He raised a hand toward my arm, unsure what to do next. "You're too nice for something like that."

I grabbed his hand and squeezed it. "Thanks, that's sweet," I said, a sucker for attention myself. I think he would have blushed if he hadn't been red already.

"You two look funny together. He's such a bear of a man, he makes you look small . . ."

And thin maybe?

". . . like a roly-poly puppy. Real cute."

I bared my teeth in a grin that made him laugh.

We'd come down to the town of Basse-Terre, and I was looking for a place to park on the crowded beachfront in front of the marketplace.

"Come on, you don't want to be stick-thin like Ellen," Tommy said. "That's a real turnoff."

"Who are you kidding?" I said, as I tried to maneuver into a narrow spot. "You can't keep your eyes off her." Parking makes me aggressive. I'm lousy at it.

"No way. For me a woman has to look warm and soft. You know . . . nurturing. Yeah, nurturing. I like that word."

Was he putting me on? I had about two millimeters

132

to spare on each side of the Peugeot—I'd make it.

"I want her to look like she can cuddle you to death."

Metal met metal with a dragged-out groan. I hit the brakes and cursed in pure Roman.

"Sorry, I didn't mean that," Tommy said, misunderstanding. "I didn't mean to bring up death again. I just wanted . . ." Tommy gulped like a fish on a pier.

"What Tommy, what did you want?" I snapped, furious with myself. His puffball eyelids split apart with effort. Two small, reddened eyes peeked at me.

"I've, well, I've fallen in love with you. I'm sorry."

Oh mamma!

I let him park while I scribbled a note for the owner of the dented Citroen. Tommy slipped the car right in, and by the time he locked up, I was in the middle of the crowded covered marketplace, feverishly interested in whatever met my eye. I didn't know what to say to him, what to do. I was having a hard time believing him. I could have sworn he'd been crazy for Ellen. Why was I always getting things wrong?

Out of the corner of my eye, I saw him pitter-patter toward me, shrouded in his layers of cloth, ready to face the Sahara or me.

"I've got an errand to run," I said, cowardly staring at a long, thin pineapple, while a stream of hips and elbows jostled me.

"Bottle pineapples they call those," Tommy said, following me as I pushed through aisles flanked by long tables of vegetables, fruits, and open bags of spices. "Did you know this town's never had any luck? It calls itself the capital, but the real center's Pointe-à-Pitre. I mean, they were dumb enough to build it at the base of the volcano and in . . ."

"I need to go alone, Tommy."

133

He stopped, swaying slightly on his small feet. "Sure thing. I'll wait here."

I walked away.

"Your friend Bob must be really upset about that woman's death."

That stopped me. "Why are you saying that?"

"They were friends. The week before you all came, they'd meet after his afternoon aerobic class. She'd be without the kid, waiting by that one gazebo on the beach. He'd come down and parade his muscles for a while with a towel around his neck. Then he'd jog to the end of the beach and she'd follow. I was on the mini golf course trying to practice my swing, so I had a real good view."

"Why are you telling me this?" I didn't like what I'd heard; I didn't like his sanctimonious tone.

"You have a crush on him. I thought you should know."

So my horny thoughts had shown through like tight panties. "You're very observant, Tommy," I said, trying to keep the resentment out of my voice. Nick was lying—now Bob. *Basta.*

"Yep, observant, that's me." For a moment his puffy eyes looked soulful. "What else can I do?"

I left, mentally wishing him someone's love. I didn't have it in me to offer mine.

FOURTEEN

There were three fabric stores behind the market. I got lucky in the second one. A young girl, rolling up yards of purple and green madras on a cardboard tube twice her height, told me to go down the side street to the first door on the right. Zaza lived in the back of the third floor.

"What do you want? Who told you where I lived?" Zaza asked me in rapid French, holding the door barely open. I saw half a dark eye, a snippet of tanned cheek, a strand of blue-black hair. I explained that I'd been the one to find Iguana. She opened the door at the sound of her friend's name and let me into a small room, her pointed face registering no welcome.

"Are you willing to talk about her?" I asked in English, my French abandoning me at the sight of the mess: a wall of dust motes framed a double bed covered in faded black cotton and topped by cushions that had once been bright. An unsteady pile of *France-Antilles,* the local paper, had been ditched in one corner. Half a dozen unmatched sandals lay strewn on the wide plank floor that still bore traces of sea-blue paint. The walls were bare, except for a few random nails stuck into thick layers of yellowing stucco. To the left, was an open door that gave me a view of a kitchen sink stacked with unwashed pots. The smell of the sea and the sun from the window didn't dispel the sense of sadness that came over me. The transient quality of the place reminded me of my first year in America, living in my cramped studio apartment, scrimping, lonely, scared that my gamble wasn't going to pay off, that freedom from a bad marriage was only an idea I'd read about in some romance.

"I just want to know more about her," I said, now feeling a stronger connection to these expatriate women. "I can't just let it go at finding her dead."

Zaza lit an unfiltered Camel from a flattened pack in her pocket. She looked like a neat black cat in her black jeans, her black T-shirt knotted under her breasts to show tanned ribs and a tight, flat stomach. Her hair, parted in the middle and cut bluntly around her ears, was dull with dye.

"She was a friend," Zaza said. "That's all there is to say." As she bit her top lip, her face looked angry rather than sad. The only makeup she wore was dense black mascara on her long lashes. "She is now gone."

She walked into a narrow corridor, and I followed, not sure whether she wanted me to or not. She kicked some towels that were lying on the floor into a tiny, cluttered bathroom, flicked the ash of her cigarette in the toilet, then closed the door and walked ahead.

"I guess I want to know more about her friendship with Eric. He's working with me and now he's disappeared." The news didn't faze her. I followed her into a small bedroom the size of the other, except this room was covered with posters of Notre Dame, the Eiffel Tower, a *bateau mouche* creeping along the Seine at sunset. Zaza went straight to the open suitcase on the bed and started throwing clothes inside, the cigarette firm between her teeth. All the bathing suits, pareus, and sundresses she'd been selling on the beach were strewn on the bed along with some narrow black dresses that had to be hers.

"I know nothing of Eric," Zaza said in English. "I wish to know nothing. If he is gone, the better for the world."

"Do you think he killed Iguana?"

"Shhh, *le petit*." Zaza stretched out on the bed and reached over to the other side of the bed. Lundi was blinking up at her from a bare crib mattress on the floor.

"Ciao, bello." I wiggled fingers at him. Whatever sadness this place had churned up was gone at the sight of that dirty face still full of sleep. "What's he doing here?"

"Where else should he be? Iguana lived here. This is her bedroom." She lifted Lundi up on the bed and propped him down on a pillow.

"He stayed with *Commissaire* Beaujoie for a bit," I said. Lundi ignored me even though I was waving both hands by now.

"Ah, no, the wife. She is crazy that one. Marcel could not stay with her."

"What do you mean by crazy?"

"Folle. Crazy, that is the word, no?"

I nodded. Had it been Madame Beaujoie on the phone? She'd been so desperate. What was it that Beaujoie had said on the beach of Sainte-Anne? Something about it being bad to hold what you couldn't keep.

"Do they have a son?"

"Ah, no! I hope not. If you are crazy, you must not have children, eh? But who knows the truth? Crazy, unhappy—sometimes it is the same thing. Iguana was so unhappy she was crazy sometimes." Zaza started to pack again, rolling her clothes in tight sausage-like

137

packages. Another suitcase was at the foot of the bed, so full she had tied rope around it.

"What made her unhappy?"

"I told the *Commissaire,* I will tell you. She wanted to go back to France, and she wanted money. Iguana worried about Marcel, his future. With money, she said she could buy him a new papa." Zaza waggled a hand in sign of protest. "Oh ooh! Not a great papa if he allows himself to be bought. Iguana had no logic . . . with this *idée fixe* in her head about wanting so much money, then talking of advertising, 'advertising is bad, advertising can bring death.' She was good, she was crazy and now she is gone." Zaza slammed the suitcase shut. Lundi laughed at the noise, drumming his hands on a pillow.

"Tomorrow I take him to his grandmother. *Commissaire* Beaujoie has lent me the money. I take Marcel and Iguana back to France. That is what she wanted. Her friends, we offered her money. It was enough for the trip, but not enough for her. So now she goes in a box."

Eric was expecting money and Iguana was trying to find it. Was there a connection?

"What about the boy's father?" Advertising? What did advertising have to do with her death?

"That's what the *Commissaire* would like to know. One day Marcel will want to know. Eric perhaps. I think Eric but then perhaps not." Lundi was standing now. Zaza pulled at his ankles, and he fell back on the pillows, laughing. Oh god, I thought, what will happen to him when he understands? His mother murdered and maybe his father . . . Eric, was Eric alive?

"Are you coming back?" It was easier to deal with her.

"Here I have friends, I have my work, a place to go every day." She curled up on the bed in one quick

138

movement, a cat nesting. "But I don't know. Here there is death and too much sun. Cancer—all the magazines talk of cancer. I pack everything in case. Also now I cannot afford two rooms."

"Who killed her, Zaza? You must have some idea? What about Coco? He was a friend of Iguana's. What does he say?"

Someone knocked on the entrance door. Knocked and kicked by the sound of it. Zaza uncurled slowly and sauntered to the door, as if the sound of someone breaking the door down was nothing unusual. I instinctively grabbed Lundi.

"God damn it! Why didn't you open right away?" It was Eric, alive and screaming.

Zaza screamed back in French. All I could understand was that she wanted him out. I didn't know whether to run out there and scream at him myself or stay with Lundi, who was now smacking his lips and pulling my hair.

"Where is it?" He dropped his voice. "She stole it from me. I want it back." I decided to stay put and eavesdrop.

"She stole nothing. You have not been here in months. There is nothing of yours here."

I heard what I thought was the refrigerator door opening. I sneaked a look in an old mirror resting on a table covered with shoe boxes full of lingerie. Next to the reflection of the Eiffel Tower, I could see Eric's back, opening kitchen doors, cupboards. "I'm gonna get outta here the minute I find it, so leave me alone, okay?" Find what? Not money; there was no money to find. Drugs? Was he a drug addict?

Eric jumped with a quick snapping motion of his knees, as if he'd been jabbed. "Damn that bitch!" He slammed a drawer shut with his fist, and turned. I didn't have time to step out of the mirror's reflection.

"Hey there, what'cha doin' here?" He beamed a grin at me as if I were his favorite sight. The left side of his face was blood red and had obviously been used as a punching bag. One eye was shut, the other popped out as usual, the eyeball darting from side to side.

"What happened to you?" I asked. "Why didn't you let us know you were still alive?"

"You look like you're sorry I am. Hey, kid, what's doing?" He snapped a finger at Lundi who strained out of my arms to touch him. Eric started throwing clothes around the bed. Lundi, ignored, started to cry.

"There's nothing here," Zaza said, pulling a black and gold stretch skirt out of his hands.

"Are you going to tell me what happened?" I bounced Lundi in my arms, trying to shush him. This is how it had all started, with the kid crying.

"Nothin' much. A little gambling that didn't pay off. Sorry about that, but I see you got home all right. I also hear my boat showed up so no sweat, you didn't lose out. Anyway, you had lousy weather this morning." He'd moved over to the shoe boxes on the table, punching a fist in each one.

"Get out of here, Eric!" Zaza threw a sandal at him. "Nothing of yours is here."

"Shall I call the police?" I offered, looking around for a phone.

"Ah, no!" Zaza looked at me as if I'd suggested a quick threesome. Lundi kept crying. Eric kept searching, opening the roped suitcase and scattering its contents on the floor, lifting the mattress, getting on his hands and knees to look under the bed. For what?

"May we help with the search?" I asked, in my best reform school headmistress tone. Zaza had taken Lundi who'd shut up on contact, which had given my annoyance an extra edge. "Are we looking for little packets of white powder or what?"

140

He pushed past me and opened the bathroom door. "One day you're gonna get that long nose of yours shortened."

I should have fired him after that comment, but of course I didn't, because I was too curious to know why he was turning the place upside down. Leaning against the dresser, I watched him sit down on the bathroom floor and sort through a pile of *Vogues, Elles,* and *Marie Claires.*

"Interested in women's fashions?" I was about to ask when I noticed a rolled-up magazine jammed underneath the curved bottom of the mirror's frame, as if to help prop it up. You could only see it standing sideways to the dresser.

"I've got a magazine collection that's worth a ton of bucks," Eric was saying now, fumbling through towels and rolls of toilet paper.

I'd seen them in his office—dirty piles of *Playboy, Penthouse, Adventure Life* with torn covers and curled pages. Hardly a collector's dream.

"Iguana took a few. She was mad at me. You know how women get." He was grinning again. I don't know how he did it with that face. Compared to him, Tommy looked like Tom Cruise. "Ruins the collection."

Lundi was walking around the bed, on his own again, crying again. Zaza tried to pick up the mess Eric had left. I started helping, but she pushed my hand away.

"Are you sure you don't want me to call the police?" I whispered. I offered to run downstairs. I hadn't been able to spot a phone.

"No, please go away. *Je t'en prie.* It's all right. There is nothing here. He will go away. He has already calmed down. Leave. You make it worse."

I glanced over at Lundi, who was now howling as if he were passing a kidney stone. I reached into my bag

141

and dangled Club beads. He grabbed the whole necklace and started sucking.

"Greedy." I kissed him goodbye on his forehead. Zaza's head was hidden behind the upraised lid of her suitcase. Eric was behind the bathroom door. The perfect moment. I scooped my hand behind the mirror and pulled, hunching my shoulders for fear the mirror would come crashing down. It didn't. I dropped the rolled-up magazine into my open bag and looked up to see a huge man loom in the mirror.

I lurched around, whipping my bag behind my back like any kid caught in the act. He nodded politely, waiting to be asked in. I recognized him as one of the gang of eight I'd seen last night at the cockfight. He was wearing the same bright yellow shirt. When I realized he hadn't witnessed my theft, he became as reassuring as a Guardian Angel standing by a dark subway entrance.

"You have a visitor," I said.

Zaza looked up from her suitcase and waved him in. *"Salut, Rudi."*

"They heard yelling downstairs," Rudi said, stepping into that first small bedroom, dwarfing it instantly. "They sent me to check."

We all heard Eric groan.

"Good luck, Zaza." I gave Lundi a last big hug. *"Enchantée* to meet you," I told Rudi as I eased out of the door. "And by the way, Eric," I yelled back into the apartment. "Consider yourself fired!"

I zoomed down the stairs like a shoplifter being chased by security. As I stumbled out into the side street, I smacked head-on into Tommy. I screamed and dropped my purse. He dropped a bag full of mangoes.

"This is my week for collisions," I said, sinking down fast to hide a small rolled plastic bag that gaped up at

142

me along with the rest of my junk. I scooped everything back into my purse while I fanned Eric's *Adventure Life* under Tommy's nose to distract him.

"I've never looked through these war fantasy magazines, have you?"

"That was supposed to be lunch," he said, ignoring the magazine and looking down at the orange and red splatter on his sneakers.

"I'm so sorry."

"I'd just bought these for us when I saw Eric. I knew you were looking for him so I followed." He tried to smile, but the bloat in his cheeks resisted the push. "I didn't expect to get you."

Mamma, he sounded lovelorn. What was I going to tell him?

"I'm sorry, Tommy . . . I . . ." I didn't enjoy disappointing him, and I felt so stupid about not having caught on earlier. I'd probably even egged him on with my attempts to boost his morale. "Look, Tommy, I had no idea. What I mean is . . . I'm already in love with someone."

"Yeah, I know, Bob."

"No, not Bob." The sun had come out, washed clean by the rain, brilliant, aiming straight for my eyes. "Someone in New York." Shading my face with the magazine, I spotted Beaujoie ambling toward us, dressed in a white shirt and dark blue suit as if he'd just come from a wedding. I called out and waved, happy to get out of a sticky situation.

"Ka ou fè," he greeted in Creole, holding his signature handkerchief over his forehead like an ice bag.

"Oh . . . the bear," Tommy said, disappointment in his voice.

Beaujoie trundled closer, and I introduced Tommy who didn't extend a hand. "I thought you'd never

143

show up for our appointment," I said, looking him straight in the eye. Beaujoie picked up his cue without even an eyelash flickering.

"Young man, will you be *gentil* and allow me to remove Mademoiselle Griffo? There are many things I must ask her."

"She's just told me she's not mine to give." Tommy was pressing the only two intact mangoes left to his chest, his towel hanging slack on his arm. "Official business, huh? She's your star witness, I guess. It's all right really. I'll eat my mangoes out by the waterfront. Want me to wait?"

"No, Tommy, take the car and tour all you want. We may take hours."

"You guys are on to something, huh? Well, thanks for trusting me with the car."

"That is a bad case of sun poisoning," Beaujoie said, pointing a finger at Tommy's face. "You should cover yourself. It is dangerous."

Tommy made a funny, choking sound with his throat. "I guess this town isn't the only one with bad luck, huh, Simona?"

I knew he wasn't talking about his allergies. "I'm sorry, Tommy." What else could I say?

FIFTEEN

We sat down at a corner table of Langou's, "where the women are beautiful and the food is good" according to Langou himself, a dark lizard of a man in his eighties who whisked rapidly between tables with plates stringing down his arms like oversized buttons.

Having finally caught my breath after tearing up the hills in Beaujoie's toy Renault as if we were winning the Monte Carlo Rally in a Porsche, I said, "Here's what I found."

I used the magazine to lift the package onto his empty plate. Beaujoie reached over to the sideboard to swipe a naked green bottle, unscrewed the top, and poured two glasses half full with rum.

"This is what Eric was really after," I said, gloating a little. I'd already told him about Eric barging into Zaza's apartment.

Beaujoie took a gulp of rum, then unfolded a clean handkerchief from his breast pocket.

"I'm afraid you'll find a lot of my fingerprints on it too. I dropped it and shoved it back in my purse real quick. I didn't want Tommy to see it. It was my very own BIG CLUE, something to be shared only with my sleuthing companion.

145

Unwrapping the roll with his handkerchief, Beaujoie opened the plastic bag and sniffed inside as if he were one of those DEA dogs I'd seen at Kennedy Airport.

"Is it cocaine?"

"I doubt it is flour." He rerolled the bag and slipped both handkerchief and package in his pocket. He looked unimpressed.

"Well, what do you think?" I was annoyed. I guess I'd expected a smacking "bravo." "Is Eric hooked or is he a private dealer?" I'd figured there was about a cup of white powder in that bag. Julia Child translates eight ounces into about two hundred and thirty grams, and I'd read somewhere that suppliers asked twenty thousand dollars for a kilo of coke. We were looking at approximately five thousand dollars worth, IF it was cocaine.

"People on Guadeloupe have no use for powdered drugs. We have our own." He drained his glass. I didn't touch mine.

"What about the people coming from the Métro?"

"A few sniffs have come in with the tourists. In a shoe, inside a portable radio, once inside the stuffing of a bra. All in all, Customs has found very little."

"I thought it might be a motive for murder." It didn't take much these days. Last year some teenagers in Connecticut had killed a man for eighteen dollars' worth of Chinese takeout. "Eric has talked about money coming in, that soon he'll be able to buy any distillery he wants."

"Not with this amount of drugs."

"Couldn't it be one of many such packages?"

"Perhaps, but there was no need to kill her to claim this one. What defense did Iguana have against him? Not her friend Zaza, who is as thin as a newly sprouted root?"

"Rudi . . ." I interrupted myself as I looked down to

146

see Langou, his head looking like an oversized nutmeg, grinning at me. His chin barely cleared the tabletop.

"Ka ou fè, Commissaire." He dropped four plates in front of us, each holding a stuffed sea shell, then darted toward three knapsacked hikers standing in the entrance. "Here one eats what the kitchen supplies," he shouted in toothless French.

"A man called Rudi came upstairs ready to play knight in shining armor," I said. "I'd already seen him last night at the cockfight with a gang of young men." Someone had asked him about Coco's whereabouts.

"Iguana might have had protectors," I said. "Coco and his friends, for instance."

Langou rushed by again, this time depositing bottled water and white wine.

Beaujoie's eyes steadied on mine. "I must thank you for accepting to lunch with me. I enjoy our tête-à-têtes."

"I've been trying to get hold of you." I expected him to say something about my phone call to his house late last night, but instead he looked down at his well-ironed blue suit.

"I have come from being informed by my superiors that I will single-handedly destroy our venerable tourist trade if I do not find Iguana's murderer. They wish for me to arrest Eric Kanzer, but I hesitate."

"I finally fired him, thank God."

"Innocent until proven guilty, is that not the American way?"

"I'm Italian and our way is 'To trust is good, not to trust is better.' Anyway, he's guilty of extreme rudeness to everyone except Ellen, and he should have called this morning to tell us he was still alive."

Beaujoie was contemplating the two plates in front of him as if he were determining where justice lay. He waved a fork at the rich orange stuffing of one shell. "Crab, spices, onions mixed with yams. A Langou specialty." The fork shifted to shell number two. "Crab, milder spices. Less good in my opinion. Try the orange one first. It speaks for the Islands."

I obliged. The first taste was delicious, then the Fourth of July went off in my mouth and I gagged, tears gushing into my eyes. Nodding approval, Beaujoie offered me a handkerchief. He seemed to have an endless supply for all occasions.

"As a spokes-dish it lacks a little umph," I said, wiping my eyes and fanning my mouth, dumbly pleased by this burning ritual of food sharing. I felt initiated.

"Eric might be the killer," Beaujoie said before clamping his mouth down on a forkful of the stuff. He chewed, swallowed, and stayed dry-eyed.

"He was on the scene. He knew where she was meeting you. He has had a relationship with the victim. He may even be the father of her child. Thanks to you we discover that in the victim's apartment there is a package, probably containing drugs, wrapped in a magazine that he claims to wish with some urgency. That package was not in the apartment when my men searched yesterday. As to the magazine, may I?" He dropped a pink palm on the table. I handed the magazine over.

After a quick look at the front cover—a lifelike drawing of an American soldier gripping a machine gun in the desert—he leafed through the pages, stopping to study the ads in the back. Paratroopers were wanted to jump in Sri Lanka; a sound detector multiplied sound four thousand times; T-shirts came in Qaddafi yellow or Desert Shield sand; guns, all sizes and shapes of guns, were begging to be bought.

Beaujoie checked a list from his pocket. "One issue of *Adventure Life,* dated October of last year," he read squinting, holding the list far from his eyes. "Accounted for by my men. The package is new, the package is probably what he is after."

I smiled as if he'd come up with the most original of thoughts, then looked down at my crab. The important debate was hellfire by food or starvation.

Beaujoie put the list back in his pocket. "A magazine glorifying guns, violence, war," he said, throwing the magazine on the table. "What idiocy. What shame!"

"Eric has a stack of these back in his office. You'd think Vietnam would have been enough for him." I took another bite of Brimstone crab and dabbed my eyes. Maybe my fat would burn off along with my mouth.

"He was never there, we checked. He was 4F, I believe it is called." He filled his wine glass. "That may explain his passion for this sewage."

Paul was going to give me a Happiness Look on that information for sure.

"Why are you hesitating about his arrest? No hard evidence?"

"I have this picture. Eric is there with Iguana and the child," Beaujoie wiped the length of his vast face with a hand, as if it were a washcloth, "but he is to one side. He does not fit in the cutout of the murderer. Perhaps the catalyst, but not the murderer. He would not use a machete, I think. A gun yes. He poses as an American war hero. He has a passion for guns. His magazine is as full as an egg with gun advertisements."

"It was also as full as a crab claw with knife ads." Actually I'd only spotted a Legionnaires Survival Boot knife ad, but his visionary way of doing police work was throwing me. Greenhouse had convinced me the police stuck to the facts, not fantasy like I did.

Beaujoie plunged a fork into the crab shell I'd offered him. "I have no evidence against him. Against anyone."

"What about her beach friends, the vendors?"

"All her friends, including Zaza, were at a sunset to sunrise party down in the town of Basse-Terre with the mayor's son, a good friend of theirs. He vouches for them. The mayor's son!" Beaujoie widened his eyes. "In any case, we question the band, the servants. With discretion. A slow process, but then we are only on the second day of the investigation."

"What about lovers? Eric said she had a lot of lovers."

"That we know of, three in as many years. Very few, judging by today's morality. AIDS has not brought sense to the young. They take such risks, they . . ." he looked out the window at a bridge, covered with purple morning glories, that stretched over a narrow, green gulch. Behind Beaujoie, a small waterfall looked as if it were spilling on his shoulder.

"She was not lucky in love, *la petite*." He shifted and I saw the waterfall pour onto wet black boulders. "A Parisian who came here to die of cancer; a black student from Mozambique who returned home without her; and Eric. Those were the important lovers. I cannot know about the one-night romances." He extracted his faithful handkerchief and kneaded it against his palm. "Who is the father of the boy? We can rule out the student from Mozambique, that is all. I am a good policeman, but I am not that good." His eyes wandered back into the wide room with bare stucco walls and tables covered in checkered oilcloth. Maybe he was wondering if Lundi's father was there among the half-dozen men eating and drinking, or the two men playing dominoes in a corner.

"It only takes fifteen minutes to make a baby, maybe less," he said.

"Sometimes a lifetime is not enough," I said.

Beaujoie raised his arm, snapping fingers, calling for

Langou. He spoke in rapid Creole, suddenly angry. He mistook my contrite face for surprise.

"We cannot wait forever for the main course!"

"Of course not," I said, mortified. I hadn't remembered the woman on the phone pleading for her son. His wife. Had they lost a son? Had they ever had one? Had I blurted those very words because I wanted him to tell me?

A girl came rushing to our table, her face averted, stiffly holding out two clean plates and a platter heaped with *Poulet Colombo,* an Island specialty.

I played hostess and served him two chicken halves, firmly believing in food as a peacemaker.

"Was Coco Iguana's lover?" I asked to distract him.

"Coco admits only to friendship. The other friends concur." He ate in silence.

I picked at my chicken, vaguely remembering I was supposed to stop eating for the rest of my life.

"Have you questioned people at the Club?" I munched on a wing for cover. "The G.O.s for example?" I was thinking of Tommy's jealous tidbit about Bob meeting Iguana every afternoon. I told Beaujoie, feeling unpleasantly gossipy. "He might know something more about Iguana," I ventured, thinking they may even have been lovers. It would explain why Bob had lied in front of Nick about knowing "any of those peddlers," as he'd put it. I couldn't bring myself to voice that possibility. What kind of man flirts with a woman within hours of his lover's death?

"I have spoken with G.O.s, with G.M.s. So many words to sift through. It is like an archeological dig covered in layers of sand and rocks." He was eating his chicken politely, between sentences, his knife and fork carefully preparing small bites. "I met with your group of friends in Gosier quite by accident. I took the

151

opportunity to ask them a few questions."

By accident? Why did I have the uncomfortable feeling, that despite his gentle ways, he was zeroing in on us?

"Monsieur Paul was worried for Mademoiselle Ellen, worried about the rocks that were thrown."

I dropped the wing bones, sucked clean, and went for a drumstick.

"I sent them to the *Panthère Rose* for lunch. Excellent. I used to dine there on special occasions."

A happy memory seemed to waft over his round, pleasant face, erasing for a moment the appearance of solid strength his size gave him. I pictured Madame Beaujoie in a flowered dress, wearing a hat perhaps, sitting at an outside table at night, toasting a birthday or an anniversary with a younger, thinner Beaujoie, dressed as he was now, in wedding blue. Both of them happy.

It was my turn to be a visionary.

"What do you know of Paul Langston?" Beaujoie asked me, after setting aside his half-eaten chicken. He seemed to have lost his appetite.

"Very little, except that he's good at his job. The days of knowing family histories are long gone. In America no one seems to live in the same city for long. Job mobility, they call it. Do you know what IBM stands for? I've Been Moved. Why are you asking about Paul?"

"That man is too much in love. It has made him angry."

"He likes to brood." I waved my drumstick for courage. "Listen, what about Bob? Could he have been one of Iguana's lovers?" It didn't sound so bad out loud after all. I mean it could have been an over-and-done-with-let's-stay-friends affair. I thought of Nick wearing my skirt, lipstick, her nose pressed against the

152

telephone booth, looking happy. I wanted her to stay that way.

"He is not on the official list. You care for this Bob?"

"I just . . ." I looked down at what was left of the drumstick. Why was I eating and why was I playing Cupid, sending Nick and Bob off jogging into an unblemished dawn? And what about Nick? Should I tell Beaujoie she lied about not knowing Lundi, about never having been here before. I put the drumstick down. I couldn't do it. I couldn't rat like Tommy. Lies don't necessarily lead to murder, I told myself. Nick had nothing to do with Iguana's death.

"Bob Halsey seems a nice young man," Beaujoie said. "Is he a friend of the heart?"

"No," I said. Greenhouse's gentle face appeared right there at the window, with the waterfall falling down through his face as though he were a real reflection, not just a vision my need had conjured up. I even turned around to check if he were really there. Bob and Greenhouse. Their faces merged in my mind.

"No, Bob is not a friend of the heart, but he does remind me of someone I know in New York. They don't look anything alike—Bob is far handsomer—but they have the same clean, honest expressions." That's the first thing I'd noticed about Greenhouse. Well, actually the first had been his eyes. With twenty feet between us, I'd noticed his smiling eyes.

"They both have what I call the American look," I said. "As good and satisfying as apple pie made with real sugar. It's funny how something as intangible as a perception can connect two very different people."

"On his second voyage across the Atlantic," Beaujoie said, "Christopher Columbus discovered a small island near the eastern tip of Guadeloupe. He named it La Désirade, the desired, thinking perhaps he had found a gem in the ocean. Instead it was a waterless stretch of land full of cactus and iguana. For many years it was used as a leper colony." He cast serious black-olive eyes on my face. "Perceptions can be false."

"You mean to trust is good, not to trust is better. Well, I know I claimed that was my Italian credo, but to tell you the truth I always forget it. 'Everything makes broth' is a saying much more my style. I like the idea that everything we do, everything that happens to us, doesn't go wasted."

Beaujoie kneaded his handkerchief. "In French we say, *tout fait ventre*—everything makes belly. The thought may be reassuring, but you must admit that sometimes that 'everything' gives belly aches."

"Yes, I'll admit that," I said looking away at the waterfall behind his shoulder not to see the pain that was on his face.

"What force of nature met up with Eric's face?" I asked after a silence. "Coco?"

"That is one affair I shall ignore until there is an official complaint." Beaujoie pushed aside the too sweet *mousse chocolat* Langou had brought us. "There is a full moon tonight, and Papa La Bouche will tell stories on the beach to the Sainte-Anne children. Tonight it will be the moonfish story, one of my favorites. Unfortunately it is a story Madame Beaujoie does not like. I would enjoy another woman's opinion. Perhaps after your performance?"

"I called your house last night."

"I know. I hope my wife did not upset you."

"I am only sorry I upset her."

"Thank you. She is better today." He turned toward the wide beaded curtain that hid the kitchen. "What keeps you so young, Langou?" Beaujoie called out. "What is your secret?"

Langou popped his nutmeg head between beaded strings of green glass. "Women," he said and blew

154

kisses into the room.

"To Madame Beaujoie," Beaujoie said quietly, turning back to raise his wine glass at the view outside the window.

"May you both keep well," I said, clinking my glass against his.

A smile came to his face, as fragile as nostalgia.

SIXTEEN

When Beaujoie dropped me off at the Club, it was pouring again. This time it was the usual ten-minute afternoon shower, and I was beginning to suspect it was a Club ruse to get the sunbathers running to the bar. So like the French to make contact with the Higher Power.

I found Nick and Bob in shorts and sleeveless T-shirts, wet with sweat and rain, lunging at each other on the steaming basketball court. Bob bounced the ball between Nick's legs, turned on one foot, and caught it as it came up behind her. She spun around, punched the ball sideways, and leaped after it with a kick of her furlong legs. They looked great together, evenly matched, graceful, their faces lit up by the enjoyment of exercise and what looked to me very much like foreplay the aerobic way.

"Nick should be a G.O.," Manou said, stopping to watch at the edge of the court. "They would hire her *toute de suite.*"

"No way." Bob threw the ball at Manou. I caught it and looped it over to Nick. "I don't like competition," he yelled and careened into her.

"They look good together those two, eh?" Manou

winked at me. "Your friend Tommy left this for you."
She lifted her lime green camisole and unhooked
something from the beltline of her silk paisley boxer
shorts. She handed me a set of car keys. "He tried to get
a refund for the hours you did not use the car, but
couldn't. He suggests you take a long drive not to waste
the money, and if you wish company, he is waiting by
the bar."

"Thanks."

Manou gave me a rueful smile as if she understood
my predicament, and lifted her hair to tie it above her
head in an unruly mass that instantly reminded me of
the dust mop my grandmother used to make out of the
unraveled black wool of old "church" sweaters. Out of
respect for the dead Christ, my grandmother always
wore black on her daily visits to chilly marble-lined
chapels—that meant a lot of sweaters and a lot of dust
mops. I'd even brought one with me to New York
which I used only on the anniversary of her death. The
resemblance made me warm up to Manou.

"How does one become a G.O.?" I asked.

"It's enough to contact a Club Med office and send a
résumé. Knowledge of languages is important, a special
talent with sports or theater helps, but there are many
things you can do. The cuisine, the bank, the boutique,
the excursions. There is something for everyone."

"Where's the rest of the gang, Nick?" I called out.
Bob was holding the ball way above his head. She was
reaching for it, tilting her body forward, her lips level
with his chin. They were *not* playing basketball, and
that court was not steaming from God's weather.

"We're back, we're back," HM said, sauntering by
with a palm fronds hat covering half his face. "Gosier
was fabulous even in the rain, and Paul got some neat
close-ups of Ellen anyway. That *Commissaire* guy sent
us to a fantastic place for lunch. You missed out, kid."

157

HM sipped from a long pink drink and watched Nick and Bob chase each other from one basket to the other.

"It is not all good to be a G.O., you must know," Manou was saying. "The Club discourages boyfriends and girlfriends even among ourselves. 'It distracts from the work of giving a G.M. a good time,'" she quoted, sounding like some Surgeon General's warning.

"Hey, Nick's on. About time, too," HM said. "She fought Paul tooth and nail about coming down here and now look at her—she is *hot*. My money's on her."

"What do you mean?" I asked.

"There are a lot of lonely women who come," Manou said, thinking I was talking to her. "They want attention. If they see a G.O. with his girlfriend, they feel even more lonely."

HM smacked his lips. "What about lonely men? Who takes care of them?"

Manou tossed her head. "I flirt a little. The rest is my business, not the Club's."

"Not what I meant at all," HM said with a wink at me. "To answer your question, Jerry told me Nick just didn't want to come. Paul got so mad he threatened to fire her. BEAU SUN is everyone's big break, he wasn't going to let Nick screw it up." He lifted his chin to stare at Manou's head.

"Sweetheart, you ought to let me in your hair. It needs a little rummaging. And as for that gorgeous G.O. thumping that ball out there," HM turned to follow Bob with his eyes, "I hope he doesn't consider what he's been doing on the court with Nick part of his job, because I'll dye that blond head of his deep purple."

I looked at Nick. She'd stopped playing now. The sun, low behind her, projected a long, gawky shadow toward us. What was it about this place that she didn't like? Did it connect with Iguana?

"HM, you wish to become a G.O.?" Manou said, her hands tugging her black curls. "We open a beauty parlor for you. Good idea, no? But you would not stay long, I know. Americans become G.O.s for a few seasons, for fun. In Europe it is a career. To become the Chef du Village is very good."

Nick had walked up to the edge of the court. "Is there a chefesse?" she asked. Bob shot baskets alone.

Manou gave a cocky smile. "Not yet, but Corsica has given France an emperor, she may yet give France a *chefesse du village.*"

"Did Beaujoie ask a lot of questions?" I said. Was I trying to warn Nick?

"Naw, but I'd watch out for him," HM said. "He's like a crab. You know, walks sideways? He doesn't really ask. He fixes you with that dark moon face of his, his eyes screwed on yours. I talked. Can you figure, I even told him the first time I realized I was gay. I was twelve years old, and I fell in love with this skinny teacher fresh from Columbia Teachers College. He was scared shitless of us kids, and I wanted to protect him. We're talking Bronx jungle here. What that's got to do with that woman's death, I don't know, but he sure seemed interested. Wanted to know all about our backgrounds." HM slurped the last of his pink drink. "Paul got real annoyed and wouldn't answer, but then Paul's really something these days, right, Nick?"

"He's okay." Nick's face was blank.

"HM, I am free for half an hour," Manou said, shaking her hair. "Make the magic!"

HM wrapped an arm around Manou's shoulder. "Come this waaay, oh sweetness of my heart. I've been waiting to get my hands on this mess you call hair since I first saw you." They went off in the direction of his room.

Nick caught me looking at her. "Paul told me to tell

you he and Jerry are taking pictures at Castles' Point," she said. "He's arranged for the sailboat to come back in the morning to take us all to Marie-Galante, Eric or no Eric."

"Good. I fired Eric. He's battered, but still alive and unpleasant as ever. Where's Ellen?"

"I don't know. In her room, I guess. I hope Paul and Jerry are careful. Those rocks can be real dangerous at high tide." She turned to look at the sun. "Which is about now."

"Nick, what's going on? You know an awful lot about this place. Come on, open up, tell me the truth." Don't let me think you're involved in a murder.

She kept looking at the sun.

"Hey, Nick, why don't you consider being a G.O. for a while?" Bob asked, dribbling the ball our way. "Great travel, fun. We might even end up in the same Club. It's gotta beat living in Rotsville."

"Did Beaujoie come around here asking questions?" I said. Did I have the right to ask Nick point-blank why she was lying?

"The morning after the murder, sure," Bob said, glancing down at my bag, spread open on the grass. "Not today."

I couldn't in front of Bob.

"You don't mind if I look through this, do you?" Bob asked, picking up Eric's *Adventure Life*. "I thought you'd be reading Italian *Vogue*. Not this stuff. Sometimes these magazines have ads or articles on endurance races in funky places. I've always thought of doing that some day."

Nick looked over Bob's shoulder as he leafed through, avoiding my eyes. "Some magazine like this one got blamed for a man's murder," she said. "The publisher ended up losing fifteen million dollars in court. They'd printed a gun-for-hire ad."

"They stopped doing that six years ago. These ads are harmless," Bob said.

Nick made a face. "I'm going back to the room to shower. You have to be at the theater at eight, Simona."

Gun-for-hire. I remembered Tommy saying something about an independence movement; Eric vehemently denying its existence; Coco's friends, Rudi and the other men, strutting into the cockfight like warriors.

"I've got to go, Bob." I picked up my purse off the grass.

Bob smiled and handed the magazine back. "No endurance races in that one."

"Try Outward Bound." I hurried off to HM's room.

"You're an excursion G.O., you know things about this place. What have you heard of an independence movement?" I stared at Manou. HM had gelled her hair into a slick cap down to her ears, then curled the rest into long corkscrew curls. The focus now was only on her green eyes, her tanned unblemished complexion, and her cheekbones. She was stunning.

"They say there is a small group . . . I like this," she said, tilting her head this way and that. "Nothing of importance."

"No lipstick, just a trace of blush under the cheekbones," HM said, his hands hovering over her head. "Nothing must distract from those eyes. Have you ever seen anything like 'em? The color of kiwis!"

"It was a stronger movement five or six years ago," Manou said, letting go of her image in the mirror. "But independence is not practical. Over half the revenue of the island comes from French aid and employment. It is like Corsica with these fanatics who think they can bomb themselves away from France. If there is no tourism and no French money, how are we to live? You tell me that? How?" She was shaking her hair free in anger. "It is the wrong politics."

"Manou!" HM rushed for his comb.

Papa La Bouche had mentioned politics when he'd talked about his son. "Is Coco involved?"

"Coco cuts coconuts and the G.M.s take pictures. That is all I know." Manou tilted her head back and let HM comb her hair down. "HM, soothe me." She closed her eyes and started singing in a throaty Eartha Kitt voice. "Do do your voodoo on little Manou."

"Which reminds me," HM said. "Eric showed up five minutes ago. He took Ellen to one of those black magic people in Sainte-Anne."

I must have sweated off five pounds sprinting to the car in thirty seconds flat.

SEVENTEEN

I found them north of the main road, on a narrow street flanked by one-story concrete houses with wooden verandas painted in bright pastel colors. Eric's jeep was parked in a dirt alleyway next to a tailor's shop painted bright turquoise. Squeezing past the jeep, I saw a thirty-yard stretch of tall grass that led to a row of scrawny banana palms, behind which sat a one-window shack made of sheets of corrugated tin nailed onto wooden planks. Empty, rusting metal drums lay gathered on one side of the yard like giant sleeping dogs. Above them, a coconut hung from one of the banana trees bearing a name—M. QUICKO—scrawled in white paint. I thought of shrunken heads and hurried up the dirt path to knock at the tall yellow door that had once belonged to a larger house.

A black woman with hair dyed bright orange opened the door and let me into a small, spotless room that held a folding deck chair, a crate on which a ten inch color TV was tuned to a girl singing a French love song, and a yellowing black-framed photograph of a severe-looking, gray-mustached man. M. Quicko senior, founder of the family business? The smell of cloves clogged thought; the heat of the room was like quick cement mix—instant immobility.

"He is busy now," she said automatically. "Come back in a half an hour."

"I'm looking for a friend." I mouthed the words carefully, afraid they would evaporate before leaving my mouth. The woman looked as cool as a moka float.

Eric stepped out from behind a faded flowered curtain, the buckles of his combat boots jangling. He was wearing his I'M A F...HERO T-shirt. F for failed or fired.

"Where's Ellen?"

"Well, if it isn't Miss Long Nose. Ellen's just fine. She's with Monsieur Quicko, the best magic man on the island." His face looked less swollen, but he still wasn't a pretty sight. The bright red of his battered cheek had settled to a raw liver color.

"It is you who need magic," the orange-haired woman said, jerking her chin at Eric.

"Like hell I do." Eric grabbed my shoulder and tried to push me out.

"Ellen, are you all right?" I called out, clutching the doorjamb.

Ellen poked her head from one side of the curtain, releasing a stronger waft of cloves. "This is interesting," she said. "Could you both wait outside?" She gave a smile of apology.

I yanked Eric's hand off my shoulder and walked out. I was furious with him for touching me and angry at Ellen for trusting him.

"This is Ellen's free time," Eric said, leaning against one of the empty metal drums. "It's got nothing to do with the job, so why'd'ya show up?" He tore off a banana leaf and started fanning himself.

I walked as far away from him as I could, feeling stupid for having rushed off after Ellen as if she were on fire. In the gagging heat of that shack, she'd looked as wonderful as ever—not one bead of sweat on her. I inhaled the breeze from the ocean. It felt as good as opening my freezer door in a New York July.

"Did you find your magazine?" I said.

"Yep. And my pal Rudi helped me look." He gave me a big infuriating grin. "You should have stayed. We ended up partying. A Bon Voyage for Zaza and the kid. They're on the four-thirty flight for Paris tomorrow."

"Is he your son?"

"Shit, you're unbelievable!"

"You bring out the best in me."

He shrugged. "So what if I'm Pop. The kid's goin'." I could have sworn I heard regret in his voice.

"The boy's going to need a father and maybe you could use a son. You might learn to be kind."

"Kind doesn't get you far. I got plans. Gonna fly me to the States soon for a job. As I told you, some real money's comin' up. I'm just waitin' to hear. And I'm not comin' back either. I'm going to dump the distillery back in the old man's lap. Let him keep gluin' labels on empty bottles 'til he's belly up. Not me! I got me a better life just waitin'." He sounded like a different Eric, even though he was spewing the usual bombast. His nervous energy was gone; his voice was flattened out, as if he'd stopped believing in his own words.

"What about your label, the one in that great-looking frame? You were so proud of it." I was almost feeling sorry for him.

"That label's just painted paper. Now the frame's gonna go with me. I like to think of it as a job trophy. That piece of silver's the kinda thing my mother would have liked." He laughed. It was the same old cackle. "If I'd ever known her, that is."

"What made you change your mind? Last night's beating? Is that why you're leaving?" I walked over and

165

joined him on the metal drum.

"It takes more than a nab or two to bring a vet down." At that moment I did feel sorry for him, but he misread my face. "You still think I killed Iguana, don't you? You think I suck so I gotta be the killer. Well, I killed a few people in my life, that's part of war, but I didn't kill her." He leaned into me and jabbed a finger in my arm. That's when I realized what had softened him up, made him sound almost decent. He was drunk. From the reek, I could have torched his mouth with a match.

"Maybe I roughed her up a couple a times. She got on my nerves, but she was an okay gal. I shouldna bad-mouthed her. It's not fair to the kid."

What about it not being fair to her, I wanted to ask but Ellen had come out of the shack. She was carrying a Grey Poupon jar full of a dark liquid as if it were the secret formula for Coca-Cola. She blinked in the sunlight.

"Hey, hon, how'd it go?" Eric said, standing up without wavering. He sure could hold his liquor. "I see you got your brew."

"I think I got a little scared in there," Ellen said, taking a deep breath. "The heat was overpowering, and that smell was awful."

"Yeah, cloves. That's the smell of a poison they squeeze out of some local fruit. Is that what you got there?"

The orange-haired woman was standing at the door, staring at me. She probably thought I wanted to be next.

"You aren't goin' to use that on me, are you?" Eric pointed to the jar.

"Nooo, this isn't poison."

"What is it then?" I said. The woman kept waving at me from the threshold, wanting me to come in. I'm

166

superstitious, I check my horoscope once in a while, in bad times I toss coins and read my *I Ching,* but black magic is a bit far out for me.

"No thanks, really," I said to the woman. "I'm not a believer."

"Oh, go, Simona. It's fun. He said my future's going to be lovely."

"No, merci."

"I'm okay," she said, sensing I didn't want to leave her alone. "No one's going to eat me up. God, you're worse than my father."

"Gratis," the woman said, her hand still rotating like a windmill. *"C'est important."*

"We'll wait for you," Ellen said, giving me a push. "It's free. Give him a try."

"Why wait for her? She's got her own car."

The woman at the door lifted a forefinger. *"Une minute seulement."*

"Sixty seconds, that's the long, happy life you deserve." Eric was sounding more like his old self.

"Simona, I'm fine!" Ellen was getting mad.

"Okay," I said. "For one free minute I'll listen to my future."

I never got to see him. The orange-haired woman was the one who wanted to talk. And not about my future either.

"Be careful for Mademoiselle," she said in slow French, her voice low. "Her aura is bad." In that heat anybody's aura was bound to stink.

"Bad how?" I checked out the one window just to make sure. Eric and Ellen were standing close to each other. He was reaching out his hand, and she was shaking her head. She was smiling, that's what counted.

"Bad things will happen."

"What? Where? Let me talk to Monsieur Quicko."

"No, no. I am the one who sees. She is beautiful and fragile, be careful for her. For Monsieur Eric it is too late."

"What's too late?" This was sounding like gullible tourist gibberish. "What are you talking about?"

She dropped a red bean in my hand. "It must come from someone close to her. Hold it in your hand, transfer your warmth, then give it to her. It will protect her."

"From what? What is this?"

"This is for Monsieur Eric. He would not accept it from me. Put it near him when he will not notice. It may help." She opened her palm to show me a small, black silk pouch. A silver crucifix dangled from one of its strings. "It may still help."

I instinctively brought the pouch to my nose. It smelled of garlic, not cloves.

"Watch over them both," she whispered. I took a quick look at the windows. What I saw made me fly out the door.

Eric was hugging Ellen, pushing his face into her neck, his hand tearing at her blouse. Ellen screamed.

"Get your hands off her," I yelled, jumping on his back. "Get out of here. I never want to see you again. You are fired, doubly fired. Fired off this earth!"

"Simona, I can take care of myself!" Ellen yelled back at me, instantly furious.

Eric snarled, "Who the fuck do you think you are?" But he let go of Ellen and threw me off his back as if I were a leech.

"Damnit, why has everyone elected himself my protector? Why can't I live my own life? What did the agency do, Simona? Give you a mandate to stop any man from touching me? Is that going to help sell more cosmetics?"

"You screamed."

168

"It was the surprise. I didn't mean for anyone to come leaping to my defense. He was just trying to kiss me, for chrissakes."

"While he tore at your blouse!" Her hand shot up to button her shirt.

"It's no big deal," she said.

I gave up trying to understand. "I'm sorry," I said. "I guess I got carried away. I knew Eric was drunk and this woman was giving me some voodoo mumbo jumbo. It's just that, well, I am responsible for you, Ellen. And even if you get a kick from some guy mauling you, some awful things have happened here. I'm nervous and I've got a job to do. You're our most precious commodity. I hate to put it this way, but it's the truth. I have to make sure nothing happens to you." I found myself fingering the red bean in my hand.

"I hate this." Ellen dropped down on the grass. Behind her, Eric kept himself busy stuffing his T-shirt back in his jeans. "I'm a healthy, twenty-three-year-old woman. I don't have to be babied. I'm not going to jump out of a window like my mother. She had her problems, they're not mine. Why can't anyone understand that? My father got so scared he locked me up in Omaha with my aunt. She used to sneak into school to watch me. Even when I was in high school, there she was behind some locker, sure I was going to flirt with some boy and next thing she'd know I'd be a whore, a druggie, or both. That's what she called my mother once, to Dad's face. She spelled it out so I wouldn't understand. D-R-U-G-G-E-D O-U-T W-H-O-R-E. Try it, it's a real mouthful. And she was a lousy speller. She left out one G." She tugged at a weed. "I wasn't even allowed to date unless she came along. Then you called offering the possibility of modeling. Wow, New York! Finally be with my Dad, out of her clutches. Then he started. You know how he hated my modeling.

Then the agency turned out to be another chaperone. Scriba makes a pass and out he goes. Paul handles me as if I were dry ice. Eric tries to kiss me and you fire him. God, sometimes I think I'd love to be ugly. Then if someone kissed me, everyone would be grateful."

"You'd hate it after about thirty seconds."

Ellen stopped tugging weeds and let out a long sigh. "You're right, I would. And I'm getting a little too self-absorbed." She looked up at me. "It's just that all this stuff keeps churning up, and I want to think of myself as Miss Strong." She gave me a quick, contrite smile. "Thanks."

I nodded. "By the way, I fired Eric this morning. It had nothing to do with you."

"Let's just say I gave notice," Eric said, his eyes sliding to her. "I got things happenin' hon! More important things, you know, for my career. I'm off, outta the Caribbean. That deal I told you guys about is comin' through. I was just tryin' to give you a little bit of sugar to remember me by." He raised his arms and came leering at her. "Why don't we ignore the boss lady and start where we left off."

She shot up off the ground fast, throwing a fistful of weeds at him. "I don't care what your life's been like. You are never to force yourself on a woman again!" With that she picked up her jar and walked away. Eric stayed put, looking completely baffled. After a beat, I ran after her, and as I squeezed past Eric's jeep, I dropped the silk pouch in his back seat. I was mad, but not mean enough to deprive him of his good luck charm.

"Come on, Ellen, I'll drive you back." Without another word, we got into my rented Peugeot and drove off.

*   *   *

170

We were two hundred yards from the Club turnoff when Eric's jeep zoomed up next to Ellen's rolled-down window.

He turned toward us, anger crammed in every crease of his face, his hair blowing straight back, as if the wind were trying to drag him away from us. I put my foot on the accelerator, but he kept up.

"You fuckin' bitch!" he yelled. "You're going to pay for this!" He flung his arm out and something black flew past Ellen's face.

She let out a gasp, flattening herself against the car door. "Is it a bug?"

Eric's jeep careened past us and I veered into the turnoff.

"Maybe it's something nastier than a bug," I said and reached between my seat and the hand brake.

"Whaaat?"

"A hex." I dangled Eric's black pouch in front of her.

"Eric just hexed us?"

"Someone may just have hexed Eric." I waved my Club bracelet at the guard and he let the car through. "And I'm the idiot who dropped this pouch in his jeep. No wonder he was mad." I parked the car in the drive-in circle.

"Someone in the gambling racket is trying to scare him," Ellen said, slipping out of the car. "That's why he disappeared last night, did he tell you? Some men dragged him off and beat him up to make him pay his debts."

What kind of debts? I wondered. I didn't believe the gambling excuse. This had to be something bigger, more dishonorable. At the cockfight no one had met his eyes, as if they knew he was to be punished. I opened my hand. With the sheen of the silk opaqued by dust, the pouch looked as harmless as a crinkled, black fig. The crucifix was no larger than a thumbtack. Was it

171

really a hex? I got out of the car and dropped the pouch into my purse, along with the supposed good luck bean. I didn't like the idea I'd been conned.

"Ellen, what's in that jar?" I was now suspicious of everything. Ellen screwed her face up in a determined expression and I turned to see Paul with his camera bag amble down the stairs of the main building.

Ellen went to meet him, stopping by the fish pond to swing the jar as if she were ringing a bell. By the look on her face she was ready to rip.

"Hi, Ellen," Paul said, smiling pleasantly. "I was worried about you. Thought you'd be resting but you weren't in your room."

"No, I wasn't resting my little face for your camera."

"I can see that." He scanned her with his eyes, stopping where her shirt was torn at the neck. The smile disappeared.

"You focus that Pentax on my face and all you think is sun cream, sun oil, presun, after sun. Do you ever see me? No, I'm just the mannequin! 'Smile, Ellen.' 'Smile, for chrissakes!' 'How can we sell a product without a smile?'

"Well, I'm not going to smile for your damn camera, or for suntan creams or perfumes, or anything else!" Her voice was loud now, full of anger and frustration. "I'm going to smile for people. For real people who have feelings!"

I put my hand on her shoulder. She wavered and looked down at the jar in her hand. "Oh, what's the use," she said, flinging it in the fish pond.

"What happened?" Paul was looking straight at me, blame on his face.

Ellen grabbed his chin and forced him to look at her. "Ask me, not her! It's nothing to worry about anyway. Eric decided I needed the warmth of a human hand on my body and made a pass."

172

He flicked her hand away. "Did he do that to your shirt?"

She pushed her face close, egging him on. I wanted to hug her, stop her, but I didn't dare interfere again. "Yes, Eric tore at me in a fit of uncontrollable passion!"

"That bastard!" Paul unzipped his bag and started fumbling inside it, his jaw set to smash stone.

"Maybe I like uncontrollable passion, did you ever think of that?"

Paul stopped cold.

Ellen looked at him for a long moment, her face as still as his. "God, you're stupid," she said and walked away.

I'd been stupid, too, never having realized she was in love. Both in love with each other and both determined not to show it. How stupid all of us can be.

Paul turned to me for explanations. I couldn't tell him the truth; Ellen would never forgive me.

"Maybe you two need to talk," was all I said.

EIGHTEEN

"Your beau's at the stage door," Tommy whispered backstage, knocking on the flat that was giving me some privacy.

"Who?" I asked, peeling my Charleston outfit off my sweat-dripping body. For a dizzy, out of breath second I thought Greenhouse had materialized out of the sand. Skipping dinner does nothing for a muddy head.

"What beau?"

"Beaujoie." Tommy chuckled.

"Cute, real cute." I wiped myself dry with a towel and dropped a hide-all navy trapeze dress over my head.

"I mean it," Tommy said. "He's wedged himself in the doorway so no one can pass. All that's missing are the roses."

I walked out. One of the spots on stage angled left, dropping a shaft of light in the wing where Tommy was standing in a bathing suit, wearing his top hat and gingerly dabbing his face with the BEAU SUN cream I'd given him. His "I'm a Man," number was next. He pointed behind me.

Beaujoie, filling the width and height of the stage door, nodded as he saw me and swept an arm out toward the sand. He was offering me a promenade by the water.

"Is this a hex?" I asked him as we walked by a lighted circle of empty chairs and tables. I opened my palm to show him Eric's pouch. The tiny crucifix glittered like a sliver of glass.

Beaujoie brought my palm to his face and smelled the pouch. I noticed he was careful not to touch it.

"Garlic," he announced after repeated sniffs. "Garlic is used to keep evil away, not to bring it on. The combination of the crucifix and garlic can only mean an offer of protection." I slipped the pouch in my pocket where the red bean was still buried, pleased I hadn't been conned after all.

"The black silk must have made Eric think of death."

"He is afraid, that one. Who gave it to you?"

I told Beaujoie of my visit to Mr. Quicko, about the orange-haired woman and Eric's reaction, leaving out the incident between Eric and Ellen. That was her story to tell, not mine.

"You went to a very good *quimboiseur*." We had started walking west again, past the nudist cove, to where Papa La Bouche gathered the Sainte-Anne children to tell them folktales under the full moon. Beaujoie had offered me his arm and now held his hands folded on the peak of his stomach.

"*Quimboiseur* is a word that comes from our slave days. Doctors, who did not understand the slaves' dialect, would give them medicine and say, 'here, drink this.' *Tiens, bois* ça. The doctors soon became the *tiens-boiseurs*, which then changed to *quimboiseurs*. From doctor to magic man is an easy step. Now they do good things and very bad things."

Beaujoie stopped to look up at the moon. It glowed white and fat, like the Times Square ball about to drop into the New Year. I wondered briefly what the new day was going to bring. I hadn't been able to talk to

Ellen after her outburst. She hadn't answered my knocks at her door, nor had she shown up for dinner, and when I caught her backstage she'd put me off, saying we could talk later. Apart from wanting to make sure she was going to show up for tomorrow's shoot, I'd hoped to drop a few reassuring hints about Paul's feelings toward her.

Fifty feet farther down the beach, the old man was sitting cross-legged under his poinciana, his French sailor's hat slipping down over one ear. Smaller heads and shoulders surrounded Papa, looking like cutouts propped up in the sand. One boy wore a jagged crown that had fallen over an eye. A long-necked girl sat up tall, her wide white hat sheltering the heads around her like a benign mushroom.

"Papa la Bouche invited Ellen to listen to his stories," I said, wondering if she was there.

"I passed her on my way to pick you up," Beaujoie said, "looking as if she had stepped out of a fairy tale. She had not changed her dancing costume." He started walking again. "You sound worried."

"I would like her 'under my eyes.'"

"She is a very independent spirit, I would say."

"That she is."

"What was it Mademoiselle Ellen wanted from Monsieur Quicko? Not a hex, I hope."

"No, no, just her fortune told." And maybe a love potion. I'd retrieved the mustard jar from the pond and taken it to my room.

"Do you believe black magic works?" I asked, hearing a round of applause coming from the theater.

"It is the belief in the head that makes things happen."

"Do you think Eric is in danger?"

"Of more beatings, perhaps. Your little package contained cocaine, as we both thought. Eric Kanzer

176

was questioned at length early this evening. After much shouting, he declared he knows nothing of drugs."

"What did Zaza say about the cocaine?"

"She denies knowing of its existence, of course."

"You don't believe her then."

Instead of answering, Beaujoie took my hand. "Do not worry," he whispered, his breath noisier than his words. "Listen."

We had reached the edge of a circle of a dozen seated children dressed in Carnival costumes. Papa leaned against the tree trunk, the wrinkled darkness of his skin blending into the bark. Beyond the tree, I could see the long row of collapsed Windsurfers, pointing to a sequined Sainte-Anne in the distance. The blue Windsurfer that had hidden Iguana's body was gone, I noticed, leaving a gap no more ominous than a missing tooth. Was the power of her death already waning or was Beaujoie's heavy presence at the tip of my arm that reassuring? I turned back to Papa who was telling his story in soft Creole, the words rolling into each other to form an impenetrable wall of soft, foamy sounds. As he spoke, he shifted sand from one hand to the other, as if establishing his own time. The air around him was as motionless as the children.

"He is telling the moonfish story that Madame Beaujoie dislikes so much," Beaujoie whispered, leading me back a few steps so that we wouldn't disturb. "In ancient times, the moon was married to the sun, but one day she got bored and dropped down to earth to play . . ."

A woman screamed. Beaujoie ran with surprising swiftness into the thicket of trees that lined the beach. After a moment of stunned recognition, I ran after him, yelling, invoking God and Ellen in the same torn breath.

She appeared, ghostly white and wavering between

177

the trunks of trees, holding her tutu to her neck, her toe shoes dangling from her free arm.

"Oh God, Ellen," I said again, tears rolling down my cheeks from the sheer relief of seeing her alive.

Beaujoie wrapped an arm around her and half-carried her out onto the beach. Blood dripped down her satin bodice. In the moonlight, it looked black.

"Watch her," he said, letting go and plunging back into the trees. Ellen dropped to the sand, her eyes wide, her face gaunt. I took her hand. She was quivering.

"What happened?" I forced myself to sound calm even though my stomach felt like it was doing a bungee plunge. I dabbed the hem of my dress against the cut on one side of her neck.

"I was looking for Paul." Her voice was flat, barely audible.

A few young heads bobbed around me; hands pressed against my back, seeking the reassuring feel of a grown-up body. I leaned into them.

"*Mamaille, viens ici.*" Papa La Bouche called them back. "I have not finished my story."

"*Un cygne blessé,*" a little girl whispered. A wounded swan. Thank God, only wounded.

"I wanted to apologize," Ellen said, watching the children run back to Papa's fairy tale. "I just wanted to apologize."

My stomach plummeted. "Are you saying Paul did this?"

"Noooo. Not Paul." She slapped the air in frustration. "I saw someone moving." She pushed my hands away. "I'm all right. I'm all right. Please!"

"Ellen, you're bleeding!"

"After my dance, he came up to me and told me I'd been good. 'You were wonderful,' he said, with this awed kind of look on his face. I was so flabbergasted I didn't say anything, and then Nick started undoing my bodice, and he walked off. I tied myself together again and went after him. I couldn't find him, so I came out here. I saw someone through those trees. I thought it might be Paul, so I walked over calling his name. Then, then he . . ." she sat up. "I felt a sharp sting on my neck." She looked behind her shoulder as if expecting to see something. "I know this sounds funny, but I could swear I smelled cloves."

"I found no one," Beaujoie said, lumbering back, a handkerchief disappearing into a pocket of his jacket. He hunkered down beside Ellen and tilted her head to one side. "Two small cuts. Not deep. I have summoned the Club guards. They will call my men. The matter will be looked into."

I heard the reassuring sound of commands piercing the static of a walkie-talkie nearby. They were going to start a search. The thicket of trees was only about a hundred feet deep and, on the western side, flanked by a gravel path that bordered the Club grounds and ran directly from the beach to the main road. On the eastern side, the trees ended at a stream that fed into the ocean.

"He's probably swimming all the way to Sainte-Anne," I said.

"Or pedaling his way on a bicycle," Beaujoie said. "Or he may have simply disappeared momentarily among the six hundred G.M.s staying at the Club." Pressing a folded handkerchief against her neck, he propped Ellen up against his shoulder. *"Viens, ma petite,* the Club nurse must see you and after a 'ti' punch, you will tell us your story." He began walking her back to the Club.

Ellen pulled at his arm. "I can walk by myself!"

Beaujoie released Ellen, surprise on his face. Ellen wavered for a minute, keeping his handkerchief to her neck.

179

"It wasn't Paul. I don't know who it was, but it wasn't Paul."

Eric. Eric getting his revenge. "You bitch! You'll pay for this," he'd yelled into our car. I'd assumed he'd been talking to me because I'd put the silk pouch in his jeep. For all he knew, Ellen might have done it.

"He didn't put his hand over my mouth," Ellen was saying. "Isn't that odd? He just grabbed my waist, and then that sting." She stopped walking and held her hand out as if to balance herself. Beaujoie offered her the crook of his arm.

"And then that odd smell of cloves," Ellen said, slipping her arm inside his.

"Eric told us there's some poison that smells like cloves," I said.

"There are no mancenillier trees in this vicinity." Beaujoie led Ellen toward the stairs of the main building. I followed. There weren't many people walking around. The show was over and most G.M.s were in the bar waiting for the disco to open at midnight.

"If you had been touched by the mancenillier poison you would be aware of the fact. It is so strong that if you stand under its fruit while it rains, the drops will burn your skin and even blind you. It is more likely the Club kitchen cooked with cloves tonight."

"Why does it have to be someone from the Club?" I asked.

Ellen moaned.

"It begins to hurt more, does it not?" Beaujoie said softly, patting Ellen's hand. She said nothing.

He turned to me. "I do not let sentiment eliminate possibilities. The Club may be a paradise on earth, but we cannot expect it to admit only saints. I will ask what was on the dinner menu. Ah, Mademoiselle Nick, I believe perhaps she will be of help."

180

We had reached the main pavilion where Bob held his exercise classes in the morning. At the far end, Nick was leaning against one of the concrete columns as if waiting for someone. She was barefoot and wearing her crumpled bermuda shorts again.

"Hey, Nick," I called out, "Ellen's had a little accident."

"Have you seen Paul?" Ellen asked. Nick came forward reluctantly, shaking her head.

"What accident?" Bob was coming up the stairs behind us, balancing a two-foot high speaker on one shoulder. "Had to lend my stuff for the show tonight. You were both great on stage, by the way. What accident are you talking about? Anybody get hurt?"

"Have you seen Paul?" Ellen repeated.

"Not since he stormed out the stage door after your number."

"Oh my Lord, Ellen! What happened to you?" Nick's hand shot out to Ellen's bloodstained bodice.

"I cut myself with a sea shell," Ellen said.

"On your neck? Hey, what's going on?" Bob lowered the speaker to the tile floor. "What are the police doing here?" He looked straight at Beaujoie.

"Nick, please take Mademoiselle Ellen to your room and stay with her while Monsieur Bob will see to the nurse." Beaujoie was business brusque now that Bob had labeled him "police."

Ellen took off, toe shoes slung over her shoulder, while Nick stayed behind only long enough to watch Bob take the stairs two at a time.

Beaujoie turned toward the balcony and the ocean. "The Club guard has already called my men. Someone will watch her."

"Why my room?"

"That is where she is not expected to be."

"You think he's going to try again?"

181

"I am not sure he or she wishes to harm her any further, but I must be careful."

"All right, we'll be gender fair, but do you think he or she was trying to kill her?"

"A killer does not let his victim scream."

"I'm sure it's Eric." I told him quickly about the incident in Mr. Quicko's yard and Eric's threat.

"You found something back there, didn't you?" I said. "You put it in your pocket. What is it? What did you find?" He hesitated.

"Please, I'm responsible for her. I have to decide whether it's safe for her to stay here or not."

He slowly reached in his jacket pocket. He unwrapped the crumpled handkerchief with almost reluctant care, as if it held a delectable bonbon he was forbidden to eat.

I saw a minuscule halo of blood, then another handkerchief fold was removed. Four inches of narrow, curved steel glinted at me.

"The cockfight!"

"A gaff. The blade that is tied to the cock's left leg to help him kill his enemy. Do not touch it." Beaujoie pulled my hand away. "It is very sharp."

"Eric took us to the cockfight."

"These can be easily bought anywhere on the island."

"You will pick him up?"

"I will, but I also wish to speak to Monsieur Paul, who causes Mademoiselle Ellen such anxiety."

"You don't suspect him of anything, do you? Those two are in love."

"I wish to reassure Mademoiselle by finding him."

Sure, and ask a few questions while you're at it. I gave him Paul's room number, two doors down from Ellen's room and left to check on Ellen.

She was sitting by the open window, still in her tutu, a clean square bandage now taped to her neck. The nurse was cleaning up in the bathroom, and Nick was on the bed, knees drawn up, looking like nobody's sweetheart.

"It wasn't Eric," Ellen said, as if reading my thoughts. She kept her gaze fixed out the window, toward the mini golf course and the cove beyond. Far to the left, Papa's poinciana tree left a long shadow in the white sand. The children and Papa had gone.

"Come on, he threatened us. Who else could it be?"

"Eric isn't part of the Club."

"What's that mean?"

She turned to look at me, her face drained of any expression. "Whoever it was, was wearing one of those." I looked down at the ribbon I'd tied to my wrist the first day we'd come to the Club. A blue ribbon with CLUB MEDITERRANEE stitched on it, a ribbon all G.M.s were supposed to wear to let the guards know we belonged. A different color every week. Even the G.O.s wore them. I turned to Nick. She was wearing hers.

"Are you sure?"

"I felt the knot. When he grabbed my waist, my hand went down to push him away. He cut me before I could do anything. That's when I screamed. It's not Eric."

"Why are you so good to that man?"

"He's had bad luck. Bad foster homes, bad jobs. He was even 4F. He finally told me that today. He really wanted to be a soldier. He thought the Army would make him into a somebody. We can't know what it's like to have that kind of bad luck." With her exhausted face, Ellen looked plain, and suddenly I felt more comfortable with her. I realized her beauty had always put me off.

"Bad luck made my mother do desperate, ugly things," Ellen said. "She couldn't stop even after my father came along and tried to help her. I looked at Eric and thought of my mother, that's all."

"You're a pretty wonderful person," I said, hugging her. "Did I ever tell you that?"

"Thanks."

"But if it isn't Eric, then who?"

"I don't even know if it was a man or a woman. It doesn't take much strength to grip me. I only weigh one hundred and fifteen pounds." She looked down at her bare wrists. "I did feel that ribbon, though. I'm sure of that."

"You better tell Beaujoie then."

"I want to talk to Paul first."

"Has Paul anything to do with this?"

"Nooo!"

The nurse hurried out of the bathroom, a tall African-American woman dressed in shorts and a T-shirt.

"Are you all right?" she asked Ellen, giving me a blistering look.

"Yes!" Ellen turned her back to us and stared out the window.

The nurse glanced at Nick, who was still huddled in a corner of her bed.

"Would you like a sedative to help you sleep?"

"Thanks. I'm okay."

The nurse nodded and left the room.

"What's wrong?" I'd been too worried about Ellen to pay much attention to Nick.

"Zilch compared to what Ellen's been through."

"Zilch sounds like something to me."

"Well, for one I'm not very good at playing the lady with skirts and makeup and stuff. It's just not me. But that's not really it either." She looked at me, her head resting on her knees. "It's that murder back in Lincoln. I can't get it out of my head."

Ellen turned around. "What murder in Lincoln? When?"

184

"A couple got killed." Nick sat up, apparently glad for the attention. "Eight years ago, when I was a junior in high school. I remember because I had to quit the basketball team after the killings. My father wanted me home right after school. The police thought it started as a burglary, and then the couple surprised him or something. I didn't really know them, except I used to walk by their house after basketball practice with Sandy, my lab, and the man was either mowing his lawn or trying to make this frisky black and white mutt heel. Sometimes I'd catch the wife peeping out from the kitchen window, but if she saw me, she'd jump back real quick."

"It's odd how the three of us have been close to violent death," Ellen said in a quiet voice. "Do you think the men in our crew have similar stories?"

"I hope not," Nick said. "It's pretty awful and what's worse in my case is that I just think of that poor mutt, not the couple. I keep remembering the picture in the paper. One of his ears was flopped back and you could see this big bloody hole." Nick pressed her lips together. "I'm sorry. Someone just attacked Ellen and I think about this murdered mutt. Sorry."

"Iguana's death has triggered bad memories for me, too." Ellen said.

To each his own nightmares, I thought, reminded of the sight of Iguana's split head. I could understand Ellen's—her mother's suicide was not something she could ever forget—but I didn't have much patience with Nick's. I went to the door, wanting to get on with things. Whether Ellen liked it or not, Beaujoie had to know about the Club ribbon, and I had to talk to Paul about the possibility of canceling the rest of the shoot.

"You two keep each other company. Ellen, use my bathrobe if you want, but don't move until Beaujoie's man shows up. I'll send Paul in when I get him. Who

185

knows, he might be thirsty and tired." I pointed to the Grey Poupon mustard jar on my night table. "I hear love potions can get a zombie to dance the night away."

"With Eric, it wasn't all kindness on my part," Ellen said. "I played up to him to get Paul jealous. It's not something I'm proud of." Regret was clear on her face.

"Try this instead." I tossed her the red bean. "Guaranteed to bring good luck!"

NINETEEN

Le Coquillage was packed with bodies dancing the *biguine,* hip bone grinding hip bone, chins rubbing each other, torsos sweeping forward and back in a dizzying mating ritual. I hesitated at the door.

Beaujoie had sent me to this Sainte-Anne disco after we gave up trying to find Paul at the Club. "It is Wednesday," he said, dangling the keys to the Renault that Roared. "Meat market night at *Le Coquillage.* Many G.M.s and G.O.s find it amusing. Perhaps he is there, taking pictures of our local dance. If he is, bring him back."

So there I was, scouring the dark room. There was no camera flash, no body parts that looked like Paul's. Martine, the 'ti' punch girl, danced by me, looking exotic in a satiny yellow halter top and groin skirt, with her purple and blue bird makeup streaked to perfection on her face. Her partner was a man old enough to be her grandfather, who scooped his pelvis against her as if she were a pint of ice cream. I plunged in, jamming myself between tables, chairs, and firm asses, being picked up by a handsome hunk who leaned back on one leg, shaking the other toward me as if it were the latest in introductions. The music, loud enough to shatter skulls, had an irresistable beat and I couldn't help flashing my partner a smile and doing a quick hip shake to the right, and two to the left while craning my neck to spot Paul. Above the barrel-wood bar Mickey and Minnie Mouse held hands under a string of Christmas lights and watched the active foreplay. Walt would roll over if he knew. Just as my hip was about to come loose, I saw Don the Texas tennis G.O. come out of the men's room. I pushed myself after him.

"Did you bring any G.M.s here?" I shouted.

"They're out back, takin' a breather," he yelled, his breath smelling of bubble gum.

I thanked him and spilled out into the moonlit front entrance, feeling as if I'd just been ejected into the coolness and freedom of outer space. There were a few white plastic tables strewn across a concrete clearing. Couples sat, smoked, and looked at the full moon or the beach which was only a couple of hundred yards in front of us. The moon left a gleaming skin over the crinkled water. The yellow neon sign flickered LE COQUILLAGE as if it, too, was not immune to the beat of the music.

There was no Paul. "Out back," Don had said and I circled the building walking under an awning of red hibiscus. A small group of G.M.s and G.O.s were talking and laughing in the backyard, holding cool beer bottles against their necks.

"Did a guy named Paul come with you?" I asked. A plump brunette with a peeling nose pointed behind her.

Paul was at a corner table, an empty beer bottle in front of him. He sat with the heavy immobility of a drunk. I noticed he hadn't brought his camera.

"Paul, we've got to go back," I said. "Ellen's been attacked."

He rocked in his chair and lifted the empty bottle to his lips. No "how is she?" or "what happened?"

"Come on, Paul. I'll take you home."

"It's that bastard," he mumbled, not looking up. "You should have fired him."

"I did, this morning."

"What'd he do, kiss her? She likes that. 'Uncontrollable passion,' that sends her."

"Oh, get real, Paul, and on your feet. He cut her, okay?" I pulled at his arm. "They weren't deep cuts, but it was still awful, so sober up. You and I have to make some quick decisions here. Besides she needs you."

He shook his head, seemingly not digesting the information. "You're going to fuck up my ad campaign."

"That's what we have to decide. Just how bad all this is."

"Ellen hurt!" He shot out of his chair and hurried to the beach.

"For her you can fuck up my career," he announced, his head thrown back to look at the moon. I scuttled after him. He walked awfully straight for a drunk.

"Just how many beers have you had, Paul?"

"For her, anything." He wrapped his arm around my neck in an octopus grip. "I can't catch her anyway. I shoot and shoot, but that sweet fragility just doesn't show up on film." Well, he stank of beer, that much was certain.

"I shot four rolls, and what do I get? No poetry, no romance, just a sterile white dot. I'm just not good enough!"

He was having an acute attack of groin ache.

"Let's go get some sleep, Paul. We'll talk in the morning."

"And you're sweet. I've always meant to tell you—real sweet—but I'm no good with words."

"Or with actions for that matter."

"I was going to punch that bastard out. I was all set to do that. I looked for him . . . the Club, that rum-making place of his, the jeep park, all over." He chuckled. "Erit the ferret, damn slippery." I was steering him to Beaujoie's car, the weight of his arm and half his body bearing on my neck. "She looked great. Didn't she look great on stage? A swan, fragile, young—a David Hamilton nymphet." He waved an arm at the moon. "Diaphanous."

I leaned him against the car and unlocked the door. "Can you get in by yourself?"

He jerked up. "She needs me?"

"Not in a drunken stupor. Come on, get in and let's go."

"Can't you see? She needs me." He dropped down into the seat. "Oh, god, I think I'm drunk with love."

"Merda di toro!" was my only comment. That's a literal translation of bullshit.

I slowed down to cross a large wet patch on the side road that led to the Club. Just beyond a line of eucalyptus trees, I could see the lights of Barracuda, a small restaurant where we'd heard some great jazz our first night on the island. There was no music now, just a burst of loud laughter. And a cackle.

I braked and turned off the motor.

"Shit, are we stuck?"

"Shh, I thought I heard something."

"Ellen?"

"No, someone else." I slipped out of the car, my sandals oozing into the mud. There was no repeated laughter, just the subdued murmur of restaurant conversation. Was he there? I had to check.

"Stay here," I said to Paul and started making my way across the grassy field. If Eric was there, I would stand guard while Paul ran back to the Club to call the police. But he mustn't see me. I scanned my surroundings. About thirty feet behind Barracuda, a shed sat like an abandoned gift box. I could hide in its shadow and still see the windows of the restaurant. I started running down the slope of the field, excited by the prospect of finding Eric, of getting him in the hands of the police.

Ellen had to be wrong—she'd been frightened, she'd touched the wrists holding her only for a second. She'd probably felt a shirt cuff—not a ribbon.

Eric had to be our man.

A woman started laughing and I ran faster, propelled by the need to hear that cackle again, to be sure Eric was there.

I tripped as I ran by the back of the shed, the ground turning black as I crossed into the rectangle of shadow. I fell on my bare knees and hands. Another cow, I thought, sitting back abruptly, afraid I'd get another blast of fermenting breath in my face. After the first moment of surprise I felt my hands wet on my thighs. I yanked them up and away from me. Mud or cow dung, freshly hatched. Damn! To make it worse everybody was laughing at Barracuda, but no cackle. Maybe no Eric. And no cow that I could see or hear in the darkness behind the shed. I leaned over into the moonlit field to rub my hands against some clean damp grass. Why did I fall?

A clean hand, palm up, lay no more than three feet from me. Its wrist was cut off by the sharp line of shadow cast by the shed. For some reason I didn't scream. It was too absurd. For a few seconds I defended myself with the thought that the hand belonged to a drunk, sleeping it off. But I didn't believe myself. Without daring to look at what might still show on my now dry hands, I ran back to the car.

Paul's head was thrown back, mouth open. He was out cold. I reached into the glove compartment, praying for a flashlight. I threw out crumpled paper cups, loose sheets of paper, folded handkerchiefs onto Paul's lap, never thinking I could run for help to the Club guard only a few hundred feet away or to the restaurant. I felt as if my chest had been pierced with an icicle and the only way to get rid of that paralyzing pain was to be efficient, in control. Go back to the source, I told myself. Examine.

There was no flashlight. I got into the car, backed out of the mud hole, and lurched directly into second gear, squeezing between two eucalyptuses. I bumped down the slope, the headlights swimming on waves of grazed grass. When my headlights stroked the shadow of the shed, I slowed to a crawl.

The lights picked up the combat boots first, sticking up like old tree stumps. Then the worn jeans, the HERO T-shirt. I slammed on the brakes and Paul groaned. Eric was lying on his back, his head twisted to one side. One arm hugged his waist, the other was flung out toward the restaurant. He might have been fast asleep, except that his eyes were open, and a dark red liquid oozed from his ear. Getting out of the car, I reached in my pocket. I broke the strings of the black silk pouch and dropped the crucifix in his open palm.

TWENTY

At seven the next morning, I sat in my usual restaurant gazebo overlooking the beach and fed a croissant to a raven black Carib grackle. Ellen and Nick were still fast asleep in my room, with a policeman pretending he was one of the cleaning staff standing outside. Paul was snoring in his room. I felt like the Roadrunner's coyote—bulldozed, exploded, shot at, bouldered—in other words, out of it.

I'd stayed up all night getting in the police's way as they questioned the people at Barracuda and canvassed the fields, the beach, the thicket of trees for the gun that killed Eric. The local doctor, who also doubled as medical examiner, sleepily declared he'd been shot in the ear at close range. I carefully avoided looking at what had happened to the other side of Eric's head. Two people in the restaurant had heard a shot around ten, but since it was Carnival and children lit firecrackers all the time, they'd thought nothing of it. The other clients had been having too much of a good time to notice anything except the emptying glasses in front of them. Beaujoie had pointed out that Ellen was still on stage at ten o'clock. It looked like she'd been right all along—Eric was not the person who'd attacked her.

That fact zapped me between the eyes. I couldn't understand who else would want to harm her. No one at the Club had known her before, so there didn't seem to be any plausible reason to attack her. Unless it was someone in our shoot crew. I thought of Paul, "drunk with love." He'd never had the courage to touch her, afraid of her reaction, afraid of losing his all-important job. Was cutting her neck his crazy way of giving vent to his real feelings? That sounded like a bunch of *merda di toro*. What about Nick wreaking revenge on Ellen for all us ordinary-looking women who, in her breathtaking presence, felt like we'd grown three heads and six feet? M.D.T. there too. HM had temper tantrums if you didn't like the way he'd done you up, but since Ellen always complimented him on his work he had no reason to shush her up. That left Jerry, who didn't seem to care enough about anything except keeping Paul's equipment in order and having a good time. That wrapped up the crew in my view and left me none the wiser as to the identity of Ellen's attacker. As far as the murderer was concerned, I was drowning in the ocean.

A female grackle landed on my plate for her share of breakfast. She was small, all gray with black legs, with none of the male's slick, satiny sheen. My art director boss, whom I should have been trying to get on the phone right that minute, would have said her minimalist fashion was hopelessly outdated. I thought her drabness sweet. Somehow she made me think of Tommy, the one less noticed, thrust aside. I waved the male away and uncovered the slice of pineapple I'd been saving for her.

Was Tommy a possible attacker? I'd been so sure he was in love with Ellen, and I did hate being wrong again and again. She hadn't paid any attention to him, which could have hurt him terribly. He could have cut her out

194

of spite, as a childish, sick way of saying "So there!" Come to think of it, he'd been avoiding her lately, showing up only when I was alone. But that was consistent with his declaration of love to me, wasn't it? It was easy to pick on Tommy, just because he was . . . well, so nerdy. Not very fair of me, just as I hadn't been fair with Eric, disliking him so much I was ready to blame him for every crime.

"Is Nick still sleeping? I got to talk to her." My birds flew away and Bob sat down. "What are you guys doing today? You're not going off to the islands, are you? Not after what happened last night." He looked anxious, which did nothing to make him less handsome.

"As soon as I talk to my boss, I'll tell you." I looked at my watch. It was six-twenty in New York. Let him sleep and let me have a few more minutes before trying to convince him to scratch the rest of the shoot and let us come home.

"How soon are you going to call him?" Something was definitely making him edgy.

I hadn't thought of Bob as a possible attacker. Maybe I'd let his looks get in the way, which made me the female counterpart of a pecker-brain.

All right, he was definitely a possible, simply because he'd been around. But I couldn't, for all the food I'd love to eat, think of a good reason why he'd want to harm Ellen.

"Why do you have to talk to Nick?" I asked.

"I made fun of that skirt she was wearing and she got real uptight. It looked so dumb on her. The lipstick, too. She looks sharp with nothing on her face except her."

"Did you tell her that?" The male grackle swooped down over my pineapple and started pecking. The female hovered by the railing.

"I didn't get a chance. Then I really screwed up by telling her I've been nipped by dogs enough times while jogging to know they suck."

"Them's fighting words." I got up. Let them work it out by themselves. I was tired of lending an ear to the lovelorn. I was tired of sitting in a gazebo feeding the birds and my fancy, avoiding my boss, avoiding the ugly thought that was lurking as black and persistent as the grackle on my plate. I was tired period.

"Hey, you really think you're leaving today?" Bob asked. "What about my modeling for the ad tomorrow at Carbet Falls? I kind of liked the idea of that extra money."

Bob was just gorgeous and self-absorbed, I decided. His face had nothing of Greenhouse's honesty.

"I had to work hard to get the Chef du Village to okay it. For some reason he's had it in for me from the day I got here. Today I was supposed to have the whole afternoon off, instead I've got to play tennis because they're one short. That guy really pisses me off!"

"You've got a rough life!"

"You don't understand. He sends out real bad vibes. You think Nick will be back by four?"

"I don't know when Nick's going to be back," I shooed the male away. "But two murders and two attacks on Ellen should have given you enough bad vibes to sizzle your pretty, blond brain!" The grackle huffed up his feathers in anger, then strutted back to the pineapple, glaring at me with his lemon drop eyes. The ugly thought came back with him.

What if Ellen's attacker and the murderer were one and the same?

"Two murders and she could be next! I want her out of here," I yelled over the phone. My boss was still in

196

bed, in his luxurious SoHo loft, probably with his lover, our client, next to him. "No, the police don't know anything specific yet, but it's the second time she's been hurt. No, Paul is leaving it up to me and Ellen's a real trooper. She wants to stay but that doesn't mean it's a wise deci . . . What do you mean we have to finish or we'll lose the client? What? Oh, great, he's furious because the agency's raising its percentage, meanwhile his exclusive model might end up strangled in a mud hole. Tell him . . . no . . . listen, tell him . . ."

The phone went dead. No, not disconnected; dead. Hang up dead. The boss's last words had been, "Finish the campaign and keep her safe!" Real simple with a murderer on the loose.

"'Morning, you look like you could use a hug or a downer. I could give you both."

"Oh, Tommy, not now." He was standing outside the phone room, a swaddled lump blocking my way. "I've got to get the gang ready to go on the shoot." I dodged around him and started down the corridor.

"Good, you're not leaving then." He was following me. I was in such a bad mood I wanted to swat him.

"I can see you're not used to having anyone take care of you, Simona. You're being rude now, but you don't really mean it."

I stopped at that.

"It's just that you've got your guard up," he said. "That's from being hurt and living alone. I get like that sometimes, too. You really should love yourself a little more or at least let me do it for you."

"Thanks, Tommy. It's just that it's been a bad night."

"If I come to New York, will you see me?" He waved a hand over his face, which today was pocked with popped blisters, looking worse than ever. "I don't always look like this."

"You shouldn't have put that makeup on again."

"How could I say no to singing in a show? You were the best, though. Much better than Ellen or any of the others."

"Tommy, I already have a boyfriend."

"That can always change." He pressed his cheeks down with both hands. "Things change all the time."

I ran off, embarrassed.

Nick, Ellen, and Paul were all in my room, breakfast goodies spread out on one bed, gloom and doom on all three faces. I thought I'd walked in on a college dorm party where all the students had just flunked their mid-terms. At least the policeman smiled at me. Dressed in the brown uniform worn by the cleaning personnel, he was sitting in the open window, legs dangling over the ledge. A reassuring gun butt stuck out of his belt in the back.

"Have they found the gun?" Paul asked, pulling at the strap of the camera bag. He looked as though a bear had hibernated on his face for the winter. He sure didn't weather hangovers well.

"Not as of five-thirty this morning. Come on guys, we're off. New York says the shoot's still on. The boat's due in ten minutes. Marie-Galante, then Les Saintes. We've lost a day so high sun or not, you're going to have to do your best, Paul. Shade her with scrims, banana leaves, whatever, but shoot your ass off. Then tomorrow morning Carbet Falls and home we go."

Paul reached over and held Ellen's hand. "Do you feel up to this?"

Ah ha! Now they were touching in public. Big improvement. Maybe we'd start getting some happiness around here.

"Ellen, I'm sorry," I said. "I know you're upset about Eric but up to it or not, we're shooting *and* getting out

198

of here. How's your neck?"

"Fine. Can we call off the guard now? I'm in no danger." I noticed she rolled the red bean in the fingers of her free hand.

"Don't argue. This gentleman with a gun is going to be your shadow from now until that American Eagle plane door closes on your back. No independence shit today, okay? You don't even go to the bathroom without him."

"Hey, what's gotten into you?" Nick asked, beginning to fill a bag with the perfectly ironed T-shirts and pareus Ellen was going to wear for the ads. "Eat something, will you?"

"I wish food would do it. I haven't slept in twenty-four hours and I'm scared. To top it off, I had to deal with those idiots in New York." I opened my mouth wide and let out a long, silent scream. "Much better, thanks." Not that anyone had worried about what I'd gone through, except Tommy. "By the way, Nick, Bob wants to see you."

Nick was in our closet now, pulling down some more clothes from a shelf. She reached up for a large sun hat, and a book came tumbling down.

"Do Jerry and HM know?" Paul said.

"They're already on the beach waiting for the boat." I stooped down to pick up the book, beating Nick to it. I looked at her in surprise. It was the Italian mystery Nick's bookseller friend had set aside for me. I'd forgotten all about it.

"I was going to give it to you when we got back to New York," Nick said in a low voice, dropping down on her haunches. "Can you wait that long?"

"For the book or for some answers?"

"The book you can read on the plane." Nick's eyes darted to Paul and Ellen still sitting on the bed, holding hands and looking like star-crossed lovers. "Trust me."

With two people dead? "I need to know, Nick."

"When we get back this afternoon. When we're alone."

"No, now."

She lifted a pile of bright colored bikinis from a shelf to her right and stood up, without answering me. That's how much clout I had.

"What's that?" she asked. Eric's *Adventure Life* dropped from the bottom of the pile onto her foot. "Why did you put that here?"

"I didn't. I left it on the left shelf, where I keep my things." I picked up the magazine and flipped through it. I was too worried about confronting Nick to notice anything at first. Then I flipped through it again, more as a nervous gesture than anything else. The Legionnaires Survival Boot knife ad wasn't there. I went back to the beginning of the magazine and turned the pages slowly this time. Page eighty-six was followed by page eighty-nine.

"Did any of you tear a page from here?"

Denials all around, even from the policeman.

"Well, someone's been in here, because when I put this magazine in my room yesterday afternoon, it had all its pages. Remember, Nick, that full page knife ad?

"No. I just remember it's a boring magazine."

"I don't like this." I sat down on the tile floor and stretched the magazine apart. My finger ran down a ripped strip still attached to the spine. My throat tightened. I'd had my New York apartment broken into once, and I still had nightmares about unknown hands rifling through my things.

"Someone went through my camera bag," Paul said, jerking it up on his knees.

"Are you missing anything?" I asked.

Ellen rested her chin on his shoulder as he unzipped his bag.

"No, nothing." He played with a roll of film, his scowl deepening. Either Ellen's chin was playing havoc with his testosterone or he wasn't a very good liar.

"If nothing was taken," I said, "how can you tell someone went through your bag?"

"I can tell. Never mind, I might be wrong."

"Well, I'm not wrong about this magazine. Nick, did you and Ellen stay here all night?"

"We didn't budge. Besides, first we had Beaujoie for company, then he was right outside." She pointed a thumb toward the policeman's back. "Paul brought breakfast. I didn't lock the door yesterday afternoon, though."

"Nick, that was dumb!" Paul said. "You have all the shoot clothes in here."

"Well, Club Med's always been famous for its open door policy. I didn't expect to find locked doors and I was coming right back."

"What did you expect to find, army surplus tents set up on the beach with us helping to cook?" Paul stood up, slinging his bag over his shoulder. "That's how they started, you know. Come on, let's just get out of here and get to work."

"Did you come right back?" I asked.

"Well, no, I met Bob and we got to talking, and then I was late for the show."

"Come on, let's motivate," Paul said. Ellen had joined him at the door with the policeman in tow.

"I'm not coming," I said. Something Iguana had told Zaza had just surfaced through my deadened brain cells. Advertising, she'd said advertising could bring death. And the page torn from *Adventure Life* had been in the back, in the ad section.

"You don't need me," I said. "I still have to set up some things for tomorrow's shoot—double-checking with the Club about Bob modeling, getting another van, the food, things like that."

Paul shrugged and started to lead Ellen out by her elbow. She hung back.

"Thanks for that bean," she said, giving me one of her knee-buckling smiles. Sometime during the night, those two had finally gotten together. I gave her a thumbs up sign and the minute she was out the door, I raised my finger at the policeman.

"Do not leave that woman for an instant," I told him in my worst imperious French.

"Do not worry," he answered in beautiful Calypso English. "The Commissaire has already warned me M'zelle Ellen is my wife, my daughter, my sister, *and* my mother." He crossed himself with a grin. "With me she will be as safe as Our Lady of Guadeloupe de Extremadura."

TWENTY-ONE

I was sitting in the Pointe-à-Pitre harbor under the full blast of the sun, perched on a bollard—one of those mastodontic iron mushrooms ships get moored on. The *Tropicale,* a Carnival Cruise Line ship, loomed in front of me with its five-story height and city-block length. Behind me, the small, crowded fish market was in full smell. The lobster man, in a low, far-carrying voice, called out *"Lang, lang, langouste ici,"* with the same persistence of a priest tolling his church bells to save our souls. Two small boats sold fish directly from their decks. One fisherman balanced a brass scale on a forefinger while a little boy tried to wrap newspaper around a round, fat fish that looked like it had been plucked from Papa's moonfish story. They were fishermen from other islands who weren't allowed to land and compete with the Guadeloupan fish sellers. Four blocks back, Beaujoie was due in his office in ten minutes. I'd driven to Pointe-à-Pitre half an hour ago to tell him about the missing page and share the suspicion that Eric hadn't been looking only for cocaine when he'd started ransacking Zaza's apartment, that this magazine I was holding in my hand was somehow important. Who besides Eric might have reason to tear out that page? I couldn't come up with anyone except the cleaning woman who might have thought the magazine was a throwaway, but she'd sworn she hadn't even been in our room since yesterday morning and I'd believed her. I propped the sliding *Adventure Life* back on my lap and read through the ads one more time.

Combat assault vests, slingshots, detective badges, private investigators. I paid particular attention to the classified ads, two or three lines of small print that reminded me of the personals in *New York* magazine I'd sometimes studied in the past four months to feel I was not the only "lonely" in town. Under FIREARMS & ACCESSORIES, a P.O. Box number in Texas offered military rifles fifty percent below retail. "Why pay more?" it read.

Under FOR SALE there were only two ads before the missing page. An Army sergeant was selling genuine Iraqi sand. A retired police detective in Denver offered lessons in electronic spying. What was that missing page hiding? I had no idea. I looked back at the fish market. The lobster man was doing a brisk business. Beside him a teenage boy was arguing with the madras-wrapped codfish woman, who kept patting the boy's arm as if she were flattening a cutlet. His mother probably, I thought, as she called out to the woman in the stall next to hers, laughing at the rising anger of the boy. The words "Independence Movement," stumbled into my head, nudged by the sight of that boy being denied something.

Was this magazine, promising adventure, somehow connected to the movement? If so, what had Eric's role been?

I almost ran the four blocks to the police station on Rue Gambetti, ready to spew my thoughts on

Beaujoie's desk. At the entrance I found the same policeman, still leaning his chair against the stuccoed wall, with what seemed the same unlit cigarette, one end now completely wet, propped in one corner of his smiling mouth.

"Le Commissaire ne viendra pas ce matin."

"When's he going to come then?"

"When is what I ask, too," Papa La Bouche's voice came from the dark doorway to the right of the policeman's shoulder, his cane poking the sidewalk as if to test its solidity. "He arrests my son on nothing, only vague ideas from his imagination, and then he vanishes." Papa's head emerged, crouched low on his shoulders, with none of last night's storytelling pride. "The full moon brings madness. To us all. Madness."

The policeman swung forward, the front legs of his chair squishing into the heat-softened asphalt with a dull smack.

"Coco should have held his madness a few more days," he said. "The American was flying away on Sunday."

"Where to?" I said.

The policeman examined the soggy end of his cigarette and shook his head.

"Come on, where was he going?"

"Don't bother with him," Papa said, waving at me to follow him down the street. "His brain is as flat as the ass on that chair."

Papa carefully placed one foot after another on the worn-down center of each cobblestone. He was dressed in a black suit with a starched white shirt and a black tie. An old suit, judging by the oversized lapels—not worn very much. A funeral suit, I thought, remembering his wife had died. Only the black fedora was

205

missing. The shoes were his usual mud-stained work boots.

"Have you children?" he asked, as he leaned against a shady wall, tapping his cane against his boot.

"No."

"Do not. They bring too much pain. Gather children around you, other people's children. Then it is good."

"Does Coco's arrest have anything to do with Eric's death?"

Papa spit between his feet. "A well-deserved death. The police think they have a motive. Fifty thousand dollars. They say my son gave Eric fifty thousand dollars for American rifles. Where does that hay-eating head of my son's get fifty thousand dollars? Eh? You tell me that? My son has no money and if he does have some, it would be in francs, no? We are in France here. It is absurd. Then they say no rifles appeared so my son, out of anger, killed him."

"What evidence do the police have?"

"Would you believe? A receipt. My son kept a receipt. Hay, that's what he should eat, like the ass he is! Written out in his hand, signed by that other dead ass. Found by the police this morning on the handle of his *sabe,* the one that killed that poor woman. Under many coils of black tape." He had started walking again, his small, bald head jutting out from the stiff white collar like a turtle eager to head out to sea. Anger was giving him strength. "Is illegality now such a farce that we sign receipts?"

"Why would Coco kill someone who owes him fifty thousand dollars worth of guns?" It's like smacking your foot with your own hoe, as my father liked to remind me whenever anger got the better of me.

"It is a police mistake," Papa said, waving away a child offering a coin for a story.

If Coco had killed Eric, had he also killed Iguana? Could her death have been a warning for Eric to produce the rifles he'd been paid for? But Beaujoie had said Coco had a fool-proof alibi.

Papa stopped his slow walk. We had come to *Place de la Victoire,* an oasis of tropical greenery that faced the sea. On one side, a long white building elegantly dressed in bright green shutters housed Police Headquarters.

"They used to guillotine criminals here in other times," he said, waving a cane toward a green square of lawn under a poinciana. "My son is an ass, yes. A killer, no." He turned back to me, his mouth twisted as if he'd been fed something foul. "Do you have a car?"

"Yes."

"Good, take me to the distillery."

"I was hoping to talk to Beaujoie."

"He will not come back today. He has his problems, too."

"What kind of problems?"

"To have children brings pain, not to have them can also bring pain."

"Did he and Madame Beaujoie lose a child?"

"Twelve miscarriages." His mouth relaxed, softening his face. "Now Solitude is left with a wind blowing in her heart like an island hurricane. A wind that devastates reason." He leaned back against the soaring height of a royal palm and closed his eyes. "Now bring the car, I am tired."

"My son would not kill with a gun. A gun is the foreigner's tool." We were crossing the Salty River, with its dab of an isle littered with birds, on our way to the distillery in Jarry. "You whites want to be efficient

207

above all else, kill many in a hurry. But such noise! In Karukéra, we kill with silent weapons. A *sabe* or arrows."

"Karukéra?"

"The Caraib name for our island. It means 'Beautiful Waters.' Once we used arrows poisoned with the sap of the mancenillier tree. That is how the Arawaks killed the Caraib."

"It didn't work, from what I've read."

"The Caraib were too fierce, the Arawaks too gentle. My son thinks himself a Caraib, but in the soul he is Arawak."

"What chances does his independence movement have?"

"It is not a movement, only a ripple in the sand. A few men with arrogant dreams for brains. What kind of war can be waged against a country like France with fifty thousand dollars worth of rifles?" He rapped the windshield hard with his cane. "My son might as well have bought water pistols!" Finally he was admitting Coco's involvement.

"Where'd he get the money?"

"He has no money of his own. I think the cockfights, perhaps. My son leads a handful of men who do not understand that dignity can be found only in honest work." He lifted the cane again, fury tightening his face. "Dignity is everything to a man."

"So's my windshield," I said, knocking his arm back down before he shattered glass.

We had turned into the dirt road and were now coming close to the distillery. Once the cane settled on Papa's lap, I concentrated on the road. About two hundred feet ahead a man was throwing something into a pile of what looked like burnt rubble in front of the distillery. I speeded up and braked next to a charred, two-legged desk that hunkered down to the ground like a wounded horse. The young boy I had caught sleeping in the courtyard yesterday was sweeping broken bottles from the entrance gate. Wide black streaks licked the wall above the office window, which was now a gaping black rectangle without wood or glass. The pungent smell of gasoline and burnt matter rasped at the back of my throat.

"When did this happen?" I said, nonplussed by the sight.

"Eric! Last night he signs the ownership papers back to me, and then he comes back to set fire to my office. All my sample bottles exploded, the accounting books now ashes." Papa lifted himself out of the car and stood in front of the pile of rubble. "This is what is left of my father's desk!" He lifted his cane above his head and brought it down on the desk top with a resounding whack. The desk crumbled like burnt toast.

I got out of the car, my stomach churning. "What happened to the magazines?" I started kicking through the mess. "All of Eric's magazines. Are they gone?"

"Where is my chair? Did my chair burn, too?" Papa yelled.

The young boy leaned on his broom and looked at me sleepily. "Paper burns."

I crouched down and started picking out unrecognizable objects, sorting through ashes—black flakes that danced up in the air as I touched them, their significance destroyed so that they floated lighter than tissue paper—broken, sooty tools, short lengths of charred rope, tin cans still warm to the touch. Why burn the office?

"Was there any insurance?"

Eric's bodyguard, the rifleman, wheeled out a blackened skeleton of coils that had once been an armchair.

The stuffing had all burnt away, except in the back where it had probably been protected by a wall.

"There has never been money for insurance," Papa said, pushing down on his cane to lower himself onto the chair.

Did Eric burn the place out of spite? But if he'd wanted to be mean, he wouldn't have given the distillery back free of charge in the first place. After another kick, an unbroken bottle rolled down between my feet. From inside its neck, I carefully pulled out a glossy magazine photograph of a gartered thigh. No other paper had survived.

The fire had something to do with the magazines, of that I was sure. He'd found the page he wanted in my closet, had left me the rest of the magazine probably thinking I wouldn't notice anything missing, or if and when I did it would be too late to matter. And he'd destroyed the rest. Why?

"What do the police think?" I asked Papa.

"Beaujoie was not there and the others . . ." Papa set his chin out in a stubborn-child jut. ". . . It is the murderer they care about, not the arsonist." Papa turned back to the entranceway, and I followed his gaze to catch the rifleman, unshaven, dirty, staring at me with squinting, mean eyes, as if deciding whether to use me for target practice or not. Luckily, he was without his gun this time.

And then it hit me. Guns, that's why. Eric had been paid fifty thousand dollars to get Coco and his men guns, and *Adventure Life* provided guns. "Fifty percent off the retail price. Why pay more?"

"Eric is dead. Who will you work for now?" I asked the rifleman.

"He was good with the fire," Papa said, pushing arthritic fingers into his closed eyes like compresses.

"He will stay if he likes."

The rifleman looked doubtful.

"Do the police think Coco killed Iguana, too?" I asked.

"No. My son was her friend. Cristophe Beaujoie does not believe he killed her, they told me. Besides, my son has a good alibi. Cristophe Beaujoie is very puzzled, I think."

So was I. Opening the car door, I sat down sideways in the driver's seat. I couldn't accept the idea of two murderers being on the loose at the same time. And why the hell was Ellen attacked?

"Did the police find the gun yet?" the rifleman asked, stepping in front of Papa's chair.

Out of the corner of my eye, I noticed the LE SOLEIL label on a crate by the entrance gate.

"Yes, yes," Papa said, waving him aside. "They found it this morning on the drive to the Club. In the crook of an eucalyptus branch."

The discovery of the gun didn't interest me. For some reason, my eyes kept turning back to that label.

"What make was it?" the rifleman asked.

"I don't know what make. What importance does it have? My son would never use a gun!"

I remembered the KANZER RUM label Eric was going to use, painted by a Key West artist. I also remembered Papa's threat.

"You will be dead before you change my son's label!"

What if Coco was innocent, as Papa claimed? What if Eric had changed his mind about transferring the distillery ownership back to Papa? What if the man in front of me, staring back at me with small, sharp eyes, looking like a wrinkled, angry child, his feet dangling from his favorite chair—what if *he* was the real killer?

211

"How and when did Eric transfer ownership?" I asked him.

"In the early evening, he signed a piece of paper."

"Which did not burn with the rest of the office?"

"Which did not burn with the rest of the office." He reached into a pocket of his pants and slipped the French sailor's hat on his head at an angle.

"Can I see the paper?"

A sly smile spread over Papa's face. "Do you wish me to tell you the story of the devil woman who ate curious children?"

I pointed to the sun which was smack-dab in the middle of the sky. "I thought daylight stories would turn us both into baskets?"

"Touché," he said. I looked at this possible killer with the red pom-pom drooping like a wilted flower on top of his head. A proud, angry man. But also mischievous and kind. How could anyone who told stories to children be a murderer?

"What happened to that beautiful frame that hung on a wall in the office, the one with Eric's new label?" I asked. "Did it melt down?"

The rifleman shook his head. "We stopped the fire before it reached that wall."

"Where is it then?"

"The wall was blank."

"Eric brought it," Papa said, "Eric took it back."

"Did you see him do it?"

"No."

The boy threw his broom down, waking up from his stupor. "It is good I came back at midnight. The fire would have burned the whole place. I think I deserve a raise."

"Midnight!" I stood up and bumped my head on the door frame. "Eric was killed at ten o'clock!"

"A timing device!" the boy said with a snap of his fingers. "Like in the movies."

"Timing devices are complicated and don't always work," I said, rubbing the top of my head. "Besides, why bother? This place is desolate. No one would have seen him. If he was afraid of a possible explosion, all he had to do was lay out a length of gasoline-sopped rope, light a match, and zoom off in his jeep. Your arsonist wasn't Eric."

"Who else would burn an old office where mice come to lap up spilled rum?" Papa asked.

If I knew that, I was willing to bet I'd know who the murderer was, too.

TWENTY-TWO

Once I got back to the Club, I called the police station, left a message for Beaujoie to phone me as soon as he could, and settled down to eat lunch on the beach. I looked up at the blue, clear dome of sky. It was a glossy, travel magazine day, perfect for ads and scrapbook photos. Ellen, Nick, and the gang were probably on their way to one of the Les Saintes islands, getting ready for a picnic lunch of chicken and tomatoes on crunchy baguettes, ice cold white wine, and assorted *petits gâteaux* for dessert—all of the above to be consumed in the shade of a spectacular coconut grove. I looked down at my low-fat yogurt and one papaya. Think of Greenhouse, I told myself, think of a late Sunday night of enjoying the warm, tingling sight of him, all the time hoping he's going to reach over and touch a hip—a slim hip, well, slimmer at least. I dug my toes in, wiggling them to find the damp, cooler sand and suddenly felt unreasonably happy. It was the weather and the beauty of this place, I decided, which didn't allow unpleasant thoughts to linger. And my simple need to stop thinking of murder.

Bob stepped on a wooden pedestal in the middle of the beach to summon the G.M.s for a noon health sweat doing *les exercises africains*. Nick and Bob would make peace, I was sure; HM and Jerry had become a couple; Ellen and Paul had just discovered each other; and I had Greenhouse to look forward to. Of course, if Sunday night turned out to be a fiasco, I might end up like that princess Beaujoie had told me about on the ride home after lunch yesterday. Princess Caroline had died of heartbreak waiting for her *chevalier* to come back, while he, learning of her death, roamed the streets of his hometown in France, wrapped in a pale blue silk cloak with his hair knotted in a chignon exactly as she had worn it, covered by lace. I'd laughed and told Beaujoie the *chevalier* would have fit right in the Halloween Parade in Greenwich Village, but he'd looked at me with those large, intense, questioning eyes of his, making me confess I had a "love" back in New York. I thought I'd noticed doubt in those eyes, but I shook the bad thought off, blaming the spices that were still simmering in my mouth.

Manou, trim and great-looking in a bikini, with her hair still slicked in the "HM do," dropped down at my side just as the jungle rhythm of "Co . . . co . . . co . . . Comanchero" started beating out of the loud-speakers. Bob, wearing Hawaiian print jams, called out for one and all to join him in glorifying the sun with a few hip and arm gyrations.

"If I try to writhe like he does," I said, biting into the papaya, "I'll wiggle like a mound of moldy jello. God, I hate this stuff!" I spit yellow goo into my empty yogurt cup.

"Then why do you eat it?" Manou asked, as she spread what seemed like liters of coconut oil on her deeply tanned skin.

"It supposedly contains some enzyme that eats your fat or some such scientific hogwash. How do you stay so slim?" Manou's glistening skin looked crackly and browned to perfection, just like a freshly roasted chicken.

"I don't like food very much," she answered. "I have a message for you."

"From Beaujoie?"

"From New York. You are to go to the airport. Your boss arrives on the Air France 17:50 from San Juan."

Porco Giuda! I jumped up as if a crab had chomped into me. I have nothing against my boss, except when he is obstinate, opinionated, disagrees with me, and thinks I can't handle the job.

"Judas Pig!" I yelled to the sun, wiggling all my pounds to the jungle beat in ferocious frustration.

I went upstairs to my room, took a fast shower, and started writing a note to Beaujoie. In it I explained my theory about Eric planning to buy guns through some ad in *Adventure Life,* how somehow he'd found out I had the magazine—Rudi might have seen me at the mirror and told him or told Zaza. Mentioning Zaza reminded me I wanted to get to the airport to catch her and Lundi before they took off for Paris. I hurried through my note, writing how I thought Eric had stolen into my room and torn the incriminating ad. And then I stopped again and thought about the word "incriminating." Why should Eric worry about the ad? It wasn't proof of anything. He'd never delivered, and Coco and his men couldn't go to the police to denounce him without ending up in jail themselves. If he'd been so brash as to sign a receipt, why bother tearing off the page? Unless it wasn't Eric who'd done the page stealing, just as it hadn't been Eric who had set Papa's office on fire. Beaujoie had to get in touch with the magazine in Clearwater, Florida, and find out what was on that missing page. The information might help

216

explain the murders. And the attacks on Ellen.

I dropped the letter and the magazine off with the same policeman leaning his chair against the station wall, with an unlit cigarette still stuck in his mouth, looking as if he were one of the natural island treasures.

Near the airport, I braked to let a child and a skinny goat cross the highway. The goat bucked his head, trying to free himself of the red paper mask the boy had slipped over his eyes. The boy laughed and waved at me.

Carnival time, I thought, waving back, wishing I, too, could find a disguise to avoid my boss.

"Do you know anything about *Adventure Life?*" I asked Zaza, who was coming out of the small duty-free shop in the departure lounge of Le Raizet Airport. I'd already done a hug and kiss routine with Lundi at the gate under the close scrutiny of a neatly dressed black man, who moved with the stiffness of a Marine in uniform. A policeman in civilian clothes for sure.

Zaza looked wonderfully brisk in a tight black cotton piqué suit, and large onyx shell earrings peeping down from her shining cap of blue-black hair. Except she was nervous. Her wide, heavily mascaraed eyes canvased the almost empty room as if she were missing someone.

"They've called your flight, Zaza. You'll be in France in a matter of hours. Come on, tell me what you know about that magazine."

"Why do you pretend?" She flipped the curtain of hair back my way. "It's not the magazine that counts. It is the *coca.*" She said the word loudly, defiantly, as if wishing the policeman at the other end of the lounge would hear her. "You gave it to the police, now it's your

217

problem." She knelt down on the scuffed linoleum floor and tried to stuff all the perfumes she'd bought in a small black straw bag. I dropped down with her, taking a few packages to help her.

"I don't care about Eric's cocaine," I said. "He's dead now. I want to know about the magazine. First of all, did you or Rudi tell Eric I had taken it?"

She looked up, her eyes narrowed. "Eric's cocaine?"

"It wasn't his?"

"I must go, the plane is leaving. Lundi is waiting."

"Whose then?" I grabbed her bag and held it tight against my chest. "Answer me, Zaza. For Iguana's sake, answer me."

Her eyes swept around the dreary-looking room and rested on Lundi, who was being cuddled by an Air France hostess. She straightened up, patting her skirt down over her thin, tanned thighs.

"I did not know you had taken anything then," she said. "Neither did Rudi. He would have stopped you. When the police came again, asking about the cocaine, Rudi understood it must have been you. I do not know if this magazine is of particular importance or why Iguana had it. She hated anything to do with war, guns, and killing. She hated Eric's war stories."

I said nothing, afraid to break that moment of sincerity with questions that might startle her to silence.

"When I found the cocaine under her mattress, I thought it would make trouble for Iguana, for the memory of her. I hid it downstairs in the fabric store. When the police left I took it back and hid it again with the magazine. I was going to return the cocaine." She pressed her nose against a package of Opium, her eyes closing. "Iguana did not like drugs and drinking. Having had a child without marriage did not make her frivolous. She was good and kind, too good. She kept it

218

only for a friend."

"Mademoiselle Zaza," the policeman called out, waving an arm while Lundi gleefully tugged at his jacket. There were only a few passengers left to board.

"To wean him," Zaza added, taking her packages from me and hurrying to the gate. I followed, still holding on to her bag.

"Now the cocaine is with the police so there is no problem, *n'est ce pas?*" She laughed, a tinkling nervous sound, like a shelf of glasses shuddering against each other after being brushed by a graceless shoulder. "Ah, I almost forgot," she said, reaching in the small pocket of her jacket and pulling out the Club beads I'd given Lundi. "I was going to leave these for you. They are worth money."

Lundi grabbed my knees as we reached the gate. I lifted him up for one last hug. "How were you going to leave them? You didn't know I was coming to the airport."

"Mademoiselle." The Air France hostess touched Zaza's elbow. Zaza showed her the boarding pass.

"Who was going to come to see you off? Iguana's friend, right? He still thinks you have the package."

Zaza turned her head sharply to the policeman who was standing just behind her, her hair slicing the air around her neck. Then she turned back, taking Lundi from me in the same, rough, panicked way Iguana had just four days ago.

"Who was supposed to come, Zaza?"

She started running through the propped-open door, on to the tarmac, her tight skirt and high heels holding her legs back. Lundi bobbed in her arms, first grimacing, then opening his mouth wide for one of his bloodcurdling screams. The plane was a couple of hundred yards out, a bloated silver fish shimmering in the still hot sun. I charged after them.

"You 'ave no ticket!" the hostess yelled. I felt the policeman sprint into motion, a dark presence moving air behind me. Ahead of me, Zaza clambered up the metal stairway. Her heels clanked. I fantasized being Flo-Jo in the one-hundred-meter dash, Lundi's screams becoming the cheering of the crowd. I'd reached the foot of the stairs when the policeman grabbed me.

"Where do you think you're going?" he asked, one hand firmly on my shoulder.

"I've got her purse!" I yelled, shoving it under his nose. He snatched it from me and started to leap up the stairs, but Zaza, with Lundi still in her arms, had clattered back down.

"Merci, merci," she said, planting kisses on both my cheeks. Lundi, who'd stopped screaming, pulled at my T-shirt.

I held up the Club beads. "A memento of Simona." He put the beads and half his fist in his mouth, with a smile in his eyes that burned my heart.

"Tell me who it was?" I asked again.

Pretending not to hear me, Zaza climbed back up the stairs with Lundi, while a steward stood by to close the plane door. The policeman led me firmly back to the departure lounge.

"I'm glad they're both safe," I said. Behind glass doors, we watched the plane coast out on the runway, flashing sunlight in our eyes as it slowly turned. The policeman, letting go of me, stood with his back as straight as an iron rod. For a moment I thought he was about to salute.

"The American, the one who was shot in the ear," the policeman said, "he didn't make his plane."

I'd forgotten about Eric buying a plane ticket for Sunday. "He always went to Florida. He had a friend in Key West."

The policeman turned a rigid shoulder, tucking his

tie under the front of his beige suit jacket with a smooth flip of his hands. "The American's ticket was to the home of a United States Strategic Air Command Base." He seemed proud of that particular knowledge.

"Where's that?"

"Omaha, Nebraska."

Once the home of Ellen Price, our star model.

TWENTY-THREE

I was totally confused again. The fact that any minute my boss was going to step into the sauna heat of the Arrivals Lounge, with its imitation beach complete with sailboat and miniature palms, wasn't helping any. He was going to rush in—impeccably dressed in tropical white linen, dark blue striped Turnbull & Asser shirt, Borsalino panama hat, exuding that crisp New York efficiency that crackled with the electricity from a too plush carpet. I could already hear him announce that the rest of the world was too slow to be believed. I took a peek at my very dim reflection in the glass door. It was melting sag all the way; nothing crisp about me.

What the hell was Eric going to do in Omaha? A male voice hiccuped some French phrases over the loudspeaker. The San Juan flight had just landed. I gave my hair a shake and stood up straight in imitation of Zaza's policeman. Straight backs *look* strong.

Passengers started coming through the gate. A family of four, loaded down with souvenirs from Disney World, was greeted with silent hugs by what looked like grandparents, in-laws, and a busload of well-behaved young cousins, nephews—a micro-world all of its own. The grandmother supervised the reunion, holding a black umbrella open over her head, as if the sun were still with her.

I craned my neck beyond the group, not seeing my boss. Eric had said something about Omaha at dinner on Monday night. I couldn't recall the exact words; I'd been too busy worrying about finding Lundi's mother. Something about having done a job there.

And then I saw him! He was wearing jeans and a green polo shirt, a battered Police Academy satchel over one shoulder. He hesitated at the gate, letting other passengers elbow past him, waiting for me to make the first move.

In four months I'd forgotten how wonderful he looked. Not tall and handsome in the Hollywood way. He had a quiet, warm face that spoke of trust and respect. And those great brown eyes that could shift in a New York minute from mule-stubborn to hot-cocoa-cozy to Playgirl-come-on. With his winter pallor, he looked a little like the belly of a sardine. Still very edible, I decided, gulping to keep my heart from shooting out of my mouth.

I walked toward him slowly, stomach sucked back to my butt, my back straighter than a ruler. A straight back *looks* thin.

"What are you doing here, Greenhouse?"

He gave me his slow grin, the one that goes straight for the groin. "I'm attending a conference on conflict management between genders."

I laughed, surprised at how incredibly happy I was to see him. "You got off to a bad start calling yourself my boss."

He lifted my hair with one hand and kissed my neck. "I wanted you here the minute I got off that plane."

223

I took his hand and rubbed it against my cheek. "What conflict?"

"We'll talk about that later."

"How long can you stay?" We were driving out of the airport in my rented Peugeot.

"I've got to fly back to Miami tomorrow morning. I left Willy with his grandmother, but he wants to do the Everglades. I offered Disney World, but he said it's not for men like us. His mother's taken him there a couple of times, so I guess he thinks that's her territory."

"Does that hurt?"

"It would be all right if I thought it wasn't hurting him so much." He slipped fingers under my hair and stroked my neck. "I didn't fly down here to talk about Willy."

That nasty feeling of rejection slipped out again from some dark corner of mine like a roach set on spoiling our dinner. After a humiliating divorce, I had plenty of hang-ups, the biggest being my need to feel a part of a small nucleus of loving human beings. I'd been seeing this man for over a year. We had wonderful compatibility under one hundred percent percale; he was a great listener during my frequent bouts of diarrhea of the mouth; but when it came to letting me in on his life, I got stonewalled. He had never introduced me to his thirteen-year-old son.

"Why did you come down here?" I said evenly, hoping he wouldn't spot the roach peeking.

"Well, let me tell you what Willy noticed—he told me all this on the flight down to Miami this morning. He said he'd examined the following evidence: an early morning phone call, followed by very loud, off-key singing in the shower that he hasn't had to listen to in at least six months," Greenhouse was listing the items on his fingers, a big grin on his face, "followed by a rejection of the cereal and orange juice he'd laid out on the kitchen table, and the hailing of a cab. I quote, 'I mean, Dad, last time we cabbed anywhere, you know, it was to Roosevelt Hospital to set my broken arm.'"

I laughed, beginning to feel that the sun was coming right back up from behind the volcano for a long, hot shine.

"Wait, the evidence isn't all in yet. We took a cab ride down to Fifty-fifth and Seventh for a mega-breakfast of blueberry cheese blintzes at Carnegie Deli. Another roll of eyes from Willie at this point. 'Daaad, cheese blintzes on a day that's not my birthday or your birthday? Come on, who is she? Julia Roberts?'" Greenhouse got suddenly serious. "And then he really stuck the knife into his old man."

I clenched the steering wheel, dreading what was going to come next. Willie saying, "Aren't you and Mom ever going to get back together?" or "Whoever she is, keep her out of my life," or something equally painful.

"He said, 'Julia Roberts no way. She's gotta be a lot older. Maybe Raquel Welch?'" He broke out smiling again and I nearly swerved off the road.

"So I told him all about you, what you did at your agency, how you'd called me from down here after four months of video blackout, how I was going to see you Sunday night and maybe we could get something going between us again. And after I got through, my very wise son looked at me with that sweet face of his and said, 'The Terminator wouldn't wait 'til Sunday. He'd get the job done *now!*'

"Then he added, 'The Terminator wouldn't take long either.' So here I am on a fourteen-hour furlough."

225

I was so relieved and happy, I felt like I'd picked up a radioactive glow.

"Do you realize you've never talked this much all the time I've known you?" I said, turning into the Club drive.

"That's to answer your question as to why I'm here. Now it's my turn to listen."

"No more monologue?"

He answered by slipping his hand from my knee to the inside of my thigh. I was ready to park the car behind a shack and consummate instantly. Then I remembered the murders. I made one of my lightning decisions not to mention anything about people being killed within a thousand-mile radius of me. Maybe not an honest way to get our new relationship going again, but wise given Greenhouse's feelings about me sticking my Roman nose in people's violent deaths. As a New York City homicide detective, he thought he saw enough murders for both of us.

Greenhouse lost control when we made love, leaving me feeling like a flapping sail, unable to grab the wind. He kissed my ear, his face contrite. "I'm sorry. Four months buildup." He started to help me, but I pushed him gently away. I wanted to wait for the real thing.

We were squeezed together on my twin bed, holding on to each other's hips, afraid we might fall off.

"Don't worry, I'll catch you before you leave," I said, sitting up so as not to feel his skin. We had the whole night in front of us. The Club had signed him in and Ellen had welcomed Nick in her room so we could be alone. I'd introduced Greenhouse to the gang at the bar. Luckily they'd had a great day of shooting and no one mentioned murder except for HM, who repeated the Princess Caroline of Les Saintes story, saying she'd "practically been murdered by that handsome brute of a Frenchman," all the while watching Jerry survey Greenhouse's body with a cocked eyebrow. Ellen's bodyguard had stepped discreetly back, pretending he was on his own.

"Are you hungry?" I asked now, rubbing my head where I'd hit it against the door frame of the car.

"Did you hurt yourself?"

"I bumped my head."

"You knew I was coming."

"How's that?"

"You bumped your head the first time we made love. You told me how it hurt, and for weeks I thought you were talking about my powerful sex."

"Sure you did." I bent down so he could kiss the bump. "I was just getting immunized for Sunday night. So, what do you say? Think you're hungry?" The restaurant was featuring "Festa Italiana" that night, and Paul had said they'd save two seats. HM had winked, saying, "Yeah, for breakfast."

"I will be soon." He squeezed one of my buttocks.

"I meant real food."

"What's unreal about this?"

I flopped back down over him, flattening my breasts against his chest. "What's unreal is that Willy told you to come and that you *did* come, for all of fourteen hours, to be with me."

"You know what else he told me?"

"No, what else? I want to know everything." I kissed his nose. It was great, lying on top of him, both of us naked, and him talking about his son. I mean, if that isn't being part of a nucleus, what is?

"He told me about a girlfriend. He's had a girlfriend for the whole fall semester who he wasn't going to tell

227

me about because he thought I was 'off women.'"

"Does he talk to her, does he let her into his life?"

"He lets her tell him what to wear."

"That's going a little far."

"He's going to have to work that one out himself. I just told him I wasn't going to butt in, but anytime he wanted advice, I'd be there."

"Some advice you're going to give." I stuck my nose behind his ear and inhaled pure, wonderful Greenhouse, the best perfume in the world.

"I offered you for the female point of view."

"I love you," slipped out as easy as an exhale.

His hand slipped over the back of my head. "Listen, for us to work out, you're going to have to accept some things about me." He held me tight against his neck so that I couldn't look at him.

"Just wrap yourself up and deliver. I'll pay the charges."

"Don't go jumping into things like you always do. Simona, you're thirty-six years old . . ."

"Thirty-seven the eighth of March, and I want a big present."

"You've got to grow up. I feel like you're only going to love me if things go your way."

I squirmed out of his grip and slid down next to him.

"You always expect everyone to react like you do," Greenhouse said. "If you feel like talking and I don't, you're surprised. If you love a movie and I don't, you're surprised. The same with food, politics, everything it seems. Willy stopped doing that when he was eight years old."

I grabbed my T-shirt and threw it over his groin. If we were going to have a serious discussion, I couldn't have that penis curled up as quiet and cute as a sleeping kitten in front of my eyes.

228

"I'm surprised only because you don't explain. That's what gets to me. How am I ever going to really know you if you don't give me opinions, or the thinking behind them. You tell me Michelle Pfeiffer doesn't turn you on, I ask you why, you answer, she just doesn't. What kind of an answer is that?"

"You want a half hour discussion on Michelle Pfieffer?"

"She's just an example."

"Michelle Pfeiffer is a very beautiful woman."

"That's it?"

"Too thin for my tastes."

"Thank God."

"You're looking very healthy."

"All the more of me to love. Besides I wasn't supposed to see you tonight. By Sunday I was going to be thin. Well, at least thinner."

"I was referring to your tan."

"Like hell you were." I slid my hand down his side, stopping at his hip, holding on to it as if it were a rudder. It felt so good to have him again.

"Look, I'm basically a quiet man. There are some things that I like to keep to myself. Things that belong only to me. You're going to have to respect that." He put his hand over mine. "Simona, I'm not going to shut you out, but don't expect me to change into a gregarious, crazy Italian like you. I'm someone different, with my own set of genes, my own history. Maybe you just have to listen more carefully."

"I didn't ask for loud, I asked for lips moving."

"We'll give it a try." He lay back down, the T-shirt falling to the floor. The kitten was still fast asleep.

"For right now, why don't you try this?" I lifted the Dijon mustard jar that was still on my night table and unscrewed the lid. "Open your mouth."

"What is it?"

I dipped my finger in the dark brown liquid. "Trust me," I said and stuck my finger in his mouth.

He sat up abruptly, slapping my finger away and spitting into his hand. "What the hell was that?" His face was a portrait of disgust.

"Oh, God, I'm sorry." For an awful moment I thought I'd given him that poison Eric had talked about. I stuck my nose in the jar for the characteristic clove smell. What I got was the smell of iodine. So much for thinking the stuff would shoot love down his groin.

I followed Greenhouse to the bathroom. He bent over the sink to gargle and brush his teeth. I rubbed that beautiful ass of his.

"Whaelwaat?" he said, looking at me from the mirror, his mouth foaming with toothpaste.

"That was a magical island potion, prepared by none other than the famous Monsieur Quicko, guaranteed to make you fall hopelessly in love on sight." I pushed myself against his back, as he bent down again to rinse his mouth. Tincture of iodine was more like it, probably to help with Ellen's cut-up back, but telling the truth was not a priority at the moment. My hand had already reached under the sink to try to work some magic of its own.

Greenhouse turned around and kissed me, his mouth cupping my lips. I ran my tongue on his slick, minty teeth while he maneuvered me back into the shower stall, the length of his body stuck against mine.

"Ten minutes build up nicely," I said, looking down as he pushed me back against the tile.

He fiddled with the water faucet until he got perfect, warm water drizzling over him, then hugged me back into spray, kissing my wet eyes, licking drops from my mouth.

230

I reached for the soap and began to lather up the white hairs of his chest. Tiffany silver, I'd called them when I'd first seen that wonderful naked chest two summers ago in Central Park. I'd been so horny for him I'd stopped making good sense. I was just as horny now.

"What does 'four months buildup' mean, by the way?"

"None of your business." He wrapped my leg around his hip and buttock.

Lifting myself up on tiptoe with the standing leg, I dug my face in his neck. "Does it mean you didn't make love all that time?" I sucked on his ear lobe, letting one soapy hand slip down his back. "Hm? Does it, honey?"

"Yes, damn it." He grabbed my ass and held me up.

My groin curled. He slipped in hard, welcomed as the only man I was ever going to want.

"No one else?" The soap fell down on my toes.

"God, I love you," he said, and I came, as fast and deeply as he had the time before.

TWENTY-FOUR

"Look, the moon is full," Greenhouse said in what had to be the dead of night. I'd been fast asleep, plastered to his back.

"It was full yesterday," I mumbled. His left shoulder blade still smelled deliciously of sandalwood soap.

"I'm here tonight so it's full tonight!" he smacked my butt. "I'm hungry."

"Oh goody!" I propped one leg over his hip, my hand reaching down.

"Hey, I'm forty-one years old, give me a break. I meant real food this time."

"For my next man, I'm going to rob the cradle." I kissed the back of his neck and rolled over. My watch said eleven-thirty. "Kitchen's closed, but let's get dressed anyway. We'll get peanuts and popcorn at the bar, then go sit on the beach and watch the waves, listen to the frogs . . ."

"And maybe recite poetry?" He'd gotten out of bed and was now bent over trying to find his Jockey shorts.

I bit into one moonlike white cheek. "And maybe get you horny again."

"Ouch, you'll have to wait 'till Sunday for that."

"How about a repeat of that other thing?" I found

the shorts and held them behind my back, swaying my breasts to tease him.

"What other thing?"

"You know, the words."

"Oh, that. I might have to take you in on a charge of extortion."

"You can't. I'll deliver anytime."

Someone knocked hard at the door. I dropped Greenhouse's shorts.

"Simona, are you there?" Nick was jiggling the door-knob. "Wake up! You've got to wake up!"

Greenhouse swept his clothes up and ran into the bathroom. I grabbed a pillow for cover and unlocked the door. My heart was doing an ominous drumroll that reverberated down to my knees.

"Has something happened to Ellen?"

"No, it's Paul. The police are taking him down to the station. It's got something to do with Eric's murder."

"What? Wait a minute, I'll be right with you." I reached into the closet for the first thing at hand—one of the pareus reserved for the shoot.

"They're waiting at the gatehouse."

I tied the thing around me like a sarong, and told Greenhouse to follow me as soon as he was dressed.

"Is Beaujoie here?" We were walking rapidly down the baby blue corridor on our way to the stairs of the main building.

"They said he's at the station. Paul got them to wait while I fetched you."

"What do they have on Paul?"

"Paul wouldn't tell me."

"Where's Ellen?"

"Fast asleep, one guard outside her door, another guy downstairs keeping an eye on her balcony. Paul didn't want me to wake her up. Said she'd look tired for the shoot tomorrow. I wouldn't have known anything if Bob and I hadn't met up with the Chef du Village talking to Paul and these two policemen by the guardhouse."

As we reached the fish pond the Chef du Village, a big hulk of a man with scowling eyebrows, seemed to be giving Bob a lecture. He stopped when he saw us.

"Discretion," the Chef du Village said, a finger on his lips. I ignored him and ran the hundred yards to the gate. Bob started coming after me and Nick, but his boss called him back sharply.

"Bonsoir, bonsoir," I saluted both policemen who were leaning against their car, dressed in white short-sleeved shirts and dark trousers, looking as if they were about to go off for a rum punch or two with a friendly game of dominoes thrown in. They stood up and nodded back. Polite men.

Paul looked like he'd just been released from a ten-year hold in a vise. He'd dressed in a hurry, hair tousled, rumpled shirt sticking out of his jeans, eyes barely held in their sockets.

"What's going on?"

Paul ran a hand down his hair. "They want to take me in for questioning. I don't know how long it's going to take, but it'll be all right. I asked Nick to get you because whatever happens you've got to go ahead with tomorrow's shoot. Use Jerry. He's good. He's been with me two years, he'll do a great job."

"Why do these men want to question you?"

"I don't know." His eyes darted to the policemen, then back to me. "Hey, you shouldn't be wearing that." He pointed to my pareu.

I asked the policemen. Polite men, but uninformative.

"They haven't told me either," Paul said. I didn't believe him. They may not have told him, but guilty knowledge was sitting on his face as plainly as if some-

234

one had thrown one of those comedy pies at him. It's what was giving him that feral look. He was scared.

"I have to go with him," I told the taller policeman.

"No, M'zelle. Seulement Missié Langston."

"He doesn't speak any French!"

"There will be an interpreter," he said in French. "Now we must go."

"Un moment, s'il vous plaît." I raised a righteous finger and strode to the phone in the guardhouse. I dialed the police station and asked for Beaujoie. They denied he was there, and I hung up, my French not versatile enough for expletives. By now one policeman was in the driver's seat, tapping a palm against the dashboard. The taller one had his arm outstretched toward Paul, silently asking him to come.

"You're not going to tell me, Paul?" I asked, as he walked to the car, his camera bag flapping against his hip.

"Promise me you'll go ahead with the shoot."

He didn't think he was coming back too soon, that much was clear. "I'll find an American consulate, but if you don't tell me what's going on, no one can help."

"You're not calling New York, are you?"

"I don't believe this! You're being taken in for questioning about someone's murder in the middle of the night and all you're worrying about is tomorrow's shoot and your stupid career?" I tugged at his sagging camera bag. "What's the matter with you?"

He whirled away from me, his arm raised in defense. "Keep your hands off!"

"Paul! What the hell? The bag's empty!"

A hand touched my shoulder gently. Greenhouse had been standing behind me, without saying a word, knowing how I hated for him to interfere. While I'd been talking to Paul, Nick had filled him in on our two "grisly" murders and how the Police Commissioner and I had become friends. I'd been too worried about Paul to stop her. Now Greenhouse was looking at me with that reassuring face of his, no anger or criticism showing.

"Want me to go with him?" he offered in a tone that belied New York homicide cop. I wanted to hug him for his restraint.

"Thank you." I bent down to the open car window. Paul had gotten in the back seat with the tall policeman. I explained who Greenhouse was and asked them, as a courtesy to a fellow officer, to let him come. Greenhouse stepped forward and showed the driver his badge. The two Guadeloupan men conferred in mumbles.

"Okay, *mamblô,* you come." The driver reached over and opened the door on the passenger side. Paul leaned back against the seat and closed his eyes.

"Will no one talk to me?" I was annoyed at being shut out. "Greenhouse, ask Beaujoie if he got my note about the missing ad page. Tell him it relates to the fire and the independence movement." I followed him to the other side of the car. "Tell him that Zaza knows whose cocaine . . ."

"Seulement le mamblô, eh?"

"What?"

"Le mamblô, ze cop." The driver jutted a long finger toward Greenhouse. "'im only!"

I was *persona non grata.*

"Oh, hell, tell him he's no longer a friend!"

A smile tiptoed across Greenhouse's eyes. "Don't call the Consulate yet. Let's first find out what's going on." He slipped down in the seat and closed the door.

"Thanks, honey. I'll wait up." *Mamma,* I was so beside myself I was sounding like his wife of twenty years. I just stopped myself in time from calling out,

"Drive carefully." And that only because he wasn't driving.

"Okay, Nick," I said, leading her away back to the walkway. Bob and the Chef du Village were gone. "I don't know what's happening with Paul, and I'm probably not going to find out for a couple of hours, so why don't we sit by the fish pond while you tell me a story under the no-longer-full moon?"

"What do you mean?"

"You offered this morning, remember?" I sat on the hewn stone edge of the pond. I could barely make out the shape of a large motionless carp.

"Tell me about having come to Guadeloupe before and not telling us, about knowing Lundi's real name and pretending he was a complete stranger, about your mood changing from sunny to thunderstorms at the mention of going to Gosier, about not wanting to come on this shoot." My tone wasn't exactly kind, but I was scared for Paul, angry at Beaujoie, and completely overwhelmed by Greenhouse's sudden appearance bearing gifts of love and sex. Nick was the scapegoat.

"How well did you know Iguana?"

"First I've got to tell you how much I love my job." Nick stood above me, one leg hiked up on the stone brim. "I lied because I get a great charge out of dressing people. I don't mean it's just a kick. It's more like a passion." Whatever she was going to tell me had to be pretty bad from the look on her face.

"You do it very well, too."

"I started at college. These beautiful girls in my dorm would wear the dullest things, everything matching, even ribbons and shoes. So I'd start telling them how to combine colors, take risks, make a statement, woman! It was just an excuse to hang out with them at first, listen to their gushing about John or Joe and the places

237

they'd gone to while I shot baskets in the gym each night."

"What does this have to do with Guadeloupe?"

"I guess I'm just hoping you won't fire me."

"You're part of Paul's team. I couldn't do that."

"He will."

"What did you do?"

"I lied on my résumé." Nick threw a pebble in the water. The carp scooted away. "That portfolio wasn't mine. I never worked in California. After graduating from the University of Tennessee where I'd had a basketball scholarship, I came to Le Caravelle—this Club—for vacation. I didn't know what I was going to do for a job. My game wasn't good enough to go pro. My parents wanted me back in Lincoln to work in a doctor's office or something equally dull. One night I met Peter, the bookseller, and his lover. We got to be friends, and they offered to let me stay with them for the whole summer. Peter called me Nicoletta and told me I was beautiful. He's gay and I looked a little like his lover, so of course he thought I looked good, but it still felt great. I stayed through the rainy season. No tourists, everything shut down. Lazy, lazy time." She sat down next to me and swirled a hand in the water. "Then Rick told me about this clothes boutique in Gosier that had just declared bankruptcy and was being sold for nothing. I thought how neat, I can stay in this paradise and play with dresses. My grandmother had left me a little money, so I bought the place. *Chez Nicoletta,* I called it. I worked here three years, discovered I was good at buying clothes, combining them into great outfits, but I was bad about the business end. If someone couldn't afford my combos I'd give them away, just as long as that customer looked great. And I wanted to do more with my talent. I got homesick besides."

238

"How did you get hold of the portfolio you showed Paul?"

"It belonged to Hogan, Peter's lover. He was a clothes stylist based in California. He used to fly back and forth, then he tested HIV positive and he handed me the portfolio. 'Go for it Nicky,' he said. 'You're allowed a few fouls as long as the team wins. And we're your team.' He even suggested I try to get a job with Paul, because Paul was fairly new in the business and hadn't seen his work."

"Why didn't you look them up when you came down here this time? Peter sounded so surprised to see you."

"Peter kicked Hogan out of the house the same day Hogan told him about testing positive. Hogan's in Hawaii now, still okay." She crossed the fingers of both hands. "Now you know why I kept my mouth shut, and why I didn't want to go to Gosier. I was sure to meet up with someone who knew me."

"Did you know Iguana?"

"I met her on the beach a couple of times. We weren't friendly. And thank God I didn't get to meet Eric. I remembered Iguana's kid's name being Marcel because my boutique had originally been called *Marcel's Rags.*"

"No wonder he went bankrupt. So you don't know anything that might clear up the murders."

"No, I don't. And I don't have any right to this job."

"You're great at it, that gives you rights. As for that portfolio, it's too bad you're always leaving doors unlocked. Things are bound to get stolen that way."

"You mean it?"

"If I find out you're holding out more information, I'll roll you up into a ball and stuff you in a basket myself, even if I have to get on a ladder to do it. Apart from that, I mean it."

She gave me a rib-crunching squeeze. "Do you think

239

Paul's going to be all right?"

"How do I know?" I straightened up to let my lungs come unglued. I could almost hear the pop as I sucked in air. Friendship with this woman could be fatal.

"He was really upset about something during the shoot today. I don't mean he didn't do a good job, but he had to do a lot of repeats, which is unusual for him."

"Did he say what was bothering him?"

"At first I thought it had to do with Ellen. Their thing is kind of sudden, isn't it?"

"Let's just say that sometime during the night their relationship shifted from professional to meaningful. A crisis can do that."

"He couldn't take his eyes off her, they'd touch whenever they got a chance. Jerry and HM started ribbing them. I thought it was making him nervous. But then he kept asking us if we'd gone through his camera bag, or if we'd seen anybody near it. HM thought he'd lost one of his zoom lenses, but Jerry said all lenses were accounted for. He had his wallet with him, so it wasn't that."

I was so tired I pictured Paul with a razor and a mirror, cutting himself a line per nostril on a mirror. "Let's go to sleep Nick, we've got a long day tomorrow."

I walked her to Ellen's room. The guard was there, this time dressed in biker's shorts and a Club Med T-shirt, ready to be a G.M. rolling in from the disco if anybody should walk by.

"What do I tell Ellen?" Nick whispered.

"Nothing until we know more."

Nick wanted to give me another hug, but I stuck out my elbows and backed down the corridor.

Something about the camera bag was blinking before my eyes, teasing me like a firefly that goes out just when you think you've cupped it in your hand. I

240

was simply too tired to keep up the chase.

Once I got downstairs I noticed Ellen's other guard was lying down against a rubber tree, glaring at me. I turned away and walked toward the restaurant.

Iguana had mentioned advertising and death together. I'd assumed she had meant the gun ads in Eric's *Adventure Life*. Was I wrong? Was my kind of advertising connected to her death, to Eric's death? What did Paul have to do with it all?

In times of crisis I need to be near food—in a grocery store, a kitchen, a restaurant, wherever the sight and smell of food is close enough to calm my nerves. It has nothing to do with being hungry, which I was, ravenously so, in fact. Food brings me back to childhood.

The smell of burnt butter soaking up flour means my grandmother has come to visit, and we will be fed spinach lasagne stuffed with ham and peas for an entire week because she insists it is my father's *piatto preferito,* his favorite dish. The sight of pyramids of red peppers and rows of shiny eggplants brings back Saturday treks to Piazza Vittorio where I was allowed to carry the smallest of the shopping baskets so that the pork vendor could deposit in its center, one pink-paper-wrapped *ceriola de' porchetta',* a hard roll stuffed with roast pork that smelled delectably of garlic and fennel and was a cherished reward for good behavior.

After only a few months in America, my father's favorite expression became, "Food gives muscles to the soul," blending Saturday's Popeye cartoon with Sunday's Mass sermon in a maxim which he then Americanized even more by shortening it to "F.M.S."

"F.M.S. or feed my stomach," he'd say, winking at me while he forked some food out of the pot and into his mouth, flustering my mother who doesn't like men in her kitchen.

I now walked behind the long counter of the open Club restaurant that was still festooned with red, white, and green garlands of crepe paper to celebrate "La Festa Italiana." I'd been hit by Greenhouse, then Paul, now by Nick's confession—my soul needed muscle, my stomach food.

The kitchen was closed. I searched out a patrolling guard who refused to open up until I told him I was pregnant and I'd been seized by one of those inexplicable urges to cook. I silently apologized to all those pregnant women who really were seized by strange urges. The guard looked at me with compassion in his sleepy eyes, unlocking the swinging doors right away. He told me his wife, each of the four times she'd gotten pregnant, had eaten only boiled cod fish soaked in molasses. He understood.

The kitchen was a long, antiseptic-looking room, with none of the coziness I was hoping for. A row of stainless steel sinks against one glossy white wall, a row of stoves on the opposite wall, and three industrial-size refrigerators below a rectangular window. Enormous pots and pans, made of stainless steel and copper, dangled above two back-to-back wooden tables that extended down the length of the room. The place could have fed the whole island.

I found the *penne* in the adjacent storeroom, along with a bongo-size can of sun-dried tomatoes and a bottle of lovely green olive oil. I hauled plum tomatoes and arugula out of the vegetable refrigerator, grabbed mozzarella, and out loud blessed the Club's *Festa Italiana* for providing me with these decidedly non-French ingredients. I was all set. Maybe not to solve two murders or even one, but at least to cook something soothingly nourishing.

242

I spooned the drained pasta and its sauce into a large plastic container, gave the mixture a last whirl, tasted it again just to get some energy, screwed the lid on, ran back to my room, scrambled into slacks and a T-shirt, dashed to the gate, hopped into my Peugeot, and fourth-geared it straight to Pointe-à-Pitre and the local police station.

"Hi there," I said, slipping into Beaujoie's office without knocking. "I'm here to do a taste test." I placed the plastic container on his desk and unscrewed the lid under his nose. Paul scowled, slumped in a chair, and Greenhouse, sitting next to him, blinked a lot, trying to hide what I hoped was amusement. A young woman sat in a corner behind Beaujoie. The translator, presumably. "Using one as guilty and ten as innocent, how would you rate this man now standing before you?" I pointed to Paul.

"How did you enter?" Beaujoie said in English. I could see his nostrils twitch. I couldn't tell whether with anger or hunger.

"I told the guard this container held crucial evidence. When he wanted to see what was inside, I mumbled something about Mr. Quicko and the smell of cloves. Want to taste? I call it *Pasta Crisi,* good for any crisis. Can be eaten hot or cold, depending on the duration of the problem. So what is the problem?" I handed out the forks I'd stuffed in my slacks pocket. My left thigh was going to be pocked for life.

"My gun killed Eric," Paul said, studying the fork as if it too might kill someone inadvertently.

"I was afraid of that." After two bites of pasta back at the Club, my brain cells had popped open and I'd figured that the source of the trouble was whatever had been stolen from Paul's camera bag. There was no other reason I could think of for Paul barking at me for touching his empty camera bag. Or for Paul to take an empty camera bag along in the first place. The thought of a gun had slipped in when I'd thought of the magazine with all its gun ads.

Greenhouse had pulled his chair closer to the desk and started eating. "Good stuff," he said, his mouth full, his eyes carefully avoiding mine. He was a great help.

"Monsieur Langston bought a gun for the purpose, he himself alleges, of protecting Mademoiselle Ellen." The woman translated in a sleep-flattened voice.

"For Christ's sake!" Paul churned in his chair. "What would you do if someone threw rocks at your wife?"

The woman translated back, her voice was as lifeless as subtitles, and for a moment I thought I was watching an old film noir; the only things missing were flies and a slow-moving ceiling fan. The fan at least would have helped with the fish market smell the sea breeze was bringing in from the open window.

I propped myself up on the windowsill. "How'd you get a gun through New York airport security and French customs?"

"The gun was bought here," Beaujoie said, his fingers laced on the peak of his stomach. "Directly from an employee of Monsieur Kanzer."

The rifleman! That's why Paul had been talking to him outside the distillery, only a few hours after HM had tried to cover Ellen's bruised, scratched back, hoping Paul wouldn't notice. Except he had noticed and taken immediate action.

"*Alors,* you are so in love," Beaujoie shifted his attention back to Paul with a five-degree turn of his head, "you would do harm to protect her."

"Don't put words in my mouth!" Paul threw the fork

against the wall; it fell near my feet and I retrieved it, wiped it with my T-shirt, and handed it back as if it were a child's pacifier.

"Impetuous. Easily angered." Beaujoie's steady voice was overlapped by the translator, his dark drone narrowed to her tinny monotony.

"How did you know the gun belonged to Paul?" I asked, going back to the window and the breeze line. I knew the answer to that one already. The rifleman had snitched. I could still see him bent over Papa La Bouche in that burnt skeleton of an armchair, asking if they'd found the gun, what make it was.

"A .22 calibre automatic pistol. Pyrénées, Unique, Model D. At least twenty years old. Not a gun of choice for an American, but when one is in need." Beaujoie unlaced his fingers and leaned forward to fork one *penne*. "The man who sold it to him came to us with the information." He slipped the pasta in his mouth with caution.

"Do you trust him?" Introduce doubt, break down their assumptions, isn't that how it's done?

"I'm not denying it's my gun," Paul said. "I was worried and I bought it."

"Great, Paul!"

"Angry too," Beaujoie said, ignoring me. "Angry at Eric Kanzer in whom Mademoiselle Ellen was very interested, was she not?"

"A charity case." I went to the desk and shook a few *penne* into the plastic lid and handed it to Paul. *"Mangia,"* I told him, then asked, "Shouldn't we get a lawyer?" I looked across the desk at Greenhouse, who was wiping his mouth with the back of his hand. He looked unperturbed.

"I don't want a lawyer," Paul said, jabbing the lid with his fork so that pasta spilled on his lap. He popped pasta in his mouth and I noticed his fingertips were dark with ink. He'd been fingerprinted. "I didn't kill that man. I'll admit that if he'd laid his hands on Ellen one more time, I've have punched him good, but I'm not into killing anything. Look, ask Jerry, my assistant. I use friendly mouse traps in my studio, then release the damn things in the park. Simona, explain to this man. I was angry, I was frustrated. The idea that someone wanted to hurt her, I . . . I . . . forget it, what's he going to know!"

Beaujoie didn't wait for the translator. "Much. I know a painful much about love," he said in English. "Angry love, diverted love, love of love, love of what is not there. Too much." He sat back in his chair and broke into French. "But since Mademoiselle Simona was so kind as to bring us a sample of her cooking, I think we would do her a dishonor not to eat in peace." He set his red-veined eyes on my face. His face was smudged with fatigue and a deeper sadness seemed to have bored into his features. "It was clever of you, this food business." He snapped open a handkerchief, tucked it in his open shirt front, and heaved a forkful of *penne* to his mouth.

"A trick my mother taught me. She says it helps 'fill out the holes the day's punched in,' not to mention the holes in my knowledge of what's going on." I stuck to English to involve my two American friends and to keep Miss Translation awake. "It's not exactly a woman of the nineties maneuver, but it got me in here. You know, you've got one fact on your side—the gun belongs to Paul—but what about that gut instinct you listen to? If that instinct told you Eric didn't fit in the 'cutout of the murderer,' it can't now be telling you Paul pulled that trigger. Come on, let's all go home."

"We've got a shoot to do in four hours," Paul said severely, as if that fact were a matter of international importance.

"All possibilities have to be examined," Beaujoie said, before clamping down on another forkful of pasta.

As long as the food lasts, I almost said. "The gun got stolen from his camera bag," I said instead. "Paul's handed it over for prints, what else do you want?"

"Sorry about snapping at you," Paul said, handing me back an empty lid. His chin, shadowy with beard, now had red speckles of sauce. "I was afraid you'd smudge the prints."

"Any prints on the gun?"

"None." Greenhouse stood up, tucking his polo shirt back in his jeans. "Simona's right. It's time we all got some sleep. Your only case against Paul Langston is for illegal possession. You haven't proved means, the motive is very shaky. This man is an outstanding American photographer. I don't think our State Department will take the matter very lightly unless you can come up with more hard evidence. Of course, we'll advise our consulate in Martinique the minute it gets to be a decent hour. They will see to a good lawyer. Maybe we can resolve this matter by paying a fine. I hope so. Anytime you come to New York, let me know. I'll be happy to show you our way of doing things." He leaned over and proffered a hand across the desk to Beaujoie. "I hope next time we won't have to discuss murder. But then if Simona can help it, we probably will."

Beaujoie stood up, a smile crossing his lips at the last phrase. He'd never let on to me he understood English that well.

"Although we are an island that depends on tourism," he said in French, "and would not want to ruin the digestion of any State Department, however big or small, we still believe in upholding the law." The woman translated.

"You don't have a case for murder," Greenhouse said, after hearing her out.

"Not yet." Interesting match, I thought. Pretty equally weighted. Of course, I wanted US to win because I couldn't even for a minute contemplate the possibility that Paul had shot Eric in a fit of anger or whatever, but I didn't like Greenhouse's patronizing tone. Where'd he gotten that "outstanding American photographer" bit?

"No deposition to sign?"

"Madame Tribaud here will type it out in both languages, the notary will affix his stamp and signature to guarantee the correctness of the translation, and then I will ask Monsieur Langston to sign it. Sometime this afternoon. It is now already two in the morning."

Paul was already at the door, his hand slapping his hip as if feeling for the renounced camera bag. I got off my window perch to go. With the handkerchief still tucked in his shirt front, Beaujoie examined the empty pasta canister. I half expected him to crush it with his hand.

"My wife and I would enjoy the recipe." He handed it to me. "A little crisis food may help, who knows?"

"I hope so. If I don't see you again, I'll mail it to you. We're leaving Saturday morning."

"So soon? You are not upset, I hope, over this last occurrence."

"Of course I am. I thought we were partners of sorts."

"I ask forgiveness. I had heard from Mademoiselle Ellen's bodyguard that you had a visitor. I did not wish to disturb the idyll."

"You're a pretty canny guy. I better start watching out for you."

He walked us out onto the street, where the two

248

policemen were waiting, sitting in chairs tilted against the wall.

"Thank you for your note about the magazine and the connection to the fire," Beaujoie said, his width and height filling the doorway. "I have already contacted the magazine headquarters. They will fax the missing page. My men will now drive you back to the Club."

"I've got a car parked in the market place."

"They will follow then. I am in need of Paul Langston's passport. As a precaution, you understand."

"You're kidding?"

"And before you go to Carbet Falls for your work in a few hours, I will ask all of you to come by Police Headquarters for fingerprinting."

"What does the rest of the crew have to do with this? Come on, Beaujoie, what are you doing to me?" I had myself already on the phone to New York, telling the higher-ups to start advertising for BEAU JAIL.

"It is for the camera bag. To distinguish which prints are whose." He lowered his voice. "Now be wise and return to your idyll. Your New York friend looks nothing like the blond aerobics instructor. You will do much better with this one."

"Thanks to you, the rest of the night is shot."

"Not with such a moon." And he pointed to the damn thing in front of everyone. Four men craned necks back to look.

"Reminds me of one of those gauze-wrapped lemons they serve in fancy restaurants," Greenhouse said.

So far, BEAU MOON was outselling BEAU SUN by a large margin.

TWENTY-FIVE

They'd turned the basketball court lights off. The Club was soothingly shadowy, with only that moon and a few dimmed beach lights to highlight the trees and the sea. Paul had relinquished his passport and gone off to sleep; I'd checked with Ellen's corridor guard—there'd been no activity—then joined Greenhouse on the beach. We sat on two chaise longues facing the water. Fifty feet behind us, Ellen's beach guard watched.

"It's going to be okay for Paul, isn't it?"

"Hard to say. They may have other incriminating evidence. I don't think so though. Before you waltzed in with that great pasta, Paul only got asked about the gun, how he'd got hold of it, the wheres and the whens, how much he'd paid for it, what exact words had he used to ask for the gun. I got the impression that the Commissioner was more interested in the man who sold him the gun than Paul."

"There's a very small independence movement brewing. The man I call the rifleman may be part of it or may be selling them guns." I took off my sandals and dug my feet in the cooled-off sand. "Paul couldn't have killed Eric. It wouldn't make sense."

"I'll take care of calling the Consulate and explaining the situation. My flight doesn't leave until ten."

"Then you won't go to the falls with us?"

"Not enough time. I'll leave you a note with whatever response the Consulate gives us. They'll call in a lawyer who'll get in contact with the police here, then with Paul. Just make sure Paul does what they ask him to do. He seems quick-tempered."

"Broody, impatient, but I've never seen a burst of real anger."

"I have. When the Commissioner implied there was something between Ellen and Eric—this is before you came—Paul shot off a tirade about Eric exploiting Vietnam, Schwarzkopf getting five million dollars for a book, Ellen letting herself be suckered in, something about a terrible childhood. Since I didn't know any of the background, his incomplete sentences lost me. And the translator. The Commissioner kept balling a handkerchief in his hand, I guess listening. I don't know how much English he really understands, how much he pretends to understand."

"He catches on real well, I think." I tried to picture Paul ranting with anger, a gun held to Eric's ear. I couldn't. But then anger frightens me too much for me to envision it.

Greenhouse kicked his shoes off and lay back. "This Club sure beats the streets of New York. Raf sends his love, by the way." Raf was Greenhouse's partner and a good friend of mine, too. "He told me to remind you that there's a great spice market down here."

Just like Raf to make me smile when I needed it. During my independence-at-all-costs period, Raf had caught me throwing out a jar of cinnamon I kept exclusively for Greenhouse to spice his coffee the way he liked it. I hate the stuff myself.

"Probably wants a present of some hot spice for his

paella," I said, not willing to confess my dastardly deed.

"You weren't too happy with my performance back there, were you?" Greenhouse said, stretching a hand to my shoulder.

"You could tell?"

"Let's say your face was extremely expressive of disapproval."

"I don't like it when anyone pulls weight. You didn't have to bring in the State Department."

"He didn't have to haul Paul to the station at twelve o'clock at night. Those are intimidating tactics. We use them all the time."

"You blame him then?"

"Is this an argument?"

"No, a discussion."

"Good. Okay, maybe I did play ugly American a wee bit, but I was trying to get him to examine his position carefully. Besides, I was annoyed at the interruption of what was turning out to be a wonderful night. What's the man's name again?"

"Beaujoie. It means beautiful joy."

"He looked anything but."

"He has a few personal problems. Nice man."

"Probably too kind to be a good policeman."

"Are you a good policeman?"

"Think so."

"Where does that leave kindness?"

"I hope with my son, with you."

I wiped my cheek on his hand that was still on my shoulder. "Did you mean what you said in the shower or was it just the four-month buildup?"

"I meant it then, I mean it now, but I can't swear to forever and forever anymore. There's still a lot we've got to find out about each other, too." He got up and sat on the edge of my chaise, next to my hip. "Why

252

don't we just keep seeing each other and test it out?"

"The word 'test' scares me."

"Me too. Let's give it a try, though. Nothing half-assed. A go-for-the-touchdown run." He leaned over and kissed my forehead. *"Va ben?"*

"It's *va bene,* with the final 'e' pronounced 'eh'."

He lifted me up and hugged me. "There she goes correcting me. Do I need this?"

"Yes, you do." I kissed his neck. "And I need you. Do you want to sleep?"

"No. What I'd like is for you to stay out of police murder investigations."

I squirmed.

"Wait a minute, hear me out. I'm not asking you, I already know what your answer would be, anyway. I've given it some thought, and I realize you should be able to do what you want without having me put the brakes on. But you've got to get two things in that Italian marble head of yours. In my humble, albeit male opinion."

I pulled away. "Lecture time?"

"Simona, you never stop to examine a situation first." His voice was soft, caring, like no teacher I'd ever had. "You rush in, driven by some mad curiosity, or need to help, then when things turn ugly you're surprised and caught unaware. You don't think of the consequences."

"Even if I don't reason like some logistics professor sucking on a pipe, I've brought in two murderers with no help from the NYPD."

"Don't rub it in. What I want to know is, when you dumped me over the phone back in the fall, had you reasoned it out?"

"I was unhappy and I felt it was something I had to do. What was there to reason? Hey, I thought we were talking about my involvement in murder cases here,

253

not why I gained twenty pounds in four months."

"Look, the reason I don't want you anywhere near murder is not because my masculine ego is threatened. You're going to get hurt one day. I don't want that to happen."

"That's exactly how I feel about you being a New York police detective."

"You know what? At this hour of the night, with this setting, I'm willing to concede you've got a point."

"Thanks, macho-man." I moved over and pushed him down to lie next to me. "May I talk to you about these murders? Maybe you can come up with something I've overlooked."

"Hm."

"There are a lot of confusing elements here." I quickly filled him in on the events, not remembering exactly what Nick had told him. "Iguana dies just as she's screwed up the courage to do something. Zaza said she was desperate for money, so maybe she was blackmailing someone. Coco has no money, was supposedly a good friend of Iguana's and has a good alibi for the time of the murder. Eric, on the other hand, has no alibi, wasn't a friend anymore *and* accepted fifty thousand dollars to buy guns with apparently no intention of delivering. So let's suppose he killed Iguana either to stop her from telling Beaujoie or to prevent her from telling Coco he was going to pocket the money. Sounds perfect! But then Eric gets killed with Paul's gun, and someone sets fire to an office full of old magazines. That same someone tears a page out of the *Adventure Life* I'd snagged from Iguana's apartment. Then there's the five thousand dollars worth of cocaine to think about and everyone . . ." Out of the corner of my eye I saw Ellen's guard walk to the water. He had his back to me and by the way he stood he looked like he was peeing. Which was fine with me, except that he had his back to Ellen's balcony, too. I turned around, just to make sure everything was still all right.

The place really did look like a movie set, the moon providing the lighting this time. At the bottom edge of the basketball court a fifty-foot palm leaned toward the water like a thirsty giraffe. I thought of Nick leaning into Bob as he held the ball high above her. The proverbial lightbulb flashed in front of me! Of course! A gun-for-hire ad just like the one Nick had talked about, an ad for which *Soldier of Fortune* had been sued. That's what had been torn from *Adventure Life*. Eric, the Failed Hero. He'd have made a perfect hired killer.

"No more monologue?" Greenhouse sounded very subdued.

"Oh, sorry. Where was I?"

"Everyone . . ."

"Well, yes, everyone falling in love is what I was going to say," I waved at the guard as he took up his post again and looked up at the ceiling of stars. "In the middle of all this ugliness there's a lot of good feeling going around." There were so many stars I thought of an arsenal of firecrackers exploding. "You know what this reminds me of? My father used to rent an apartment in a beach town two hours out of Rome for the summers—Sperlonga. On Sunday nights we'd have supper on the beach. Papa was in charge of the meal and it was always the same." I took Greenhouse's hand and placed it on my knee, repeating a gesture I'd seen my mother make countless times in the darkness of those Sunday nights. "Cold breaded veal cutlet sandwiches with mustard and lettuce. We'd eat and sit back to watch the stars. My mother could never find the Big

Dipper either." My remembering brought me to Nick remembering her dead mutt, shot in the ear. Just like Eric. Weird.

And then memory served up two items that were like movie-theater-peeks at the coming attractions. One was of Nick at dinner four nights ago, the night Iguana was murdered.

"Greenhouse, you were talking about consequences before. Listen to this." I turned on my hip. His hand, which had rested on my knee, slid to the sand.

"Honey? Stan?"

He was fast asleep.

TWENTY-SIX

"What do you mean, he's called off the bodyguards?" It was six-ten, Friday morning. I'd torn myself away from Greenhouse, now sleeping in my bed, and had run down to the Club entrance to set off for our last day's shoot: Carbet Falls. I found the crew lined up, being fingerprinted on the hood of my rented Peugeot by last night's two policemen, while Tommy hovered nearby dying to find out what was going on. Paul had just informed me Ellen was going to be unprotected for the day.

"Is Beaujoie crazy or what?"

"A very important French dignitary is landing at Le Raizet in a few hours," the tall policeman mumbled as he handed HM a paper towel to wipe his hand. "We need all our police to ensure his safety. There are many of you. You can look out for her safety if you are so worried. The Commissaire does not worry."

"He's not in charge of her. What dignitary?"

"It is not for me to say."

I opened my mouth to give a healthy operatic scream, but Ellen was sitting in the front seat of the car, beaming her smile.

"I'll be fine," she said, before I could sound a note.

"Besides . . ." She held out the red bean.

"Sure." Let her believe it. I'll enlist HM to watch her like a hawk.

"Merci, très bien," I said. "Now are you policemen through mucking up people's fingers, because we're here to do some work."

"So are we." The tall policeman clicked the ink pad shut, dropped a handful of paper napkins on the hood of the car, and walked off. The other policeman had already gotten behind the wheel of his car. The wind picked up the napkins and blew them right in my face.

"Cazzo!" I yelled.

"Come on Simona, cool that temper," Bob said, lifting his shades to flash me with his swimming-pool eyes.

"Glad you reminded me." One of the two things I'd remembered on the beach with Greenhouse was Bob's anxiety yesterday. I joined Nick in the back of the van.

"Yesterday morning Bob was very anxious to talk to you. He wanted to know if you were going to be back by four."

"I wasn't." Nick was making room for Bob's Club Med satchel next to her neat pile of bathing suits and designer towels. The expression on her face said she didn't like what I was leading up to. "We didn't get back until after five."

"Too late to go to the airport for him, I guess?"

She started pulling on a white bathing suit on top of the pile as if to stretch it to a more comfortable size.

"Am I right?"

She nodded without looking at me. "He asked me not to tell anyone, but I guess I owe you one."

"Thanks, Nick. I don't think anything will come of it." I walked back to Bob, who was leaning against a black tractor on the grassy center of the driveway, part of the 'farm art' decorating the entrance. Tommy followed me.

"What are you doing up at this hour, Tommy?" I said, none too graciously, hoping to lose him. I was edgy, excited by the sharp tingling feeling a truffle dog must experience when he thinks he's close enough to start digging. I also hadn't gotten any real sleep in two nights.

"Your friend was here. I thought you might be leaving and I wouldn't get to say goodbye." He looked totally forlorn and sweet with his blotched face, reminding me of a stray mutt.

"We're not leaving until tomorrow." I had more questions to ask Nick, questions about that dead dog she couldn't forget, but I needed to wait on those until after the first setup when she could finally stand back, keep only one vigilant eye on Ellen's clothes and props, and lend me her attention.

"Come on, Simona, can't you see the guy's dying to come on the shoot?" Bob put an arm around Tommy as if they were the best of buddies. "What do you say? There's plenty of room in the van."

"No, I can't." He squirmed away from Bob. "I'd be in the way."

"No, you wouldn't," Nick said, joining in with a happy face. "You can give me a hand carrying all my stuff down those narrow paths."

"No, Tommy's mine," HM called out, heaving two black leather kits into the back of the van. "Hop in, Tommy boy, I need all the help I can get. I mean we could have picked an easier place to get to, right, Simona?"

Tommy hesitated, keeping his eyes on me.

"Sure, why not?" I said, not wanting him there at all. Tommy hurried to the van after Nick, as if afraid I'd change my mind.

259

"I'm looking forward to this," Bob said. "You'll tell me what magazines are going to carry the ads, right?"

"I saw Zaza off at the airport. She was disappointed you didn't show up."

He shook his handsome blond head, nothing showing on his face. "What are you talking about?"

"Two hundred and fifty grams of cocaine or thereabouts. I think they belong to you."

"The sun's gotten to your brain."

"I found the cocaine in Iguana's bedroom and gave it to the police."

"Are you trying to pin her murder on me?"

"I have a hunch cocaine has nothing to do with the murders, but I am trying to sift through a maze of details that are confusing the hell out of me. Iguana was a friend of yours, wasn't she?"

Bob finally hooked his eyes on mine and gave me a quick smile. "She was a good kid," he said after a pause. "I was this close to being addicted." He pinched thumb and forefinger together. "The first three months were hell. She and I would have these sessions on the beach. She'd get me to talk about myself, all the shit I'd done. Said she was going to wean me like a baby. She was a real help."

"How did she get hold of your cocaine?"

"I gave it to her stuffed in a sneaker on the beach, the first week I was here. I thought the Chef du Village was on to me. If he'd found the stuff I'd have been kicked out 'pronto.' I asked her to hide it for a while, then she started in on me and I haven't used since. I admit I wanted the stuff back after she died." He shook his head and smiled again, trying to charm. "I tried to get hold of Zaza, but she's got no phone, and the police were sniffing around her."

Paul was hooting the horn of the Peugeot and yelling at us to hurry up. HM had already driven the van off

260

loaded with Nick, Jerry, Tommy, equipment, clothes, and food.

"She sent a girl over with a message saying the stuff was gone. I was counting on finding out more yesterday. I was going to send Nick with a note.

"Are you going to tell her?" He tried his smile on me again, but this time I didn't mind the fakeness of it. He'd asked about Nick first, not the police. That made him okay in my book.

"Why don't you tell her?"

He nodded his head and slipped his glasses back on. "After the shoot. Okay with you?"

"It's your life, your relationship."

"Are you two coming?" Paul yelled.

"Try stopping us!" Bob grabbed my hand and ran me to the car at Carl Lewis speed.

For the first hour after we got to the Carbet Falls parking lot we were all kept busy, Tommy included. We unloaded clothes, food, equipment, maneuvered the load down steep paths narrowly carved on the edge of small, fern-carpeted canyons and across a quavering suspension bridge. I listened to everyone's laughter, to pretended giggles of apprehension, to HM cracking dumb jokes about "Me, Tarzan, you, Jerry," all the time staying close to Ellen and hoping she wouldn't notice.

The air was cool and humid—filled with the sound of the approaching thunder of *La Deuxième Chute*—the second fall, the most beautiful and easiest to get to—ricocheting bird calls, the crackle of broken twigs underfoot, and the tick of leaves heavy with water, hitting the ground. The mood was light, relaxed, set by Paul who was elated to be free of the police and able to do the shoot.

261

We reached a flat, rocky plateau and gaped at the curtain of white foam that crashed one hundred and ten meters down to a large pool of water sixty feet ahead of us. Luckily, it was too early for tourists, and we had the whole place to ourselves except for a naked man who, at the sight of us, walked out of the water and climbed up the side of the cliff, disappearing behind some thick, vine-drooping trees.

"Ellen's got to get under that?" Tommy said, his mouth practically hanging open.

"You can't swim real close to the Fall, the pressure's too great," Bob said. "It sucks up the air. And the water is freezing. I hope you guys want us to wade in those." He pointed left, to the hot-tub-size pools scattered in the bed of rocks. "They're warm, thanks to the volcano."

Paul had come back from an inspection tour of the immediate surroundings. "Don't worry, the Fall's just for background. Great place. Those slashes of sun across the water look almost fake, like some old Hollywood Bible movie." He picked up the tripod and tracked back to Jerry, who was already shooting the Fall from various angles.

I walked over to Nick, who had spread a large plastic sheet between two boulders and was busy making the spot her clothes and props corner.

"Remember Monday night? We were all sitting in our gazebo and somebody started talking about where everyone came from."

"All I remember about Monday night is that murder!"

"No, listen. I was looking out for Iguana and I wasn't paying much attention, but at a certain point you recognized someone. You said something like 'how familiar you look.'"

"That's when it came out that Ellen and I had lived

sixty miles from each other." She was on her knees, unfolding a white Pratesi towel with a red and black sun woven in the center.

"Whom did you recognize?"

Nick sat back on her heels. "Are you sure I said that?"

"Yes, it came back to me this morning. Paul remembers too, except he doesn't know who you were talking to. Come on, you've got to remember. It was only four days ago. Close your eyes and picture the people there." She did as I asked.

"Paul and Ellen—but you've seen them too many times for it to be them—then Eric walked in jangling his boots. Could it have been Eric?"

"Then Bob came by." Nick opened her eyes again, smiling. "I do remember being embarrassed. He was practically naked under that white paint. And very beautiful."

I heard a light tick in my head, like the sound of those leaves falling, except I wasn't prepared to listen just yet.

"I've got this crazy idea in my head about that dog and the murdered couple you've been fixating on. I think whomever you recognized Monday night reminded you or was even connected to that murder eight years ago."

Nick made a face. "Come on!"

"I said it was crazy, but it's also possible. Think of that woman who remembered her father killing her girl friend years later, when her own daughter did something to bring it all back. It doesn't have to be a face necessarily. It could be a walk, a gesture."

"I'd remember Tommy's walk, that's for sure." Tommy had changed into a long, floppy bathing suit and was hobbling over the rocks toward one of the warm pools.

"His mother must have used his feet as pin

263

cushions." Nick got up, picking up a folded sheet. Ellen was made up and ready to slip into her first bikini, a tan and gold skimpy number that echoed the packaging of the product.

"Can't you remember?"

She walked to the cliff's edge and spread the sheet over a low branch. "Not now. Come on, Ellen, wiggle yourself into this." Ellen slipped behind the sheet.

I sat on my boulder, certain that she'd recognized someone, and her subconscious had connected it back to that one violent event in her life. The facts that she did not remember saying those words convinced me all the more. She was suppressing, a therapist would say.

Eric had said he'd once done a job in Nebraska. Not 'had a job,' 'done a job,' which I found odd phrasing. And before he died, he bought a ticket to Omaha. Had his job been in Lincoln? Had Nick perhaps seen him? I thought of the gun-for-hire ad. Could I go so far as to think he'd been hired through an ad in *Adventure Life* to kill that couple?

Maybe I was beginning to wallow in *merda di toro*.

I watched as HM relished spreading body color on Bob, who had stripped down to his briefs.

"Why does he need that stuff?" I asked, suddenly annoyed by the streak of dark liquid HM had squirted on Bob's arm.

"He's not evenly tanned. And his color's wrong. Too red."

Paul and Jerry had moved over to the pool Tommy had picked for his baths. Tommy climbed out, dripping wet, apologizing to everyone, hoping he hadn't disturbed anything. Nick held back laughter while Ellen, half-submerged in the pool, leaned her head against a boulder, the red and black sun towel carefully tossed next to her.

"I bet that warm water's great for the skin," Tommy

said, dripping my way. With an eye on Ellen, I kept turning back to HM and Bob, the falling-leaf-tick coming back a little louder.

"I'm going to plunge in the cold water," Tommy said, catching my eyes wandering back to Bob.

Tommy took his watch and suntan cream out of his golf cap. "You gave me this in Pointe-à-Pitre, remember?" he said, showing me the small jar of BEAU SUN. "You've been so nice." He looked like he was going to kiss me, then changed his mind. "Hold these for me?" He pushed jar and watch in my hand and made his way to the Fall.

"Be careful," I yelled.

Time passed and pictures got shot. Bob and Ellen in the pool, Bob and Ellen leaning against dark, oily-leafed philodendrons clinging to the bark of ancient trees, Bob and Ellen sitting on a boulder, the Fall plunging down between them in the background. Tourists came on their tours of the beauties of Basse-Terre, the Falls rating a ten on everyone's scale. They stared, without disturbing. While HM watched Ellen, Tommy stood guard over HM's leather kits, and I watched over Nick's clothes. And then, a little past three, the photographing was done and I spread out lunch. I was no closer to knowing anything.

"Come to think of it," Nick whispered, between bites of her crab and avocado baguette sandwich, "I could have been thinking of Tommy. His walk does remind me of that man. Same squishy walk."

"Are you kidding me?" I nibbled my detested papaya.

"Of course I am. Well, only half kidding. The similarity is there, but come on, what's a walk mean?"

Nothing, everything, another detail to crowd the picture. That's when I decided to plunge into the comfort of the knee-deep warm pool. I was wearing a bathing suit underneath my clothes and when I lifted my skirt, Tommy's cream and watch fell out. The top of the jar broke and cream spilled on my foot. I thought nothing of it, spreading the cream over my leg. I went into the water and everything was fine until I put my hand to my face and smelled cloves. Faint, but definitely cloves. And then I felt the sting on that leg. A searing sting as if alcohol had been poured on an open wound.

"Tommy!" I yelled. "What the hell is this?" I jumped out of the pool and looked at my leg. A red splotch marked the area where I'd spread the cream. "Tommy!"

"What is it? What happened?" Everyone ran to me. Everyone except Tommy.

"Where is he?"

"I don't know," Paul said. "Are you all right?"

Ellen pointed behind her. "I saw him run back up the path just a minute ago."

"Damn him." I slipped into my sandals, pulled my T-shirt over my head and started running.

"Where are you going?" Nick yelled.

"Everybody stay with Ellen," I yelled back. I was going to catch him and pummel him into telling me what he'd put in that cream. I slowed down over the suspension bridge which still swayed from his weight.

"Tommy, wait up!" Fat chance he was going to do that. Not if he'd been the one to attack Ellen. Cloves. She'd smelled cloves. I started climbing up the slope. I wasn't in good enough shape to keep running. I helped myself up by pulling on lianas, grabbing roots as I slipped.

When I reached the top of the hill, I looked at the thick vegetation surrounding me for signs of Tommy. Ahead of me was the long flat stretch that led to the parking lot. How had he gotten away so quickly? He looked in worse shape than I was.

Of course he hadn't gotten away at all. In my rush to catch him, I'd never thought of looking behind me. He came up to me now, puffing as much as I was. He'd probably hidden behind a tree while I stumbled on.

"Does it hurt very much?" His face was a mixture of alarm and regret that competed with his blotches for space.

"Well, you should know." I moved back from the edge of the cliff. "You put it all over your face, didn't you?"

He didn't deny it. "You were kind to me. You noticed that I had burned in the sun, you gave me the jar as a present."

"You wanted more attention, is that it?"

"The sting doesn't last that long."

"Thank God for that." Where was everybody? I didn't want to stand alone with this nut. For all I knew he'd attacked Ellen *and* killed Eric and Iguana.

"Did you attack Ellen?" My curiosity always wins out on my wisdom. "Come on, Tommy, this burn on my leg deserves an answer."

"I didn't think you'd open that jar."

"I didn't. It broke. You're in love with Ellen and angry she doesn't love you back, is that it?"

He grabbed me then. "Noo! I love you. You can't accept that because you want to be loved by the likes of Bob or that Greenhouse guy." He held me by the shoulders, his face only a few inches from mine. "I'm just a fat slob to you and fat slobs aren't supposed to love you, but I love you, goddamn it!" He started shaking me, yelling at me like an enraged teenager. "You were nice to me and I got so drunk on that I wanted more. I paid Mr. Quicko to add a drop of that mancenillier juice to that jar. I wanted to make my face swell so you'd have to pity me. I wanted to get you to like me. That's all I wanted, but I don't know how to do

267

that!" He started crying and I felt sorry for him, but I wanted him to stop holding me, because if he chose to he could easily push me over the edge of the hill.

"Tommy, please let go of me!"

"You have a problem?" a very welcome voice asked in the back of my ear. I turned around to recognize the naked man who'd been swimming when we'd reached the Fall this morning. Now he was fully dressed in jeans and a white shirt.

"I'm in love with her!" Tommy blurted, letting go of me.

"Not an uncommon problem."

"He's a policeman," Tommy said, that tidbit bringing some of his composure back. "He's been going around the Club asking questions."

"You've been watching us all along?"

"Since this morning, mademoiselle. You arrived earlier than expected. I am afraid you caught me off guard. I apologize."

"Off guard!" Tommy piped in, composure totally restored. "Isn't there a law against being on duty and naked at the same time?"

"Tommy, I'm going to have to tell him about the cream."

"Shit, I'll tell him. The French understand about love." And he did, just as he'd told it to me, without the shouting or the tears. He denied attacking Ellen, he denied having even thought of killing anyone. The policeman took Tommy's arm and walked him to the parking lot. They were going to pay *une petite visite* to Beaujoie. I followed at a distance.

Tommy turned back to me when he reached a stand where an old woman churned ice in an old tin tub.

"Try her coconut snowballs," he called out, pointing. "They're the best."

268

I laughed in spite of myself. "How do you know all this stuff?"

"I'm observant, remember?"

The crew came back up, tired by the extra load they'd had to carry without me and Tommy to help. I kept explanations to a minimum, just saying I had smelled cloves in the cream and suspected Tommy attacked Ellen. I didn't tell them about his declaration of love, how his words and tears had shamed me, or about his sick bid for attention. Somehow I believed him innocent of the murders, maybe because I'm sentimental or maybe, remembering Tommy's accusation, because I assumed a man who loved me couldn't be a killer. Had Tommy attacked Ellen? Maybe. But if he wasn't in love with her, I couldn't begin to think why. Unless he was psychotic.

We piled the stuff back in the van. I paid for a round of coconut snowballs for everyone, asking for extra ice for my leg. We toasted the end of the shoot with our snowballs and piled back into the van and the car. I insisted Nick ride in the car with Bob, Ellen, and Paul. I piled in the back of the van, while Jerry drove and HM sat next to him. I threw myself on Nick's towels, propped ice on my leg, and closed my eyes, hoping for pleasant dreams of Greenhouse.

TWENTY-SEVEN

I woke up at the sound of gears screeching. The van seemed to rear and then lurch forward in a steep climb. I slid down on the uncarpeted floor and was instantly pinned to the back doors by all of our equipment. The ice I'd pressed to my leg was now sitting on my stomach.

"Hey, what's going on?"

HM turned around and laughed when he saw me, limbs akimbo, trying to untangle myself from a mass of towels and bathing suits with Paul's tripod sticking in my ribs.

"Sorry, sweetheart here isn't too good with a stick shift."

"Why are we climbing?" The front window was offering me a view of burnt tree stumps.

"Our leader's decided we celebrate the end of the shoot with a vista of the sunset from the top of the volcano. You were fast asleep so we didn't consult you. Sweet dreams?"

"Of maple-cured hams studded with cloves." I wasn't making that up.

"Want me to climb back there and give you a hand?"

"No, thanks. I'm fine." I felt something sharp dig into my thigh and I quickly shifted my weight. The offending object was a small metal comb with a gold ruffled bow attached, the ends streaming down. The tick I'd heard in the rainforest became a thud. I remembered:

A ruffle, white, fluttering, the loose end wrapped around the black handle of a machete. The ruffle trailing back to Iguana's arm. Above her elbow, a white streak that was not part of her eyelet top. A white streak as if she had brushed against something. Or someone. Someone who had painted his body white to play marble statue.

I took a deep breath as if a rush of oxygen would obliterate that horrible thought. It didn't. I looked at the Club Med bag pressed against my calf. It was Bob's. I ran my hand along its sides. It was full. Of what?

I crawled up to the front seat, pushing myself close enough against the back so that Jerry and HM would have to crane their necks to see what I was doing—an unlikely event anyway since they were busy bickering about the effects of jealousy. I hooked a foot under the seat to stay put and lifted the bag between my knees.

I had no right to do this and yet, remembering Iguana under that sail, I felt I had every right. Unzipping the bag, I started rummaging. He seemed to have brought his whole wardrobe with him: four pairs of white socks, containing nothing; a brand new pair of Nikes, empty inside; a bathing suit with no pockets; tons of sun cream that smelled only of sun cream, a pair of Porsche sunglasses, croakies in all colors, and at the very bottom, a paper bag.

I reached to pick up the bag and saw the corner of a magazine. My heart racing, I jerked it out of the bag, expecting to see an issue of *Adventure Life*. What I got

271

was *Sports Illustrated* featuring Lyle Alzedo on the cover. I rifled through it, shook it, torn between wanting to and hoping not to find a ripped, telltale page. Nothing came out.

The paper bag also held a gift box the size of a coffee table book. Heavy like a book, too, and wrapped very prettily in gold foil with a lattice of thin silver ribbons. It had to come from a very fancy shop with that wrapping. Was it a present for Nick? There was no way I could rewrap it so that it looked untouched. I shook it, then pressed it under my fingers. It wasn't a book. The middle was thinner than the sides. If I opened it what did I expect to find? More cocaine? Irrefutable proof he was guilty? I looked at Bob's new sneakers. Just do it!

Holding my breath, I slipped a finger under one end of the foil and pried the fold loose. I crunched against the seat and tried to unwrap the thing with as little noise and damage as possible. After a painstaking three minutes that felt like an hour, I uncovered the lid.

The evidence I held in my hand was not irrefutable. It was simply damning enough to make my heart turn cold. I was staring at Eric's silver frame, still tarnished, the glass smudged with dirt and fingerprints, the water-color of the KANZER RUM label gone. The first thought that came to my mind was: How the hell am I going to tell Nick!

The van stopped, then lurched. The motor died.

"Sweetheart! You're supposed to put it in neutral!"

"Why don't you shut up and put it up your ass!" Jerry jumped out and slammed the door.

"Well, I guess the volcano's erupting already!"

"We have to go back down!" I quickly wrapped the frame in my ice pack towel, scattering ice everywhere.

"Why?"

"My leg is burning up. I need a doctor."

The van's back doors opened, and I almost screamed as Bob leaned in with his usual smile.

"You carsick or something?"

I pushed the toweled frame against my leg as if it were still an ice pack, praying he wouldn't notice his bag was unzipped.

"My leg hurts."

"Aw, come on, hobble over at least to that ledge. It's so clear today you'll get to see Guadeloupe, the Saintes Islands, and even Martinique. I'll help you."

"Noo!"

"Called the Saintes because Columbus discovered them on All Saint's Day. Or so they say." That was Nick, now peeping over Bob's shoulder at me, looking like a picture of perfect happiness.

"Nick, I've got to go back. My leg really hurts. Let's all go back, please!"

HM had gotten out of the van and stood a few feet behind Nick, examining the landscape. To me it looked like we had parked at the entrance to hell. All I could see were crags of varying heights covered by gray and brown lichen. Here and there a small patch of low green plants dared to grow. Yellow, foul smelling steam came from sulphur holes buried in the rocks. A cold hell, I thought, shivering. The temperature had dropped at least fifteen degrees and the air was dripping wet.

"Are you sure this is safe?" HM turned to Bob. "I heard the last eruption was only back in 1976."

"Where's Ellen?" I screeched, scrambling out of the van, the frame safe in my hands. "I don't see Ellen!" Bob was right in front of me, but I'd been programmed to worry about Ellen, and she wasn't anywhere in sight.

"She's started the climb with Paul up 'Ladies Way,'"

273

Nick said, making a face on the last two words. "It's an hour and a half climb." She pointed to the left where a rocky path wound up the side of the volcano. A wooden sign read: *Chemin des Dames. Le sommet de la Soufrière 1467 m.*

"HM, you're supposed to stick with Ellen!"

"What for? She's with Paul and that jerk Jerry's gone right after them."

"Stop worrying about Ellen," Nick said. "She's fine."

"Jerry!" I yelled as loud as I could. He was already a hundred feet up, rounding a bend. "Bring Paul and Ellen back down." I wasn't about to leave anyone here with Bob.

"We've got to go home!" Jerry didn't even wave.

"Come on, Simona, I'll take you back in the car," Nick said. "The others can come down with the van. Paul's really set on watching this day end from up there."

"No, I'll take her," HM said. "I don't like heights anyway."

"No, everyone has to come!" I was panicked and feeling like a kid no one would listen to.

Bob started jogging up "The Ladies Way."

"Come on Nick," he yelled, with a wave of his arm. "Show 'em what a woman can do. Whoever gets to the top first, wins!"

"Wins what?" Nick was already running after him.

"Niiick!"

She stopped.

"I've got to talk to you."

"What is it?" she said, walking back. "Does it hurt that bad?"

Bob called out, "Your loss!" and kept running.

I clutched the frame against my chest. I had to tell her now.

"God, Simona, what is it? Your face looks like death!"

HM had dropped to one knee, pretending to tie his sneaker. His curiosity was as bad as mine.

"Let's go see that fabulous view," I said, taking Nick's arm and walking toward a ledge fifty feet farther up.

"I thought your leg was killing you."

"Hey sweetheart, wait up!" HM yelled, sprinting up the path. Jerry had reappeared from behind a bend farther up the volcano. "I looove youuu!"

"I had to talk to you alone, Nick."

"So talk!"

"I don't know where to start."

Nick pulled away, climbing ahead, stopping only when she reached a forty-foot, wet black crag with smoke coming out of its crevices.

I tried to run after her but the rocks were so wet, I kept slipping.

Someone yelled "Yoohoo!" and I looked up to see Ellen standing two hundred feet above us. Paul stood behind her. They both waved. Nick waved back. I gripped my towel-wrapped frame instead.

She probably wasn't going to believe me. I'd have to show her the evidence.

"I don't like playing games," Nick said when I reached her. She was standing, with hands on her hips, dangerously close to the edge of a precipice that plummeted to the rain forest three hundred feet below. Beyond was the Caribbean, with its two Lilliputian Saintes Islands and their surrounding islets. The white sun hovered over the edge of the sea, looking as if it were hesitating to take the plunge. As was I.

Ellen and Paul disappeared and Nick turned to look at the vista. "It's such a beautiful place," she said. "I

275

almost hate to leave it again." She was thinking of Bob, I thought, hating to leave him.

I touched her arm. "I've just found this in Bob's bag."

"What?" Nick turned abruptly, her elbow knocking against me. I was so nervous I jumped back, lost my footing and fell to my knees.

"God, you're clumsy!" Nick reached down to help me just as the frame fell out of my towel. I tried catching it, missing, and watched as the frame tumbled along the edge, finally catching in a shallow cleft.

Nick looked at me, then back at the frame, her face blanching. Her eyes turned hard, as if to refuse that sight. She'd recognized the frame!

I scrambled to my feet and leaned against the massive, barren crag for support. My knees were bleeding, my hands scratched and wet. "We have to go back down and tell Beaujoie. I've got no choice, Nick. I have to tell him."

"Why? That frame means nothing." Nick's face seemed to narrow, as if someone had smashed her cheekbones.

"If Bob stole this frame, it means he burned Eric's magazines, ripped the page out of the *Adventure Life* in our room, and maybe even killed Iguana. When I found her . . ."

Nick gripped my shoulders with both hands.

"Whaa . . . !" My head hit rock as she pushed me underneath the crag, down in a shallow hollow. She pressed one arm against my chest, immobilizing me, while she reached for the frame with one of her long legs, trying to kick it free and down the precipice.

"Throwing the frame down won't stop me!" I said, trying to push her away. "I've got to tell Beaujoie!"

She looked back at me, furious. And then it dawned on me. She wasn't protecting Bob!

Oh, dio mio! Not Nick! Not my roommate, my new buddy!

"I can't believe this!"

"What? Did you think I was going to let you lead me to the police like a dumb cow? They question Bob, he tells them I asked him to keep that frame for me and then they're on to me. It took me an hour to wrap that frame up so that no one would get the idea of opening it. I should have known it wouldn't stop you." She was on her knees in front of me, one hand over my mouth now, the other reaching into her bermuda shorts. "You've been sniffing around me from the beginning, sticking your snotty nose into my passport, my clothes, my life."

She glinted something before my eyes, but I was having trouble seeing. A sulphur hole was sending rotten-egg steam right into my face.

"Remember those dumb cocks? One thrust of a leg and the opponent flops down dead."

Nick let me wipe my eyes to see the six-inch gaff she was waving two inches from that nose she didn't like.

"Extra long," she said. "For tall people like me." She let go of my mouth then.

"Don't even think of screaming." She kept one arm to the side, in constant motion, as if she were playing defense on a basketball court.

"The others are going to be down any minute," I said. If I tried lunging out of that hollow, she'd be on top of me with that gaff in a second.

"The sun isn't going to set for another hour and then it'll take them another hour to get back down. We've got plenty of time."

I bent my head to one side. The crag curved over me a couple of feet leaving me no headroom. The only way out was straight ahead, which meant tackling Nick and

277

that gaff or to my left, to open sky and the precipice below. On my right, the hollow narrowed into a one-foot-high cleft spouting sulphurous fumes. Even if I had the time to crawl through, I'd never make it through with my fat.

"So what will we do with all this time? Are you going to tell me a story of how you killed Iguana and Eric?"

She slapped me with the back of her hand, a triumphant smirk coming to her face. "Still curious huh? Want to know all the details of the killings? You think that if you get me to talk long enough you'll get out of here. Why not? I've been into sports all my life. I'll give you one chance in a thousand." She sat back up on her haunches, body wavering, ready to spring in any direction, arms in motion, one still holding that curving gaff.

The thought—she's going to kill me too—finally began to hammer my skull.

"You like stories," Nick said. "I'll give you one. You can pretend it's just another one of Papa La Bouche's fairy tales if you like."

Move your ass, Simona! *Forza!*

"You're so fucking sentimental, you know, Simona? Anyone can feed you sugared crap and you'll swallow it."

If I kicked that gaff out of her hand, was I strong enough to knock her down and make a run for the car? Behind me, my hands felt for a stone, a pebble, anything to throw at her and gain a second's advantage. I didn't even get lichen, just solid, wet rock not even a bulldozer could lift.

"What you told me about yourself, was it all lies?" I asked to give myself time to think.

"I just slipped a few lies in the truth. That's the best way. The main lie was that Hogan never made it to

278

Hawaii. He didn't want to give me the portfolio. He thought he had lots of years yet to live even after testing positive. I knew better and on his last night, I borrowed Peter's sailboat and took Hogan for a nostalgic ride in the Atlantic. Come on, get rid of that look on your face. He was going to die of AIDS anyway!"

Coughing, I waved at the sulphur fumes and moved a few inches to my left. She noticed my movement, not caring. I was only getting closer to the sheer drop.

"A couple of months later I cashed in his ticket over in Martinique, using his passport. I looked enough like him to pass. Iguana said she saw me, but didn't think anything of it until much later when she spotted an ad in *Adventure Life*. That's when she figured in her clever French way that Hogan had never left the island and since he wasn't anywhere around, he had to be dead. When she saw me on the beach this trip, she was so desperate to get out of here, she threatened blackmail. She apologized and asked for fifty thousand dollars. I pretended to agree and made a date on Monday night up at that bluff above the western end of the Club. I hid Coco's machete under a bush up there in the afternoon. No one goes up there, except for Miss Beautiful Asshole Ellen, and I got rid of her fast with a couple of rocks.

"Iguana never showed on the bluff—probably chickened out—so then I waited for her where you'd told me she was going to pick up the kid. I was pretty sure she'd be early. She doted on the kid."

"Papa La Bouche was there!"

"He screwed things up for me. I was planning to swim her out to the coral reef and sink her with some rocks. I saw him coming and had to stuff her under that sail."

I moved a few more inches to my left.

279

"Are you aiming to jump?" Nick said with a smile. "It's a pretty long drop before you'll hit anything soft."

"Those fumes!" Scared as I was, it was easy to gag and let my face go red, at the same time steal another inch. What Nick didn't realize was that she was instinctively shifting left with me, just to keep in front of me where she could more easily stick that gaff in my throat.

"Why did you kill Eric?" I asked to distract her.

"He's sure no loss to mankind! He also tried the blackmail routine. Got all set to go to the States with my money. Iguana had leaned on him for money first. He paid her with a little rough stuff. Maybe that's when she told him about the ad. I don't know."

"What ad?" Another small shift.

"Hogan loved *Adventure Life* magazine, said reading that stuff made him feel like a real man. Most of Eric's collection came from him." Anger crossed her face again. "That jerk Peter was having guilt pangs. 'Hogan, darling, forgive me. If you're still alive, answer my letters, I beg you.' I didn't even know about it until Iguana mentioned it."

"I don't see how that was dangerous to you." I moved some more. Come on, Nick, follow!

She leaned her head into the hollow, holding the gaff to my collarbone. "Can't you see, you of all people? There are a lot of snoops around. That ad could stir things up, people talking about Hogan again, wondering why he wasn't writing to any of his buddies, wanting to know if AIDS had gotten to him, maybe asking around in Hawaii. So I had to get rid of the magazines. Who knows how many ads Peter had put out. And I snitched that great-looking frame. I thought, no sense in letting it melt down. I was going to use it for a shoot we're doing next month."

280

I was almost there, at the spot I wanted to be, where a five-inch shelf of rock jutted out enough to give me leverage. If she'd only lean back a little.

"Eric didn't know anything," Nick said. "But he'd have found out. That jerk had a great nose for trouble and money. I shot him in the ear just like that poor mutt. That couple was really killed, you know. I didn't lie about that, and I do have nightmares about that dog."

On a gamble I leaned forward, into the gaff. "Maybe that murder made you think killing was easy."

"It is easy," Nick said, bringing the gaff down and backing off as I'd hoped.

I assumed she wasn't planning to slit my throat. She'd only have another murder on her hands. An "accident" was much easier to explain.

"It was fun using Paul's gun," she said. "Watch him get flustered when the police found it. Ellen almost fucked that up. She barged in on me while I was trying to hide the gun in one of the trees. She's lucky I didn't cut up her face. I hate people who look that good."

"What are you going to do with me?"

"Everyone knows how clumsy you are, how the leg is really hurting you, and how you're always wearing those fancy Italian sandals. Everything's so wet up here. Real slippery. It's too bad I was nowhere near . . ."

Before she could finish, I shoved my weight against that small ledge and swung my legs across as hard and as fast as I could, whacking Nick's left side. She lost her balance, falling down on the hand holding the gaff. She screamed in pain, her body balling up. I threw myself out of the hollow, scrambling on my hands and knees to get away from her, my whole body propelled by sheer terror. I heard her lunge after me. Using all my

281

weight, I hurled a rock at her. I fell forward with the effort, toward Nick and the precipice two steps beyond.

Nick dodged the rock by twisting to one side. I saw one yellow high top slip as a rock slid away from under it. The leg flew up, then the other, the yellow sneakers bright against that twilight sky. Nick grunted, I think, or perhaps I was voicing my own surprise. She had pitched backward, half her body over the edge already, her legs kicking furiously to counter the pull of her head. Throwing myself flat on my stomach, I reached for one of those legs, forgetting for that instant that she wanted to kill me. I felt the touch of a wet sole, the tip of a shoelace.

"Niiick!" I screamed.

She was gone. The silver frame rolled down after her.

EPILOGUE

I had to cancel my Sunday dinner with Greenhouse. The crew left as planned on Saturday, with all the other departing guests. For a send-off, the G.O.s lined up on each side of the entrance walk, applauding and singing "It's good for the morale," to the rhythm of the *biguine*. I had to stay behind until all the legalities connected to Nick's death were over. Club Med couldn't have been nicer, putting me up free, plying me with food and drink, hoping, as Manou put it, "that you take home a *good* Club Med vacation." I lost five pounds in those few days, not because I wanted to. I simply couldn't eat. It's not a diet I would recommend.

Tommy left on Sunday. He confessed to Beaujoie that he'd taken the photo proofs and the negatives from the Club Med photographer to stop me from seeing two terrible pictures of me in a bathing suit. I saw him just before he left and thanked him for being so considerate. Together we tore up the pictures. He promised he won't be so self-destructive in the future, but I don't think I believe him. I suggested he get professional help, to which he laughed. He's been in therapy for years. "Who else is going to listen to me?" I was glad when he didn't ask for my address.

Bob asked to quit Club Med. He'd loved it there, but he felt he had to go back home. Last week I got a note from him telling me he's joined Narcotics Anonymous. He doesn't need it for the drug-taking, he writes. He wants the emotional support. He ended the note with, "I really thought Nick was great, and now I feel like I'm the one who took that fall."

Beaujoie's wife invited me to tea. To my surprise, she's a large, handsome woman who dressed, on that occasion, in a bright red and yellow dress. I'd expected her to be small and dress somberly, probably because I'm hooked on nineteenth-century novels where frail women suffer in gray or dark blue. Papa La Bouche was invited, too. We had tea laced with rum and coconut cookies called *Tourments d'amour* that can only be bought from the children of Les Saintes. Beaujoie and I listened while the two of them argued about the treatment of women in fairy tales. The Moonfish story came up. Madame Beaujoie doesn't think it fair that the moon be turned into a fish just because she doesn't want to go back to her husband, the sun.

Beaujoie asked her, "Isn't the moon happy with him?"

"That's not the point," Madame Beaujoie answered and I agreed, much to Beaujoie's unhappiness. Then we spoke of Carnival and how from the beginning, this particular story had been full of disguises: Nick making up a résumé, Paul hiding his feelings behind a brooding mask, Ellen hiding behind her beauty, Eric pretending he'd fought in Vietnam, Tommy pretending to have allergies, me covering up my loneliness with twenty extra pounds. Even most of the names weren't the real ones. Nick was really Elizabeth, Iguana was Lucille, Lundi's name is Marcel, and Coco's is Fabien.

When I asked Papa his name, he said, "What you are

284

in the imagination of children is all you need to be in reality."

I looked at Madame Beaujoie and thought of her painful imaginings. No mention was made of the phone call Madame Beaujoie answered that night. I don't even know if she was aware I'd been the one to call.

On my last day Beaujoie drove me to the airport. I told him about the Citroen I had dented in Basse-Terre and how the owner had never contacted me. He laughed, saying the car belonged to one of his men and I would not have to pay for anything. After all, I had been on "investigative duty" at the time.

I remembered to give him the *Pasta Crisi* recipe, which reminded him of the cloves Ellen had smelled on her attacker.

"Mademoiselle Nick must have eaten the excellent Caribbean dish of malangas and crab which the Club cuisine offered that night. It is a dish spiced heavily with cloves."

When my plane was about to leave, I hugged Beaujoie hard.

"Remember the good, digest the bad," he told me, hugging me back. "That is all we can do." Then he surprised me with a box of white cotton handkerchiefs, for which I had to pay one franc to break "the spell of tears" such a present brings. I now carry one with me at all times.

After a few days back in the office, I found out that Ellen had gone back to Omaha to visit her aunt, a duty call she'd planned all along. She might have told Eric, which could explain why he bought a ticket to Omaha, but I still wonder where Eric got the beautiful silver frame. I somehow picture it in the living room of that couple in Lincoln. Maybe it held a picture of their son with the mutt. I've asked Greenhouse to find out if the Lincoln police ever found prints of the burglar/murderer. If they did, I'm going to ask Beaujoie to send Eric's prints to them. You never know. Besides, I have a hard time letting go of certain fixations of mine. I never seem to learn from experience.

Paul's off on a shoot for another agency, this time in Sun Valley. Ellen has joined him. We don't plan to shoot any more Janick ads for at least a couple of months. I'm back into the routine of office work, figuring shoot budgets, scouting models, spouting opinions whether asked for or not. I'm glad to be back in cold, drizzling New York, but sometimes, despite all the ugliness of that week full of sun, I find myself happily singing one of the Club's end-of-show ditties. Manou would be glad to know I brought something good home. I've even sent for a Club Med catalogue, thinking that Mexico at Christmastime might be warm and romantic.

Which brings me to *il grande amore*—I forgot to buy Guadeloupan cinnamon for Greenhouse's coffee, but he had a wonderful surprise for me at the airport. He came with Willy, who's turned out to be as wonderful as Greenhouse said he was. The three of us have gone to the movies a few times. I've cooked a couple of meals at Greenhouse's apartment. It hasn't been instant love on Willy's part, but things are improving every day. Last night I got a "Hey, this pasta's awesome. Will you make it again?"

He imagined me in his future. That's a reality I like.

Pasta Crisi

Serves four as a main course

2 lbs. ripe plum tomatoes—sliced lengthwise
1/2 bunch arugula—leaves torn or cut into small pieces
2 cloves garlic—minced
1/4 tsp. red pepper flakes
1 large mozzarella—diced
8 sun-dried tomato halves—chopped
1/3 cup olive oil
1 lb. imported dried penne or spaghetti
salt and pepper to taste

Heat broiler.

In large serving bowl mix olive oil, garlic, red pepper flakes, sun-dried tomatoes, and diced mozzarella.

When broiler is very hot, line the fresh tomato slices on an aluminum-wrapped broiler pan, add salt and pepper, and broil tomatoes until their edges turn black—10 minutes approx. (If your broiler pan is not large enough to accommodate all the slices, repeat this process.)

Add broiled tomato slices to serving bowl. Add arugula. THIS SAUCE CAN BE PREPARED A FEW HOURS AHEAD OF TIME AS IT IS BEST SERVED AT ROOM TEMPERATURE.

Cook the spaghetti or penne in a large pot filled with salted boiling water. When the pasta is al dente, drain and transfer to serving bowl. Toss all the ingredients together, letting the hot pasta soften the mozzarella.

Eat and forget the crisis!